ABACULUS III

EDITED BY
DANIELLE KAHEAKU

Abaculus III

Published by Leucrota Press
P.O. Box 647, Poway, California 92074, USA

ISBN-13: 978-0-9824713-2-6
ISBN-10: 0-9824713-2-7

Cover design by Gilly.
Cover art by Chris Malidore.

First printing, November 2009.
Manufactured and printed in the United States of America.
Printed simultaneously in the UK and Canada.
http://www.leucrotapress.com

ABACULUS III

EDITED BY

DANIELLE KAHEAKU

Contents

Contents, Cont.

Introduction
BY
ERIN DURANTE

As an author, my work has always leaned toward the fantastic, the horrific, and what many would call "far out there." My love for these genres began early on when I was a child, from the first time I read Peter S. Beagle's *The Last Unicorn* and Terry Brook's the *Shannara* series, to more recent films like "Starship Troopers" and the "Lord of the Rings" movie trilogy.

But what is fantasy?

Fantasy is one of the oldest genres in literature, dating back at least to Hellenistic Greece, with the most well-known stories including "Gilgamesh" from Babylon, Homer's the Iliad and Odyssey, and the Aeneid by Virgil from the Roman Empire. Though these stories came from different lands and times, all shared the common patterns of quests, heroes, magic, gods, mythical creatures and adventure.

Now that we know what fantasy is, what is its purpose in literature?

Fantasy presupposes that the reader will like taking chances, for there are few leaps of faith more vivid than positing physical and logical worlds other than that which we experience on a daily basis. Readers enjoy the thrill of not knowing what to expect; the unknown is exciting in itself, and placing a reader in the midst of the mystery and exploits of the hero or heroine only heightens that sensation of surrealism.

Science fiction and horror are no different, and between the three genres interested readers can find nearly any adventure their heart desires between the pages of a book; from multi-species battles in deep space to high school-attending vampires, the possibilities are endless and we as a society have barely tapped into the potential these new words have to offer.

And honestly, I don't mind the lifted eyebrows, narrowed eyes, or even the few wrinkled noses I get thrown my way when I announce that I write speculative fiction. I don't get angry when I'm told that I don't write "real" literature, or that I'm not a "real" author because I haven't written a Great American Novel.

No, I don't get angry—I actually become disappointed that more readers out there have not had the chance (or refuse) to allow themselves the excitement and almost subliminal experience of completely letting go of the world around them, to release their inhibitions and immerse themselves into a great work of fiction.

In this sense, we should all take a good look at the children around us and really pay attention. They've got the idea down; between playing dress up salon with Barbies or shoot-out at Dad's bar-b-que, kids understand the idea of make-believe—and they embrace it. Roleplaying, dress up, and even their crayon doodlings are all creative outlets that let their minds wander into worlds and characters that are not "real" or the "norm." Do you see them lifting their noses at each other, or scratching their chins deciding if their card-board spaceship has been built up to code? Of course not. They run, they laugh, they wing it if their paper steering wheels break during a high-speed chase... The point is they have fun. Something a lot of adults today could afford to indulge in more often.

Well, guess what, here's your chance. Enclosed between this bright cover is a collection of some of the best science fiction, fantasy, and horror short stories from around the world. These stories are not about "real" life; you won't find anything about a boring nine-to-five schedule, or a monotonous traffic report. No, these stories are of the surreal, the outlandish, and the unknown.

So grab a blanket, curl up on your favorite couch, and dim the lights (unless you scare easily) and prepare yourself for an unforgettable experience on a fantastic ride through the imaginations of a wonderful cast of writers both new and experienced. Let yourself go as the words jump off the page and pull you in face-first, and forget about the mundane daily activities that probably need to get accomplished. Indulge yourself in a few moments of blissful escape from the world around you.

Are you ready?

Then let's go.

Erin Durante has published multiple short stories and essays, and is the author of the science fiction trilogy Damewood. *The trilogy, which includes* Demons of the Past, Stones of Time, *and* Rise of the Dark Son, *is currently being adapted to illustrated graphic novel form. She lives in San Diego with her family where she writes full time.*

THE THING IN THE TUNNELS

BY
KEVIN WALLIS

Kevin dedicates this story to Euro and Mel, for whom he will always go back into the Tunnels. He thanks them for saving their laughter until after pulling him from the snapping turtle-infested waters, although we all know the turtle wasn't as big as Euro claims.

We often learn our lessons too late, don't we? I've finally learned the futility of cowardice, how to fight fear with a well-aimed punch to its inhuman face. I've seen behind the parent-fed lies that evil doesn't exist. I found that evil. I lived those lies. And I learned to believe in monsters.

I still love Oscar. That's why I'm going in. For him.

Dear God, I'm going into the tunnels again.

"Hurry up. Our parents will kill us if they know we're outside." Oscar had already swung one leg over the bayou and into the opening of the drain pipe. He looked back at me with shining eyes, his excitement stamped across his rat-like face, his other leg dangling above the water. His white Chuck Taylors shone through the garbage bags he had wrapped around his feet and shins to protect us from whatever bugs might live in the tunnels.

"I'm coming," I said. "If you're right about this, the bodies won't go anywhere." I spoke with confidence, but the squadron of butterflies in my stomach threatened to expose my fear. Plus, Oscar's smirk told me I hadn't fooled him at all. The thought of searching for dead bodies under the ground didn't seem to faze him a bit. As for me, I figured as soon as we got this nonsense over with, we could get back to our tree and laugh at our stupidity. His explanation for thinking the bodies were in the sewers was reason enough for a chuckle.

Samantha Herkle's big sister was getting laid in Jimmy Devont's Beetle last weekend and she told me—Samantha told me, not her slutty sister—that they heard screams coming from underground, but they ignored it because Jimmy had his hand...

"You know I'm right, Howie. I'm always right. As soon as we're done we'll go hang at the tree and be heroes." He could always read my mind. "So toss me my torch and let's go."

"Call me Howie again and I'll make you eat your torch." I lit the Vaseline, Tide and gasoline mixture (with a little dissolved Styrofoam thrown in for a thicker consistency, it was our version of napalm) coated the end of a small log and handed Oscar his flame. We didn't trust flashlights in the dampness of the tunnels.

Oscar pulled a crumpled Marlboro pack from his jeans, lit a smoke on the torch's fire, and pulled his other leg into the tunnel. He threw me a "hurry up" gesture as he inhaled, and I noticed the jagged cut running along his knuckles. My heart flinched as I imagined the wound's origin, no doubt some school bully's teeth. It would heal into another battle scar, one more in a long line of injuries suffered while defending his four-foot frame from bruising fists and tyrannical tongues.

Many people doubted Oscar would survive the ninth grade, much less graduate, but they didn't know the Oscar I knew. Oscar would stare up at his enemies until he stared them down.

I reached out over the bayou water, grabbed the rim of the drain pipe, and swung into the tunnel behind my friend.

Oscar barely ducked as he ran into the darkness of the underground tunnel, but I had to shuffle along in a painful crouch to keep from bumping my head on the roof. A slow stream of water flowed down the corrugated pipe and into the bayou behind us. I placed a leg on either side of the trickling water, my legs bent awkwardly outward as I tried to balance on the curved sides of the pipe. The slippery plastic of the garbage bags I had slid over my shoes and tied firmly to thighs didn't help my balance problems.

"Oscar, wait up!" My voice rang out, smothered and metallic in the narrow pathway.

Flickering shadows danced off the tunnel walls and flashed across Oscar as he headed back towards me, distorting his small but strong stature into something trollish. The smoke from his torch had left a smudge of black ash below his nose, reminding me of Hitler's mustache.

"I don't know about this," I said. I had to raise my voice over the rumble of cars passing only a few feet above our heads. "If you really think the missing people are down here, we should just call the police."

"Come on, think about it. How many people have disappeared around here these last few months?" He turned away from me and continued deeper into the tunnel without waiting for my answer. "Lots, right? And what have the cops done about it? They've shot their wad and done nothing. No arrests, no bodies, bullshit excuses thrown at the public."

I'd seen Oscar get emotional before. As his only friend, I'd seen it a lot; when nose to chest with a would-be bully, or telling me how one day he was gonna kick his old man in the nuts and leave his deadbeat family forever. I'd seen him grinding his teeth when he thought I wasn't looking, his fists curled, his muscles tensed, probably railing against the wretched cards he'd been dealt; his diminutive frame, his mousy features, his mountains of acne, his girlish voice.

But never had I seen the raw intensity behind his eyes as he turned to me that day in the tunnels. "The cops don't deserve any glory. *We* do."

We trudged along, smoking in silence. The flow of water increased. Eventually we succumbed to the inevitable and plunged our trash-bagged legs into the muck. Soon the pipes widened into cylindrical man-holes. We took breaks here, using the sunlight streaming in through the holes in the covers to rest our ever-squinting eyes.

"They'll respect me after this," Oscar said during one of these breaks. Smoke squirted from his nostrils as he talked.

"Who will?"

"My parents. Those pricks at school. Teachers who assume my brain is as small as the rest of me. After I find the bodies, they'll respect me. They'll leave me alone."

I looked down, preferring to stare at the filthy water flow by our feet than the hope in my friend's face. I knew the armor he lived behind better than anyone, but I also saw the cracks beginning to form. This fool's quest for respect reeked of desperation.

There *had* been a lot of disappearances lately. They started with the neighborhood dogs vanishing from backyard kennels, their owners finding nothing left but busted collars and chains that appeared chewed through. Then Mr. and Mrs. McIlvaine disappeared, last seen gossiping with the rest of the town's old folk on their front porch. The only clues left behind were some patches of bloody gray hair. Several more old people vanished soon afterwards, but people really started to panic when the first kid was taken. All in all, twelve people gone.

I learned early in our friendship to never underestimate Oscar.

The smell hit us just as the pipes widened into actual tunnels. A stench like wet garbage. Here I could stand without ducking and spread my spread my arms with plenty of room to spare between fingertips and concrete wall. Our feet squelched through mud and who knew what kind of shit under the now knee-deep water. The suction created as we dislodged our feet from the muck threatened to rip our protective garbage bags away, but so far the plastic held strong. And when the reek came like a kick to the nose, we added our vomit to the gunk below.

"Jesus!" I coughed the word more than spoke it. "Enough is enough, Oscar. Let's just go." Even as I said it, I knew I would follow him if he decided to go on. It was a long way back, especially without a backup torch by your side. And I knew what he decided after one quick glance at his face through the dancing lights from our flames.

"We're getting close," he said. "I know it. I was right. Only dead bodies smell so rot—"

A rumble, aggressive and deep, rolled through the tunnel. I first thought an eighteen-wheeler had passed overhead, but the roar sounded just like that—a roar, a growl. The water trembled around our feet. White roaches scurried for safer ground over our heads. Oscar ran as fast as the water, now up to his waist, would allow.

I willed my legs forward. I *wanted* to follow my friend, but the water felt as restrictive as hardening glue, and I was paralyzed with fear. Oscar disappeared into the darkness, his flame failing to illuminate more than his tiny hand on the shaft.

His torch went out. His screams melted into the rumble until the entire tunnel rang with a shrill cacophony.

I tried to run but couldn't move. The growling—I'm sure it was a growl now—intensified, sounded hungrier somehow. I heard teeth in that growl.

Oscar's dim form appeared a few seconds after his shrieking began. He splashed towards me, half-running, half-swimming. I couldn't see his face through the darkness, but his screams rattled with panic.

Behind him, drowning the darkness of the tunnel loomed... something. It filled the width of the tunnel and seemed to scrape the ceiling as it pursued Oscar. I couldn't see if legs propelled it, churning under the water, or if it rolled like an onyx boulder. But I saw teeth. White fangs the size of my legs flashed sporadically like a subliminal hint of what was to come. One moment they hovered over Oscar's head, their sharpened points seeming to toy with the panicked boy, then they would vanish as the thing either closed its mouth or rolled over it.

It barreled towards us, a towering black mass, closing the distance between its vastness and my screaming friend. I imagined that bulk stampeding over me, teeth gnashing at my face, my screams as I'm absorbed...

"Help me, Howie!"

I should have helped him. I should have run to him, swept his small body over my shoulders, and used my stronger legs to flee the thing. We probably could have made it. Things could have worked out differently.

I turned and ran. I heard him heard him shrieking my name as the thing bore down on him.

Then I was at the narrower pipes. An eternity of hunched and frenzied sprinting passed, and I was out of the pipe's mouth and falling head-first into the bayou.

Guilt is like a crack in a mirror, marring the surface image, defilling what you see. It takes what once was whole and warps the parts until only ugliness remains. You can dodge it, look at yourself from slippery, sidelong glances, but the crack will grow. It will always find you with time.

If guilt is the crack, cowardice is the biggest fucking funhouse mirror ever created. With every look inside, a monster looks back.

The guilt consumed me. Oscar screamed in my head for weeks, a nightmare cycle that drove my self-contempt to unchecked levels. Always, lurking behind the venom, my own voice chanted: *You could've saved him. He would've saved you.*

I didn't tell the police, and I avoided my parents like a disease. I'd seen enough cop shows to know that, without any solid leads, all eyes would turn to me. I watched the newsman report yet another disappearance. I saw the FBI roll into town in their gleaming government cars. I listened to my mother try to console Oscar's hysterical parents. And I suffocated beneath my hatred until I finally made a decision.

The mouth of the tunnel bellowed silently at me in its perpetual "O." A strong and steady flow of the previous night's rain drained from the pipe into the bayou waters below. My flashlight shone on a solid wall of darkness inside.

I don't know for sure why I went back. Goosebumps rippled across my skin at the mere sight of the tunnel, and my legs protested the entire way there. All of this only fed my self-loathing. If I had pissed my pants I probably would have just killed myself.

But perhaps that's why I went.

Maybe I needed to stare into the maw of the monster's lair and revisit the ghosts of my cowardice. Maybe riding my guilt to rock bottom could quell the deprecating voices in my head.

A moan drifted from the tunnel. At first, I thought wind whipping across the pipe opening made the sound, but the air was still. Again, barely audible, like the braying of a cow on the far side of a pasture. My heart clogged my throat. My bowels loosened but mercifully held. Visions of tearing teeth stole into my mind, and once more, terror paralyzed me.

Something floated towards me, carried by the forgotten rainwater like any other piece of post-storm debris. The moaning got louder..

Oscar, I thought. Maybe the floating object was Oscar. A wounded, dying, but still *living* Oscar. He would reach for me with fang-ravaged hands, tears of gratitude spilling from his eyes, tears of forgiveness . . .

It was a shoe. Oscar's shoe, filthy brown with spots of its original white still visible and a Chuck Taylor star glaring upward like a catatonic eyeball. Sprouting from the shoe were the bloodied remains of my friend's leg.

The moaning exploded into clarity like a phantasm screaming into my ear.

Howie. Help me.

For the second time, I turned and ran from Oscar's pleas for help.

I ran until my lungs burned for air and my legs begged for mercy. Three words fueled my sobs.

Howie. Help me.

Only Oscar called me Howie.

What was he going through? Why hadn't the thing killed him? It devoured me every night in my dreams. Why wasn't Oscar rotting in its belly?

Were all the missing people still alive?

I raced through my neighborhood, rending teeth and screaming boys seeming to bear down on me from all sides. Then I was off the residential streets and crashing through the brush of the woods lining our subdivision. These woods were our sanctuary. Here we would climb our tree, a massive oak in the center of the forest, perch on our self-assigned branches, and smoke without suffering the smug, disapproving stares of adults. We would talk about neglectful parents, laugh over our imaginary sexual escapades with the school's A-list girls, and plan for the day kids like us would decide who made that list.

I skidded to a stop in front of our tree. It had once been my tree, but Oscar had earned his share of it on the day we met. That day stayed fresh in my mind, a constant reminder of why cowards, like me, blindly follow the fearless, like Oscar. I saw myself as I had been that day. In the tree, crying, climbing higher and higher to avoid the volley of rocks fired my way by the trio of slack-jawed thugs below. A thrown stone had smashed into my cheek and sent me hurtling towards the ground, bouncing off branches on the way.

Then there he was, a tornado of fists and grit, slamming into the bullies before they had a chance to advance on my bloodied, weeping self. He only came up to the chest of even the smallest of them, but all three were running full-speed away from Oscar within minutes. He extended a tiny, bruised hand, helped me to my feet, and with a grin from ear to huge ear, told me to quit crying and help him climb this big-ass tree.

After that, we were inseparable. I followed in the wake of the tsunami he rode through life, while my nonjudgmental friendship kept him from riding over the edge.

He had saved me. Now he needed my help. But fighting a gang of bullies wasn't the same as charging into the den of a child-devouring monster. I knew I should call the authorities, but by the time I convinced them I wasn't crazy or playing a prank, Oscar might not be much more than stomach acid.

I pocketed my flashlight, grabbed a branch, and propelled my body up the tree. I didn't think—muscle memory guided me—as I settled into my claimed space among the boughs. Thick, abrasive leaves scratched at me, and my swipes to clear them away soon escalated into full-strength punches. My own skin felt constrictive.

A ball of pressure expanded inside my skull, all my frustration and anger and fear, begging to be released, but my head kept it caged. So I struck the tree, again, again, wrapping my hands around the bark, imagining it was my own neck, shaking and striking until the body parts started to fall.

Old fears of taunting punks and hurled rocks flooded back when the first severed limb fell from the foliage above me and struck my forehead. But as I saw the dismembered leg pinball off the branches and crash to the ground, I remembered all the new fears in my life.

Arms that looked chewed off at the elbow, hands missing digits, pale severed feet, an ear, globs of unknown anatomy, it all rained down on me. I held my breath, afraid to feel facial parts bounce off my tongue should I dare to scream. But a shrill siren of terror still managed to escape my mouth.

A hand landed in my lap, and the tree was still once more. I wriggled my hips, trying to dislodge the gray, ashen hand from my lap without touching it. The wounds at the severed wrist told its story. I could see the teeth biting through the limb, hear the snapping bones and screams, death cries in the voices of the missing. I heard my own fear-drenched voice in those screams. I heard Oscar yelping in the joy of the fight as he smashed his fists into my tormentors' faces.

He never would have abandoned me.

I fell more than climbed down the tree. My head bounced off the kneecap of an ice-cold leg, but I didn't feel any pain.

I'm coming, Oscar. I didn't think it—thought was too evolved a function for my torpid mind—but I *felt* it. I knew where I was going, and why I went, but I could not put it into words had I tried, not then, not now. The primitive need to fight and protect took over, burying my cowardice beneath logic-defying audacity.

I ran.

I don't recall my second flight to the tunnels that day. My basest instincts had control. Had I been capable of coherence, I never would have gone back in. I plunged forward like a mindless beast, my flashlight flickering a weak yellow into the dark.

The stench nearly crippled me. The rotten smell of death

greeted me as soon as I swung into the drain pipe. I vomited, splattering my shoes with gunk as I was forced to hunch over while running. The pipes seemed smaller than I remembered, tighter, pressing down...

Help me, Howie.

Alive. Oscar was alive.

The pipe opened into the full-sized tunnels. The glow from my flashlight winked off the concrete walls and black water as I sloshed ahead.

Oscar's cries grew louder.

Terror started to creep past my mindlessness as I realized I had no idea what to do once I reached Oscar. Or the monster. Or both. I could only hope the thing had left its prey to hunt. Just give me time to throw Oscar over my back and escape before it got hungry again.

But I found them before I had time to form a plan. Sprawled across the left entrance of a fork in the tunnel, the beast filled the corridor like a mammoth ball of solidified oil. Beside it, grinning, sat my friend.

"Finally, Howie. Thought you'd forgotten about me."

His voice was a raspy croak, pebbles raked over sandpaper. I shined my light on his face, ignoring the monster and its gleaming teeth for the moment. The creature's wet breathing filled the dank air with the reek of old blood and buried things, but the shock of Oscar's appearance monopolized my attention. Streaks of filth littered Oscar's face, but the skin visible around the grime was cadaver-pale. His lips, apparently trying to smile, seemed stretched outward by unseen hooks until only a maniacal semblance of a grin remained.

His eyes burned with joy.

"I knew you'd go to the tree, Howie," Oscar said.

Behind him, the monster rumbled. I was vaguely aware of its slick, black flesh, its child-sized teeth glistening like icicles, but I couldn't move my light from Oscar's face to get a better look. Oscar grinned.

"You always run to the tree when you're scared."

"Os..." My voice failed.

"Sorry for the surprises I left you in the tree—believe me, it was a bitch lugging all that crap up there in the middle of the night—but I'd given up hope that you'd come without a little push." Oscar's hand crept upward as he talked, settling on the tunnel-thing's hide with a lover's caress. "I shouldn't have risked being seen, but I had to get you back here. I had to push you over that edge. Obviously the shoe wasn't enough."

Oscar raised his legs one at a time out of the water, revealing two bare, but quite intact, feet.

I stuttered like a simpleton.

Oscar laughed. "You think I'm the only kid with size eight feet? My friend here gave me plenty of legs to choose from."

The smirk vanished under a veil of sober sincerity. "It had me, Howie. While you ran, it caught me, held me down... and saw me. It *saw* me. We locked eyes, and my fear just melted away. It *gets* me. We're the same, he and I. It was like I looked in a mirror and saw myself for the first time, without all the fear and loathing I live with every day." I started to protest, but my tongue seemed pasted to my palette.

"He has to take them," Oscar said. "He has to eat. He didn't ask to be made like this. He would change if he could. But you can only change so much before you're a lie."

He looked back at the thing and stroked one of its fangs. The monster remained wrapped in blackness despite the weakening glow from my flashlight. Its breathing morphed into what I first mistook for a purr as Oscar caressed its teeth, but I heard the anger and anticipation of hunger in that rumble. Its teeth seemed to grow as it opened its mouth wider with an almost boastful slowness, elongating to span the entire distance from ceiling to the water's surface.

"We are how we're born, aren't we?" Oscar whispered.

I wasn't sure who he was speaking to, but I didn't care. I took a few steps backwards. I was so tired, but I prepared once more to run for my life.

"Stay with me," Oscar continued. "We'll never be abused again. Down here we have all the power. We protect each other. I feed him, luring all those blind fuckers towards him so he won't be seen. We go topside and take who we want. *We* make the rules now."

I shook my head, feeling tears mix with my sweat. I mumbled "no" over and over.

"It's okay," Oscar said. His scar of a grin had returned. He reached below the water and brought something out, something gray and bloody and bony. "He shares his food."

I ran from the tunnels for the last time, not bothering to shine my light ahead of me. Echoes of Oscar's laughter pursued me, but the tunnel-thing did not. I heard Oscar shout, giving me one last piece of brotherly advice, then all I heard were my own screams.

That was three years ago.

He still calls to me. I find myself at the tunnel's entrance often, his voice beckoning. Or maybe it's all in my head.

The disappearances slacked off for a while—maybe Oscar and his pet grew bored with the same flavor—but I still hear the sporadic reports of a missing child two counties over, a lost mother several miles down the road, a farmer whose cattle have vanished overnight.

My guilt still weighs on me, but not enough to ignore Oscar's last words of warning as I fled the tunnels. Five simple words, but they've dictated the scope of my life these last few years.

If you tell, you're next.

Solutions often bite with sharper teeth than the original problems, don't they? You see, I'm not scared anymore. Oscar taught me that. I remember too well the spark of insanity I had always seen in his eyes, a spark I had mistaken for the spirit of a fighter. That spark had become an inferno, and I've seen where his fear led him. I've seen it, but I can't accept it.

I pull my newly acquired pistol from my waistband and click off the safety. Whether he's lifeless in my arms or walking by my side once again, I'm taking him out of the tunnels.

Because, God help me, I'm going in again.

God's Laugh
BY
Jessica Dall

A soon to be graduate of American University in Washington D.C., Jessica has been writing from a very young age and has published one novel between working as Leucrota's Acquisitions Editor and a freelance writer.

Beauty allows for a dangerous sort of tyranny that comes with its own distraction, hiding until there is no chance of escape. Emma Moirae was beautiful. It was a necessity of her trade. Blonde sixteen-year-olds weren't exactly known for their crime sprees. It was just a fact, and perception was all that mattered. She wasn't sixteen, but that was immaterial. She was the youngest of three Moirae sisters, but that wasn't saying much. They'd all look the same as they did, as they had for decades, until they passed their job on to the next generation of Moirae girls.

When it came to their jobs, Emma believed she had gotten the short end of the stick. While Nina got to start life and Louise watched it, it was Emma's job to end it. It was an important job, of course, even an act of compassion in some cases, but still the least enjoyable. It was always shoved off on the youngest.

"Em?" Nina called from down the hall. "Come here a sec."

Emma sighed, following Nina's voice to the room they had always worked out of. Most of the time the door was locked, the few pieces of furniture in the room sitting either in shadow or in the light from the one gabled window that looked over their small backyard. They'd once owned a lamp, but it had broken several years before. They found no need to replace it. The room was their job, not their lives.

Louise was already in the room, her auburn hair pulled back into a low bun at the nape of her neck--a sure sign that she was working. She didn't bother to look up from the book she had in her lap, her hand warped into a strange shape, fingers curled under and thumb out to keep her place in the book.

Nina waved Emma over, her other hand tapping rhythmically on her knee. She had never been good at keeping that hand still. It was always itching to work.

"Is this important?" Emma crossed her arms, leaning against the doorframe. "I was filling out paperwork to start at that new school that opened down the street."

Nina shook her head. "I don't know what your fascination is with playing human."

"Better than sitting around here waiting for you two to decide you need me," Emma retorted. "What is it?"

"This kid on Elm Street." Louise finally looked up. "We think he's getting to the end of his cord."

Emma frowned. "I hate doing children."

"Don't be juvenile. You know we only take children when necessary."

"So what?" Emma picked at the corner of the wallpaper that was starting to curl with age. "This one going to be the next Hitler?"

"It's fate." Nina smiled at her own joke. "Have your verdict, Louise?"

"It's necessary."

"Agreed." Nina moved to the armoire. She pulled out a short string and handed it to Emma. "Do you want to wait until tonight or head over to Elm?"

Emma looked at the string in her hand. "I might as well go over there. He can't be more than four with a string this short. Least I can do is to try to make it humane as possible."

Louise nodded, pulling a sheet of blank paper from the back

of the book and ripping it out, pressing it on the page she had been looked at. She waited a second, pulled the sheet back and blew on the ink that had transferred, soaking straight through the paper to make an exact copy. She held it out to Emma. "Stephan Black: 36 W. Elm Street."

"Let me get my shears." Emma took the string from Nina and paper from Louise, stuffing both in her pocket before moving to the armoire and pulling a drawer open. She picked up the thigh holster she kept the silver pair of shears in, grabbed her purse and threw them in rather than strapping on the holster.

She walked downstairs quickly and moved out the front door, not bothering to say good-bye. For the most part, Emma would miss this town when they ended up moving. There was only so long three girls who perpetually looked 21, 18, and 16 could live in one town without people getting suspicious.

She took a deep breath, fading so no one would see her before turning the corner down Elm Street. Shifting her purse to her other shoulder, she staked out a spot by a tree across the street from the address Louise had given her and waited, pulling out the waxy thread from her pocket and the shears from her purse. She slipped her fingers into the rings of the shears and flexed, hearing the soft, sharp slip of the blades against each other. She continued opening and closing them, the nervous tic finally stopping when the door across the street opened, and a young boy came outside.

"Stay in the front yard!" A woman called from inside.

Emma's stomach dropped; it was always hard when she saw the person whose life she was ending. Less painful for them, though, than her cutting the cord and letting a reaper amuse itself. Reapers got bored with death far too often and the unfortunate souls too often ended up being impaled on the broom it was sweeping with or something similarly gruesome.

She waited five minutes, watching the little boy run around with a balsawood plane, his engine noises reaching her across the street. Eventually he dropped it, bored, and climbed the tree in their front yard.

He scampered up with the quick dexterity that only came with practice, hooking his legs around one of the thicker branches before dropping back, swinging his head so his torso moved back and forth like a pendulum.

Emma sighed and sat down, catching the end of the string between her legs and pulling it taunt. This was as good a situation as she could hope for if she didn't want to be sitting here all night. She glanced at the boy one last time before opening the shears and snapping them shut over the cord, severing it cleanly in two. The string unraveled, the pieces floating away before completely dissolving on the wind.

She didn't look up until she heard the soft thump of the boy hitting the ground across the street. A sweet smell hit her, that of a freshly departed soul, the smell that came when they were freed, before the body began to decay and it turned rotten.

She waited for a few seconds, looking around for anybody else who might have seen the boy, and then returned to being visible, slipping her shears back in the holster and zipping her purse shut. She pulled the paper out of her pocket, making sure it was now blank and shoved it less than carefully back in. Walking across the street calmly, she looked at the body for a long moment. The head sat at an unnatural angle, the neck snapped cleanly, probably in more than one place. She knelt down, doing her best to look distraught. "Help! Someone!"

Within a moment the front door swung open, a pretty woman surveying the scene. She looked at Emma, and then at the boy. She screamed with true panic, making Emma realize what a poor facsimile she had mustered. She really needed to work on that.

"Stephan! Stephan!"

Neighbors rushed over.

"What happened?" The first person on the scene frowned.

"I'll call an ambulance," an older man called from the other side of the house, taking one look at the scene and returning to his home.

Emma nodded, though she knew how little good that would do. The boy was dead, irreversibly by now. Any chance of reviving him had ended as soon as his string had blown away.

She looked at a younger, dark-haired man who was standing on the other side of her looking disturbingly nonplussed. The same person who had arrived first after the boy's mother.

"What happened?" he repeated.

"I don't know." Emma shook her head. "I was just walking down the street and…he must have fallen out of the tree."

The woman had completely dissolved, her body shaking as she sobbed.

It was a common enough scene with any death, especially a child's. Emma still found it oddly fascinating. She looked at the dead boy, trying to keep her perverse interest hidden.

She waited for the ambulance to come and promptly report the child DOA before leaving. She offered some generic words of condolence to the mother, brushed her jeans off from kneeling in the dirt, and moved down the street, frowning at the lack of sympathy she had mustered. She was becoming more callous. A necessity, yes. A desired trait, no.

The younger man looked at the small group for a second before going after Emma. "Oy!"

Emma hesitated, looking over her shoulder, pulling her purse tighter against her side.

"It's a good thing you found him." The man jogged a little up to her, stopping a couple feet away. "He could have been laying out here for hours. It's a quiet street." He held out his hand. "I'm Conner."

Emma gave a tight smile. Attraction was part of her job, it let her slip away from deaths, but it often seemed to backfire when it came to teenage boys. She pushed her hair back behind her ear and took his hand, shaking once before releasing it. "Emma."

"Not Antropos?"

Her smile dropped. "What do you mean?"

He smiled, glancing back at the small group a few yards away. "Walk with me?"

She nodded, walking silently with him until they couldn't hear the sobbing any more. She glanced at him out of the corner of her eyes. "Who are you?"

"Conner," he said.

"So you've said," she turned her head, "Conner what?"

He avoided her eyes. "Scythe."

"You're a reaper." She smiled. "Never seen one of you up close before."

"Well, you aren't exactly the easiest people to peg down." Conner stopped at the corner. "You are Antropos though?"

"Shouldn't you be busy?"

"Taken care of." Conner shook his head. "We're quick about it. Have to be with you killing people off left and right. I'm surprised you have time to talk to me."

Emma shrugged. "Most cords are set up on a time release. They last a certain amount of years before snapping. It's only the ones Louise has doubts about that I have to do by hand."

"Louise?"

"My sister."

"You've just updated your names then?" Conner looked her over. "Clotho, Lachesis…"

Emma laughed.

"Something funny?"

She shook her head.. "Nice meeting you," Emma moved off.

He followed her. "I've been looking for one of you for years. You think I'm just going to let you walk away now?"

"You realize I have no idea who you are," Emma rolled her eyes.

"Conner Scythe."

"I've got that part, thanks."

"I've been stationed in the suburbs here for five years, and for all that time been doing your dirty work picking up the souls you kill…I also like candle lit dinners and long walks on the beach."

She looked him over stonily.

"Come on." Conner rubbed his arm. "Ten minutes. All I ask."

Emma considered for a moment before sighing. "I'm hungry. Buy me lunch and maybe I'll try to help fill you in."

"Buy you lunch?"

"You want to talk or not?"

Conner nodded quickly. "There's a quiet place two blocks over if you want…"

Emma followed him into a small café two streets over. She held up her hand, watching the waiter deposit their food and took a bite of her burger before finally looking up. "So what do you want to know?"

He set down the fry he had halfway to his mouth, "Do you change your names often?"

She laughed again.

"I don't get why that's funny," he frowned.

"I'm Emma," she said, "Antropos has been dead for about two thousand years now. We only live for three hundred or so. We have the whole genealogy traced, Morta took over and then Skuld and so on and so forth..."

"There are more of you then?" He studied her. "Fates-in-training?"

"No," Emma shook her head, "There can only be three of us alive at a time."

Conner blinked. "I don't follow."

"We're the great-great-great-great-etc. granddaughters of the original Moirae. When we finish our term we reproduce and then they take over. We all mix our genes together and new Moirae pop out fully grown, one after the other."

"And then you die?"

"Pretty much," Emma nodded.

"So...how old are you?"

"Hundred-and-three if you want to get technical about it." She smiled. "Louise is a hundred-and-four, and Nina a hundred-and-five."

"So, not directly one after the other."

"Well there needs to be some overlap as a learning period." Emma shrugged. "I'm the youngest so I didn't know the last Moirae girls, but someone needs to tell people what to do, and we can't exactly do that when we flash age and die within three minutes of the next Moirae appearing."

"Well, you look good for your age," Conner looked her over. "You're supposed to be crones."

"Easier to get in and out of places when you look like this." She gestured briefly.

"I'd imagine."

"You can stop looking at me like that." She frowned. "The secondary sex traits are completely for show. We reproduce asexually so there's no need to attract anyone other than what's required for our job."

"So you don't have sex?"

"Why?" She raised an eyebrow. "You want to sleep with me?"

"Wouldn't be against it."

"Is that how you reaper's amuse yourselves when you aren't directing the exact time of death? Casual sex?"

"Better than sitting around waiting for you to cut and let us head off-site," he rolled his eyes. "All that death gets boring after a while."

"Which is why you are so fond of causing car crashes I'd imagine."

"Explosions are more fun in my opinion," Conner smiled. "And you leave it up to us when you just pull the scissors out."

"Shears," Emma corrected. "They sound so much more threatening that way."

He leaned back in his chair, glancing at her legs below the table. "Where are they anyway? Invisible?"

She just smirked, picking up the glass of water in front of her and taking a sip.

"You aren't going to tell me."

Her phone rang inside her purse. "Excuse me."

Conner watched her get up and move to the archway that led to the restroom. He smiled after her, making her roll her eyes and turn away.

A tall blond man took her empty seat, helping himself to some of the fries on her plate. "Planning on kicking me out of the room again tonight?"

Conner frowned. "She isn't someone I'm trying to sleep with."

The man looked up. "Why'd you bring her here then?"

Conner turned, checking to make sure that Emma was still on the phone before looking at his friend again. "She's Antropos… well, the current Antropos."

The blond looked at Emma and then back to Conner. "Antro… you found the Moirae?"

Conner nodded. "The important one at least. I mean, we get her scissors, shears, and we can stop death. Then without death…"

"We go on vacation." The blond smiled, looking back at the archway. "She's hot."

"Apparently the whole crone thing gets in the way of sneaking away from crime scenes unnoticed." Conner nodded. "That's where I found her."

"At a crime scene?"

"Well, 'accident'." Conner flexed his fingers in the air around "accident." "She was on the scene for this one for whatever reason and I got the message to grab the soul. Trucked it away and then came back to see this chick walking across the street calmly, working up enough faux-emotion to call for the mother to come out. I snuck inside the house next door and then went back out to check her out. She's not a bad actress."

"Eleven o'clock." The blond glanced behind Conner quickly, motioning with his eyes.

"Everything ok?" Conner twisted in the chair to look at Emma, seamlessly transitioning.

She slipped her phone into her purse. "Just need to go home. My seat seems to be taken anyway."

"Oh, this is just Smith." Conner waved at the blond. "He's my roommate."

"Ah." Emma looked him over. "Is he…?"

Conner shook his head.

"Well, nice to meet you." Emma nodded shortly. "I've got to get home."

Conner offered a final smile as she wandered out of the café.

"You're letting her go?" Smith frowned, watching the door swing shut again.

"I don't want her to think I'm stalking her." Conner ate a fry.

"You aren't planning to?"

"Well, I am planning to, but there's a difference between following someone and *noticeably* following someone."

"And this is why you get paid the big bucks." Smith shook his head, "How long do you plan on waiting? We don't want to lose her."

"Just a couple more seconds.".

Smith nodded, picking at the food Emma had left, glancing up after a second, "N…?"

Conner stood up before Smith could finish.

Emma was surprisingly easy to follow for a supposed minor goddess. She walked quickly, not so differently than any other teenager might walk down the street, not looking around much. Apparently she wasn't worried about being followed.

"She is really very attractive." Smith walked in step with Conner.

"Yes, so you've said." Conner sighed.

"And she's blonde."

"Reddish-blonde."

"You'd think black," Smith continued. "I mean, she's death."

"No, we're death." Conner rolled his eyes. "She's just fate."

"Either way, I'm not sure if I'm happy or disturbed that the person who ends up getting to decide whether we live or die looks like *that*."

"If you're going to get enamored with her, you can leave now." Connor let some force creep into his voice. "We're getting the shears, not trying to indulge a school-boy crush."

They paused as Emma walked up the steps of an old colonial style house, opening the front door and disappearing inside.

"So," Smith watched when Conner didn't move, "What are we going to do now?"

"I say wait for night and then get inside." Conner looked the house over, a tingle going up the back of his neck. "Great, someone else is dying."

"No rest for the wicked." Smith rolled his shoulders attempting to shake off the familiar tingle. "Want me to take this one?"

Conner nodded, "I already had one today."

"Meet back here…"

"Eleven." Conner didn't look away from the house.

The house was dark when they arrived that night, an eerie sense of calm hovering around the property.

Smith frowned, wrapping and unwrapping his arms around himself like a swimmer warming up before a race. "Are we sure we want to…"

"Don't wimp out now." Conner looked at Smith.

"Just…they're Fates right?" Smith looked at his friend. "Don't you think they know what we're going to do now?"

"I think their book only covers humans," Conner said, moving slowly up towards the house.

"I'm not sure I'm okay with just an 'I think' right now," Smith frowned.

Conner waited for Smith to make it up the front steps after him before touching the doorknob. Like any other door, the lock clicked softly, letting them inside without issue. Conner looked around the entryway that was colored pale blue moonlight.

"They don't live much different than normal humans, do they?" Smith whispered.

Conner waved for him to be quiet before moving across the hardwood floor to the stairs that ran directly parallel to the doorway.

Nothing seemed to be out of the ordinary. In fact, everything seemed incredibly normal. Things you'd find in any house that three girls lived in. A laundry basket sat on the landing at the top of the stairs, half filled with dirty clothes, a couple books sitting by the linen closet and pictures of the three girls on the wall.

Smith lifted a picture frame off the wall, turning it towards the window to take advantage of the moonlight. "Wow. They're all hot."

"Shut up," Conner hissed.

"Just look at them," Smith held up the picture.

"Yes, they're very pretty, can we keep going?"

"I'd really rather you stay there," a light voice came from the room behind them. A twenty-year-old looking woman with black hair moved into the hallway.

"I told you they were coming," another voice came. An auburn haired girl leaned against her doorframe.

"You know, I really wish you would be wrong for once." Emma sighed, standing near her sisters. "Nina, Louise, this is Conner and his friend Smith, whom I believe he said, wasn't a reaper."

"You'd think he'd know better than to lie to a Moirae." Nina shook her head. "Even if you can't foresee their lives…"

Emma glanced at her sisters before looking back at the men. She frowned at Smith, "Are you feeling all right?"

Conner sighed when Smith didn't answer. "I think the blood's diverting from his brain. Ignore him."

Nina smiled, looking at Smith. She motioned to the stairs, "Sit."

Smith didn't question her, sitting down where she motioned.

"Smith," Conner looked at him.

"Don't bother." Emma shook her head,."I told you, the aesthetics are purely for job-related purposes. Nina's got it down the best apparently. Interestingly enough, you seem more immune to it."

"I'm surprised he hasn't run yet." Louise looked him over. "I distinctly saw running."

"We can leave right now," Conner replied. "Smith, will you get back up?"

"I don't know." Nina shook her head, motioning Smith down when he started to get up, "Stay. I'm not sure that's in the cards. What do you think, Louise?"

"Don't I ever get a say in this?" Emma frowned.

Louise shook her head. "Personally, I think they came after your shears, they should get to see them."

"Listen." Conner held up his hands. "It was a stupid idea. Mea culpa. We'll just go away now."

"Well, I think there are a few things to consider here," Nina said, counting them off on her fingers. "Biggest ones being how much we can trust two men who can get through any lock, and what would be a more fitting punishment for the embodiments of death, dying or…something else."

Louise nodded, studying them silently.

"Emma," Conner looked at her.

"You're pleading with the wrong sister." Emma shook her head. "I might be the compassionate one, but it's a very strict democratic system here. They say it's two to one; it's my duty to fulfill that verdict."

"But…"

"Got to convince one of them." Emma ran her fingers over the cool, rounded silver of the shears where they were attached to the outside of her thigh.

"Can't we just get rid of them?" Louise pouted. "I'm tired."

Nina pursed her lips. "Might be a problem. Only so many reapers around."

"They're here because they don't want to do their job anymore." Emma shrugged. "I hardly think death is the worst fate for them."

"Well, what do you think?" Nina asked her.

Emma smiled and began to speak.

Emma smiled to herself, knocking on the front door of a small house at an hour much too late to be cordial. When it didn't open, she knocked again, harder this time.'

Conner answered the door, groaning when he saw who it was. "God, I change my mind. Just let me die already."

"Well, it was never your call to start with, so..." Emma pushed her hair back behind her ear, "I'm going on-site."

"It's 3a.m. Can't you just cut them and let them die in their sleep? None of us are willing to be theatrical about it when it's this late."

"Now where would the fun be in that?" Emma smiled. "Besides, weren't you the one who said 'explosions were more fun'?"

"Yeah, yeah. But I just got to sleep an hour ago."

"Well, that's your own fault," Emma shrugged, "Sooner we move, sooner you get home again."

Conner groaned, rubbing a hand over his face, "You can be mean when you want to be."

"You brought it upon yourself." Emma smiled. "You should know what you're getting into when you start messing with fates."

"I'm going to get those shears eventually." He picked up his coat from the back of a couch near the front door.

"Wouldn't help you," Emma shook her head, "We set up a security system on them now. You touch them and they'll burn you. You can test it out if you want." She smiled. "Werewolf or not..."

He looked her over. “You’re bluffing.”

She pulled the shears out of their holster, and offered them to him. “Want to try?”

He looked at the shears for a long moment. “I think I’m good.”

Emma smiled.

“So where are we going?” Conner stepped outside, pulling the door shut behind him.

“4th Street,” Emma said. “Get in the car. You’re driving.”

“Yes’m.” Conner rolled his eyes and climbed in the driver’s seat.

The Witch's Camel

BY
Josh Alletto

The witch lived right behind us in an old, one story house that sagged between its neighbors like a shy head amid high shoulders. It collapsed in on itself. The storm-cloud gray wood split in some places, buckled in others, and left the house with a scarred and bruised exter ior. The backyard, a sporadic jungle of long grass and brown dandelions, stretched out to the fence at the edge of the alley. The witch had dozens of statues made of stone, metal, barbed wire, and old glass bottles scattered in her front and back yards and on top of her house. Small rabbits with heavy iron ears, red gnomes with curly beards of steel wool, and big grey bird feeders stained with the green and yellow of dried up bird crap.

I leaned over the low fence, staring at the witch's camel and waiting for my sister, Christina, to come around from the garage with the sledgehammer. The witch's camel stood at the edge of her yard, staring back at me with its one good eye. The body was made of car parts, bumpers and fenders and spoilers, all sliced lengthwise and bent to form the rolling girth of the torso and the sagging length of the neck. The hump, a browned chunk of an old oil barrel, looked boxy and awkward. The camel's fat tongue, a peeled open soup-can, stuck out sideways, and its remaining eye, a smoothed and polished copper penny, was wide and flat. I stared at it, fascinated. Its head peeked over the fence. I was nearly bumping noses with it.

Christina called from behind me; she was struggling with the giant sledgehammer. She had to lean all the way forward to get the head to drag behind her. With every aching pull, her face crushed in at the middle.

"Get the hell over here and help me!" she said.

I eagerly jumped down from my perch on the fence and ran toward her. "Why does the Witch have all those things?" I asked.

"'Cause she's a witch, Alan. They have all sorts of evil ugly things." She rolled her bright blue eyes at me and shook her tiny head so that the frizzy black ponytail bobbed back and forth and then folded a face at me that made me regret the question.

Christina had one of those faces that looked odd and uneven on her tiny body; one of those mature looking faces that she would have to grow into. It was one of those faces that could crease and fold itself every which way to give you all sorts of looks that made you feel like dirt.

The two of us struggled with the hammer. "I don't think those things are ugly," I said. "I think they're kind of neat."

"Well, they *are* ugly," she retorted. "And stupid. And when I'm in the fourth grade you better not talk to me about baby things like that anymore." Christina very much enjoyed reminding me that she would be starting the fourth grade at the end of the summer.

We settled ourselves in the center of the alley and Christina pulled the bullet out of her pocket. She rolled it in her hand, and then placed it carefully – deliberately – onto the ground, with the head of it facing away from us.

"So that it won't go off in one of our faces," she said.

She stood in front of it and started to lift the hammer.

"You said I could do it."

She cocked her hip and threw a tiny hand over it. "Well," she said, "I'm older. So I get to do it." Curling her bottom lip into her mouth, she dared me to argue. "Besides," she added, "you're just a little midget dweeb."

"But I saw it first,"

I had seen it first. Had been the one to feel it jammed into the corner of a box we found in our hall closet. It was a worn box, soggy and stale. On the side, written in frantic black letters was: ALAN SR.'S THINGS. We dug through it, cramped inside the small closet with the door shut, a tiny light bulb dangling above our heads. We ravaged it like animals, ripping things out and tossing them to the side, his old shirts, a box of boring looking papers, and a stack of old autumn colored photographs, until we found it – a single bullet – a remnant from his days on the force.

I stomped my foot. "You said I could hit it."

"Fine," she said, "but quiet down, will ya? Someone's gonna hear." She struggled to keep her voice at a whisper. I looked down the alley. The morning mist was thick; everything was quiet.

Christina kept the head of the hammer on the ground, and pushed the handle toward me. "Make sure you don't miss," she said.

But when I reached for the hammer, Christina pulled the handle back toward her and leaned in with her free hand flat, pushing the palm against my chest. I fell backwards, hitting the ground hard and scraping my hands up on the pavement. When I looked again, she was readying herself to lift the hammer. I tried not to cry.

Her tiny arms flexed. She lifted it, her eyes fixed on the bullet. Her face reddened with the effort. The hammer came up to her shoulder, parallel with the ground, before the weight of it pulled her backwards and she had to let go before it dragged her down. The hammer crashed down and left a fresh divot in the pavement. I laughed. She snarled and shook her head.

"Shut it, dweeb." She wiped her nose on her sleeve and readied herself for another attempt, rubbing her hands together. She never took her fat blue eyes off the bullet.

The ground was cold and its dampness seeped into my t-shirt. I stood up. I didn't want to look at Christina. I felt betrayed and embarrassed. Used up. I should have known this would happen. Just when I thought Christina and I were getting along, she would turn around and push me onto the ground, or slug me in the eye. The sight of her right then made me feel like crying.

I let my eyes wander around the alley, over garages and overgrown patches of weeds, back into the shrapnel-zoo of the Witch's yard. That is when I noticed that the witch's camel was gone. It had vanished, disappeared. A painful blankness replaced it, a startling hole in the carefully chaotic patchwork of the yard. I screamed. That camel had been staring at me my entire life and now, suddenly, and for no reason, it was gone. Its absence jarred me, scared me, and I yelled out, making Christina drop the hammer again.

"Holy damn, what the hell is your problem?" She whirled on me, using the newest grown-up expression she'd learned.

I pointed to where the camel had once stood, with its tongue out and one eye open wide. Her tiny jaw dropped. One of us grabbed the bullet, leaving the hammer in the middle of the alley as we ran back into our yard, up the stairs of our back deck, crashed through the door and slammed it behind us.

We spent the rest of that day plotting and debating in the basement. Christina wanted to go back and "investigate."

"It'll be like Nancy Drew," she said.

I protested. I hated Nancy Drew. Besides, sneaking into the Witch's yard at night meant certain death. Rumors about the witch swirled through our town. Tales of quicksand and trap doors; stories of secret dungeons and poisonous plants; myths of falling boulders and evil curses, all of them lurking, waiting patiently in the thick brush that surrounded the witch's house. Some we knew to be true; some we were more skeptical of, but only one fact existed that no kid in our neighborhood would ever dispute: The witch did not live alone in that house. She had a mute. We had even heard our mother – *our mother!* – talking about it on the phone one time to our aunt Clara.

"Well, you know, Clara, she's got that mute son to deal with."

"A mute," she had explained to me, "is a mutant that can change into a normal person if it eats one every day for a year."

I was just about to say 'no way' when Christina opened her eyes really big. She was suddenly so excited about it she couldn't sit still. With that look on her face – bright and big, cheeks round, her hair pulled back tight – she actually looked pretty when, smiling, she demanded that I come with her or risk a bloody nose.

At eleven-thirty that night, I slid out of my bed and met Christina by the front door. The summer night air was cool, so we grabbed coats from the closet, both our mother's. For Christina, a light windbreaker that made her look like a flying squirrel, all the excess fabric sagging low under her arms, and for me, an old fur shawl that I wore like a bright, white cape.

Outside it was dark. The moon was clouded over and the street lamp behind our house had burned out. A light rain earlier in the day had left the air moist and filled it with rolling fog. We crept out slowly into the backyard and moved carefully along the fence toward the alley. Christina dug into the pocket of her flower petal pajama bottoms and pulled out the bullet. We stood in the dim moonlight breaking through the clouds and examined it once more.

"Remember," she said, pressing the cold metal into my palm, "only use it if you see the witch."

Without another word, she ran off, and, in one jump, vaulted herself gracefully over the fence, landing crouched in the witch's back yard. I shuffled over and knelt down next to her, and we spoke through the crisscrossing of the fence.

"I'm gonna look in the shed," she said. Set back further in the yard, up against the rear of the house, was an old, dilapidated shed, dripped down the sides with brown rust and green mold.

I squeezed the bullet in my hand until my palm started to sweat around it.

"Wish me luck." And without another word, Christina dove deeper into the yard, landing hard on her stomach and began to army-crawl toward the shed. She let her swinging elbows drag her across the thick, overgrown grass, around the gnomes and the rabbits, around the birdbaths and bird feeders.

The witch's yard was so dark and the shed set so far back that I could only make out the whiteness beneath the flower-petal pattern on Christina's pants. The blur of it moved like a ghost and my heart began to race. I opened my palm and looked at the bullet again. When I looked back up, Christina was gone.

I thought about the mute and gripped the bullet tighter. It squished in my sweaty palm as I peered back into the yard.

That's when I saw it – the haze of a soft blue light. It was dripping out at the base of the witch's house, dancing around slowly in the darkness. I watched it as it bobbed playfully, silently on the walkway that led to the side door. It looked warm and calm. I watched it for a long time before finally standing up. My eyes were glued to the light as I began climbing the fence. I was at the top with my one leg swung over, struggling to keep my balance when Christina jumped out of the darkness.

"Alan!"

Startled, I fell the rest of the way over the fence, hitting the ground with a thud. On my back, I struggled to catch my breath. I held the bullet tight to my chest. Christina leaned over me, her eyes big as ever and her smile curling little spirals at the corners.

"She cut its head off!" she said. She was elated, holding her hands together, her body shaking against the urge to jump up and down. "She cut its head off!" she repeated it with a sharpness that made her voice break and squeak too loudly.

Startled and embarrassed, she slapped her hand over her own mouth and let herself fall down beside me. She grabbed my arm, squeezed her tiny fingers around it and smiled. But I could tell by her popping eyes, round and fierce, that she was terrified. Still, she smiled.

With her close, warm against me in the wet grass, I was starting to feel better. I shimmied myself closer. We waited in silence like two taut rubber bands and it wasn't until Christina finally sighed that we were both able to let our muscles relax again. Christina started to giggle.

"Come on." She stopped giggling enough to stand up. "Let's go get it."

I shook my head and told her I wanted to stay on the ground until morning. She pulled me up anyway.

"Come on." She grunted.

"Where?"

"To go get it," she said, as if it was the normal thing to do.

I shook my head again but she pulled me along, adding, "It's fine. We've got the bullet."

We moved through the yard, crouched and creeping like hermit crabs through the wet grass.

Our mother's blue windbreaker swooshed and swayed as Christina tried desperately to move inside of it. The fur shawl I was wearing was muddy and heavy with dew. Still, we had the bullet. We kept moving.

I searched again for the blue light, but it was gone. I tapped Christina on the shoulder as I followed behind her. I wanted to ask her if she had seen it, if she knew what it was, but she just brought a finger to her lips and flapped her other hand back toward me. Then she folded it into a fist that she shook at my chin, so I stopped.

After what felt like forever, we reached the house and settled ourselves next to a basement window that was set low to the ground. We crouched next to it. Christina pointed and smiled.

Down through the window, we could see a large, scratched, worn-out worktable – bigger than either of us was tall – and on the edge, tilted to its side and staring idly off into the darkness, was the one-eyed, severed head of the witch's camel.

I shrieked, wide-eyed. Christina shot a hand up to cover my mouth. With a gruff voice she scolded me. "I'll kill ya."

I nodded that I understood and she slowly pulled her hand away. I looked through the window again. The head sat alone on the worktable, teetering on the edge. I recognized it, the soup-can-tongue, the medicine-bottle-eyelids, the round metal nostrils, but, alone, without the rest of the body pouring off of it, it no longer seemed familiar.

A single light dangled from the ceiling and swayed lazily from side to side. There were little bits of metal, plastic and other things, tiny and round, fat and square, some big like nectarines, others very small scattered on the workbench, so that only little pinpricks of light reflected their presence. Everything else in the room was merely the presence of clutter cloaked in darkness. Just looking in through the window, the room felt crowded, but all was black.

Suddenly the sound of footsteps creaking down a long staircase that was out of our view made us jump and we both turned away on either side of the window, splashing our backs up against the wall, our hands spread out to hold us there. Someone was in the basement. I saw Christina close her eyes and roll her lips as if sending up a prayer before she turned back to the window to grab a quick look, then darted back to her position against the wall. She mouthed to me at the other side.

"The mute!" She whispered it with joy and terror and fascination.

I closed my eyes, curled my lips, and then *swish-swish*, like a broom stroke I glanced in the window and then fell back again. What I had seen had only been a blur, a ghost of an image, but was no less terrifying than I had expected. A man – *a giant!* – with a bald head and a face that slanted violently to the left so that the corner of the lip hugged the chin and the weight of the slack pulled extra meat down over the eye. I shook my head again, but Christina pulled me toward her and the two of us rolled flat on our stomachs and peered through the window to watch.

The mute had on a heavy black apron and thick, worn and stained welding gloves that stretched tightly over his enormous hands. He held the head of the Witch's camel to the light, rotating it and cocking his head so that his right eye could get a better look.

I wanted to tell Christina that we should leave, run and get out of there, but she raised a finger to her lips and shook her head before I had a chance to say anything.

Then the Mute seemed to hear something coming from upstairs. His neck twisted and he let the hand with the camel's head fall, resting it on the table. After another moment he had set the head down, removed his gloves, and left the room. We heard the heavy footsteps ascend the staircase.

Before I had a chance to move, Christina leaned forward and pushed at the window. It opened easily and with only the tiniest chirp of un-oiled protest.

I shook my head no again, but Christina was already halfway in, headfirst. The rest of her body slid down into the basement like egg yolk and she was gone. In an instant, she was in the center of the room, near the heavy table, waving me in.

I climbed through the window awkwardly, feet first, my butt bumping against the glass. I kicked around slowly until my feet found solid footing on a flat shelf that was low on the wall. Letting the rest of my body slide in, my stomach scraped against the chipped up window frame and when I tried to let myself fall the rest of the way, the fur shawl flew up over the back of my head and I was stuck, the latch of the window holding onto the heavy wet cape. My face pushed against the cold concrete wall, and I hung there, kicking in the darkness.

The hands that felt around behind my head were small and familiar. Christina gently removed the clump of cheap rabbit fur that had wedged itself under the sliding lock of the swinging window. The sudden release caused me to fall into Christina's arms. She lowered me safely to the ground, then punched me in the shoulder and made a wrinkled face of complete annoyance.

The basement was packed with strips, clumps, coils and crates made out of all types of materials. Wires of every thickness, some new, some corroded and chipping heavy flakes of green and red, hung like drooping necklines from the ceiling. The rust and dust, the frigid air and chemical vapors from open cans of varnish and paint and whatever else, gave the air a chilled, mealy texture, like rotted up apples. Sticky, soft, and cold.

"Don't touch anything," Christina whispered. I nodded and she turned toward the workbench in the center of the room. "Look at all this stuff. I bet we could find something great to blow that bullet to smithereens with." Her eyes rolled with wonderment. "Cover me."

I held up the bullet and she nodded. She crept into the blackness, leaving me behind. My heart beat heavy; the air so thin that my breath came out in short gasps. I let my eyes wander over the junk and the trash, the piles and the heaps, the shelves of tin cans curved over at the top with nuts and bolts and other heavy metal shapes. As my eyes adjusted to the dark, more wonders and oddities smoked into view only to fade away, blinking themselves in and out of existence, back into the background of twisted carnage that lined every wall.

All but one, that is. A shape, a hint of bright color, was slow to appear to me in the far corner. Long and tall, but tiny too, a seven-inch shape that sat still, high up and out of place. I moved toward it without thinking. Closer and closer, all the time rolling the bullet in my hand.

I had to climb onto a low shelf near the basement's far window to finally be at eye level with it. Before me, posed rigidly on a plain wooden pedestal and encased in newly-polished glass, was the most perfectly beautiful ballerina.

The torso was pushed up straight at a low point in the back. The arms shot straight out at acute angles from the shoulders and the legs were pressed perfectly together and wrapped in fine white stockings.

Her hair was gold, fine and very real. The features, rosy and delicate, gave the impression that a complex network of muscles would at any second roll the kind, little, candy-red smirk into a full and bright smile. Much of it was still cast in shadow, though. I tapped at the side of the glass. A noise like a coin rolling, a gear shifting and then a sharp *click* hummed out of it. A bright baby-blue light, warm and safe, poured out from underneath and bobbed playfully over the ballerina as she began to turn. She spun slowly and elegantly, but seemed lopsided and unhappy.

That's when I finally noticed her hands. They were giant hands, at least three sizes too large, with fat, knotted-up knuckles and thick, heavy palms. They were so huge and grotesque, in fact, that it was a wonder they weren't the first things I noticed. Their presence seemed to weigh down the shoulders and justify what now seemed to be a look of complete surprise and embarrassment on the milky face. Still, she spun beautifully, noiselessly on the pedestal, while the warmness of the blue light winked through the sparkles of the pink tutu.

"Holy damn!" I heard Christina from across the room. She came out of the darkness and stood under the swaying light above the workbench wearing a dusty medieval knight's helmet over her head. She had the visor pulled down, her arms stretched out. Standing like that in the blue windbreaker, she looked like a peacock.

"This place is awesome!" she exclaimed and even though it was muted and muffled from inside the helmet, her voice was still way too loud. I cringed from my perch in front of the spinning ballerina. She removed her helmet and, holding it between her arm and waist, cocked an eyebrow at me.

"What's that thing?" she said, pointing above my shoulder.

"Isn't it neat?" I whispered.

"Looks pretty dumb."

I wanted to wave her over and show her how gorgeous it was and how weird the hands looked. I wanted to tell her that just because I was looking at something it didn't mean that it was dumb, just because I found something cool didn't mean she couldn't at least give it a chance. I was angry now, madder than ever and suddenly I didn't care how many times she would probably hit me. I wanted to tell her all sorts of things, yell all sorts of things, but before I could open my mouth–before I could say anything–a heavy hand fell out of the darkness behind Christina and landed on her shoulder.

She shrieked and I fell back, startled, against the shelf where my weight pulled loose the rotted nails, and brought the whole mess crashing down to the floor on top of me. There was a heavy sound, like hot breath from a dragon and then Christina struggling and shouting.

"Let me go! Let me go!"

I couldn't see anything. A heavy slab of wood had fallen on me, nearly crushing my head, stopped only by a knocked over paint can on the floor. I kicked at the debris. All the while, I heard the rustling of Christina's jacket and the kicking of her feet. I pushed and pulled my way through the pile. Nearly free, I found that my cape of tattered and stained fur was again latched on something. It pulled at my neck when I tried to stand, pressing down on my throat. I slid out of it and leaped to my feet, dropping the fur shawl on the ground.

The mute was even taller than he had seemed when we saw him through the window. His eyes, squinted and veiled in blackness, were above the hanging light. He held one of his raw, blackened hands over Christina's mouth, his free arm hanging big and beefy at his side. Christina was struggling, holding herself off the ground, both hands gripped around the mute's fat wrist. His hand covered her whole face, but through the spread fingers I could see one of her eyes, big, blue and terrified.

Again I felt the bullet; it was still in my hand, still rolling in my palm's oily sweat. Without thinking, without knowing what else to do, I held my arm back behind my head, squinted my eyes and took careful aim before launching it, straight and true, hard and fast, so that the follow-through nearly toppled me forward. The bullet glided through the air, spinning slowly.

It struck the mute in the chest, just below the neck and then fell dumbly to the floor. Christina continued to kick. I could see that her face was turning red, her eyes full of fear.

The mute's head seemed to tilt down and his dark eyes fell on the bullet rolling lazily in an awkward circle on the floor. A thick and horrifying hum came out of his mouth. He dropped Christina. She slid out of his arm and fell to the floor, hands on the ground, struggling to catch her breath.

I ran over to her. My heart was racing, icy sweat dripped from my forehead. I helped her up and we ran to the window. I started to climb, but felt a tug on my shirt. When I looked back, Christina was pointing behind us.

The mute, ignoring us completely now, was holding the bullet between his giant thumb and forefinger, admiring it in the light with a squinted eye, as though it were a diamond.

The air seemed to grow calmer then. We moved slowly as we made our escape. Careful to exit on tiptoe, helping each other up and out without a word, as though exiting the room of a fussy child finally lost to sleep.

Once out, I looked back for the blue light one last time and was able to catch a quick glimpse of it, a twirl of it before it blinked and disappeared forever. We walked casually through the yard, lifted ourselves over the fence, and ran like hell for home.

That night I could hardly sleep. I kept seeing the Mute's big fat hands in the shadows on my bedroom wall. I kept hearing his heavy breaths blowing against my window. Twice I got up and crept into the hallway. I stood in front of Christina's door and listened. I got cold and shaky. I wanted to knock on her door, but I went back into my own room and hid under the covers.

When I did finally fall asleep, I dreamed of the ballerina and the blue light. Thousands of ballerinas spun, life-size in a great room made of rusty metal. I started to walk toward one of them, the blue light dancing. The ballerina was Christina in the pink tutu. She was trapped in the rigid pose, arms out, legs together. Glass shattered. There were more of them, some of them looked like me; most were Christina. All were struggling with a worried look to move from their perfectly stiff positions. Some fell forward from the weight of the enormous hands.

The air filled with smoke. I kept my eyes on the original, on Christina. She was crying, terrified and she yelled for me to help her. She yelled and yelled and I fell backwards as she glided toward me, ghost-like now, a blur, and when I tried to get up, something caught me around the neck. I sat forward to stand but it gripped tighter and pulled me back down. She was in trouble, I could tell. Her lips moved. "Help me, you dweeb." But the sound of her voice went quiet. I didn't know how or why, but I had to get to her.

The next morning, I awoke with the sheet wrapped around my neck and both my pillows kicked onto the floor. When I went to find Christina, she was not in her room. Searching the house for her I noticed that the back door was open. In the yard, I spotted her standing in the alley, still in her pajamas. I walked over and stood next to her. She was staring into the Witch's yard, not smiling, not frowning. She held her chin high and had her head turned to one side.

She stood with her arms crossed and stared at the witch's camel. It stood like it always stood, lazy and bored, as though it had never left. I stared too. Everything was as it had been: the body made of strips of car doors, the tail a coiled spring, the right eye a smoothed, polished penny. And there, in the gaping hole where the emptiness of the missing left eye once winked darkness, was the bullet, shined up brighter than before and poked out so that its copper head pointed right at us.

Christina laughed a little. I shuffled up to the fence and slowly climbed over.

"What are you doing?" Christina hollered, but I just ignored her and stood barefoot in the wet grass before the camel and the bullet. I reached up and pulled. The bullet gave easily. I held it between my thumb and forefinger. It shone in the early morning light.

"Well, take it and let's go," Christina shouted.

The bullet seemed smaller than before, and lighter. It seemed useless to take it, so I just reached up and pushed it back into place. When I looked back to the alley Christina was already walking back toward the house.

Raven's Transformation
BY
Melissa Carmichael

Melissa's love of writing grew out of her passion for reading, her tastes leaning toward urban fantasy. Besides writing, she enjoys sketching, hiking, and riding her motorcylce. She is currently working on a novel.

My head was throbbing in time with the ticking of a nearby clock and my eyelids felt like they weighed a ton. I didn't own a clock. That was my first clue that told me I wasn't home in my bed.

Eyes still closed, I tried to sit up and clear my head at the same time. That only managed to induce a rippling wave of dizziness followed by nausea. That was my second clue. This felt like a hangover but I don't drink. I hadn't been a drinker before or even after I died.

Unlike the hundreds of poor souls that frequented the local bars and nightclubs, finding their excitement or self-worth in the bottom of a bottle, I didn't need drugs or alcohol for an adrenaline rush. I worked as an enforcer for Damien, the most powerful vampire on the east coast.

Slowly my dizziness abated and my head stopped spinning. I opened my eyes and found myself completely enveloped in darkness. I'm not afraid of the darkness. I need the darkness to survive. Now the sun, that's a different story. Just thinking about getting caught by the dawn is enough to make most vampires cringe.

After several minutes, I took a deep breath and managed to push up onto my elbows without feeling like I was going to puke. My arms trembled in protest as I straightened them. I could barely support my own weight.

I had to wait a few seconds before my night vision kicked in. It seemed like it was taking forever. Normally, my night vision is intact from the moment I wake but this wasn't a normal night. I had no idea where I was or who had brought me here.

Blurred objects gradually came into focus and my vampire eyesight navigated the darkness with no problem. My eyes met nothing familiar. I was lying in a massive bed in an oversized bedroom. That was all I was able to make out at the moment.

I ran my fingers lightly over the headboard. It was made of thick wood with deeply cut carvings in it. Over in the corner of the room was an oval, full-length mirror. Half of the bedroom was just a normal bedroom, with a bed and nightstand. The other half was set up like a study, complete with an old-fashioned secretary's desk. A floor-to-ceiling bookcase filled with leatherbound books stood behind the desk. *Where the hell was I?*

My nostrils flared, smelling the room and tasting the air. The only familiar scent was my own blood. I spotted my torn, bloody leathers hanging over the back of an old oak chair beside the bed. The hilt of my short sword was leaning against the side of the chair, still inside its leather sheath. That gave me pause. Whoever had brought me here either didn't see me as a threat or didn't want me to consider them one. Either way, that told me that they weren't intimidated by me or who I worked for.

The covers fell away as I sat up. I was naked except for the silk sheets that had been covering me.

I ran my hand gingerly over my body, counting six wounds on my torso. Most of them felt pretty superficial but a deep stab wound on my lower right abdomen was oozing blood. A scab had already started to form.

I leaned back against the headboard of the massive bed. I couldn't remember how I had gotten my wounds or who had gave them to me. Working for Damien, I figured I had probably pissed somebody off and that somebody had kicked my ass. It wasn't the first time I'd had my ass handed back to me, but it had been a while.

I'm not used to being the one getting her ass kicked. Yep, I was more of the ass-kicking type and I was pretty damn good at it.

My abdominal muscles tightened when I touched the stab wound. I was glad most of my wounds had already started to heal, but they didn't seem to be healing as fast as they normally did and that worried me. How long had I been out?

My body felt like I'd gone a couple of rounds with Mike Tyson. I knew I would survive but I needed blood. I also needed to know where I was and who brought me here.

Pushing off the bed I doubled over with a sudden sharp pain in my right side. I pressed my hands into my side panting as my eyesight went almost completely black before returning to normal.

Leaning and still clutching my side, I reached for my leathers then stopped, noting a shot glass filled to the rim with blood on the marble-topped nightstand. I picked it up, tasting its scent. I didn't recognize it and set it back down, careful not to spill any of it on me. The blood was still warm. Someone had obviously left it for me.

The dizziness and nausea were gone, but my head still throbbed. I wiped a bead of sweat from my forehead with the back of my hand and made small circles with my fingertips on my temples to soothe my headache, trying to ignore the rising craving for blood. I forced myself to focus on my present predicament.

Someone had rescued me, provided blood to feed me and taken care to ensure my safety from the dawn. But who? Why? Who would have saved me: a vampire? Another vampire house would have killed me if they had the opportunity and the guts—but not rescue me. No. This just didn't make any sense. The situation didn't feel right.

I didn't feel right for that matter. My body felt weird. It felt different, like you feel when you sit on your leg and cut off the circulation...and then the blood rushes through your leg, sending prickles and tingles down it. My whole body was tingling! I definitely needed to find answers about what was going on.

With that thought in mind, I forced myself into motion and started exploring the room. Even in the dark, I knew my host had expensive taste. The high-backed bed would have looked right at home at the Biltmore Estates I stayed in last year while handling some of my master's more delicate business deals with a rival house. Whoever lived here had money. A lot of money.

Padding barefoot across the room, I came to a pair of heavy double doors fixed with intricate carvings around the borders of figures either in battle or lust. Even with my excellent vision in pitch darkness, I couldn't tell which it was.

Surprisingly light, the doors swung open with a slight push to reveal an oversized walk-in closet, completely outfitted with clothes I would have chosen: leather jumpsuits, jeans and tons of motorcycle gear. I touched the nearest jumpsuit, admiring its supple feel under my fingertips and absent-mindedly flipped over the tag that was still attached. It was my size. I checked a second, third and fourth; they were all my size!

I quickly backed out of the closet, closing the door behind me. I needed to remember what had happened. I closed my eyes and forced my thoughts back to the night before.

Slowly, then with increasing speed, memories flashed though my mind with burning intensity until I thought my already throbbing head would explode from pressure.

My eyes shot open as I remembered being attacked. I was on a run for my master against another house. Yes… I and the other enforcers had been attacked. Nick was dead! That I knew for sure. He had been beheaded. One of the only sure ways to kill a vampire for good was to decapitate it. I remembered seeing the flash from a sword before Nick pushed me to the ground, causing the blade to miss me by inches but costing him his existence.

I clenched my jaw, my body trembling with anger as I silently swore to hunt down Nick's assassin and make him beg for a quick death. Nick had been like a brother to me. He had taught me everything I knew about being an enforcer. Yeah, whoever killed him would definitely be answering to me. When I got out of here, I'd be asking my master for a little time off to take care of some personal business.

Exacting revenge would have to wait. I would grieve for Nick later. Right now was about survival. Mine. Where were the other house enforcers that had been on the run with Nick and I? I was out of my element and alone. Now I was here. Which was where exactly?

I could feel my heart pounding in my throat as I tried to make sense of what had happened and how I was going to get out of this. I had to handle first things first. I needed blood to recover. I frowned at the blood-filled shot glass sitting on the nightstand. I didn't know its source and I wasn't about to drink it, injured or not.

I grabbed my bloodied leathers, finding comfort holding something familiar. I fingered the torn material, wondering if it would spark more memories but quickly realized there was no time for that right now. I had to put my desire for answers aside. There would be time for that later, after I got out of here and found the others.

I found my cell phone still in my right hip pocket. Damn, covered with blood and cracked to hell. That wasn't going to do me any good.

I didn't think meeting a potential enemy naked was a good idea so I slid into my jumpsuit with a practiced precision. Mid-zip I stopped.

"Oh shit!" I exclaimed. "I've got a heartbeat? How the hell can I have a heartbeat?"

I flipped the light switch on the wall over the nightstand with trembling hands. I was more concerned about my latest discovery than the safety the darkness could have provided at that point.

I crossed the room to stand in front of a full-length mirror by a window covered with closed, heavy drapes. My skin was no longer colorless, or lifeless! My long onyx hair now framed a tan, vibrant living face as it cascaded past my shoulders full of body . I didn't even look like a vampire anymore.

I held my hands in front of me; I was tan down to my fingertips. I reached out to touch the image but stopped short. I touched my face instead and found it warm and inviting. Sliding my fingertips down to the hollow of my throat I found a strong pounding pulse. The tingling I'd felt…it must have been my heart pumping, circulating blood through my body.

Panic gripped me until my tongue slid over my teeth and found that my vampire canines were still intact. Thank God! I let out a long shaky breath that I hadn't realized I had been holding.

Fear, something I hadn't felt in a very long time started to slither over me, and I backed into a corner wrapping my arms around myself. I didn't know what was happening or what this meant for me. I had never known or heard of anything like this happening to a vampire before.

Once you became a vampire, that's what you were, immortal, strong, predatory, and almost invincible, but definitely dead. Not tan with a beating heart. I had to get out of here…back to my master. He'd help me. He'd know what to do. God, I hoped so. Did I just call on God? I knew I was really freaking out. Vampires don't have souls.

The sound of soft footfalls caught my attention and my eyes turned on the bedroom door as it swung open. A slight creak from the oak door as it opened ripped a low, rumbling growl from my gut. I instinctively fell into a defensive stance.

The door revealed a slender, caramel-skinned woman with large almond-shaped amber eyes. She was dressed from head-to-toe in black leather.

"What have you done to me?" I growled.

The woman in black smiled, revealing two small pointed canines on her upper and lower teeth. She answered my question with a crooning question. "Is this any way to treat the one who saved your life?"

"Where am I?" I demanded, trying to sound sure of myself and not scared shitless of this woman who was more powerful than anyone I had ever met.

"Home," she said without further explanation.

"What are you?" I whispered.

She threw her head back and laughed; then looked at me and smiled wickedly. "I'm your new master, Raven. Because, the things I have to offer you…you won't be able to refuse. You won't want to. Now, come sit with me and take more of my blood so I can heal you completely." She exposed her throat to me.

My eyes widened as her jacket collar fell away from her neck and I saw two small puncture marks in the caramel-colored skin. They were mine.

Midnight Train
By
Brandon Ford

Novelist Brandon Ford has been putting pen to paper since the age of eight. Since then, he has published two novels, one novella, and multiple short stories in anthologies and magazines. He writes horror and suspence fiction because he is a great admirer of the genre, as well as a respect for the challenge it is to write.

Dimitri's hard, heavy footsteps stomped against the icy ground as he stalked the city streets. He heard the church bells far off in the distance. Eleven chimes of somber passing. A soothing gateway leading into another silent hour of darkness. The moon shone brightly, casting a mysterious glow of angelic white as he scanned his surroundings for precious human life ready to be snatched from grounds unexpected. Deep into the welcoming arms of insanity, death would come.

Soon, death would come. He could taste that life. Taste it on his lips and even smell it in the air. It taunted him, teased him, begged him to capture it.

A stiff wind shivered him to his withering core. Clouds of hot breath passed his lips and sifted into the night. The arctic-like chill left him pining for warmth, but relished memories pushed him onward. Still, he could see the spilt blood of his many previous victims. He could feel their quivering bodies go limp upon meeting his steel blade. Most of all, he could see that look of sheer terror in their frozen stare—a look so unmistakable. That look meant death was near… and they knew.

How many lives he'd taken, he was unsure. He'd lost count long ago. On nights like these, when that notion of merciless menace struck his very being, he could've taken three. Maybe even more. Lord knows he'd spilt the blood of at least a dozen unsuspecting victims on nights just like these.

No, only one tonight. He had to catch the midnight train—the last train back to Hemdale. Dimitri knew when morning came and his eyes opened to the sights and sounds of a brand new day, his first thoughts would lead him back over the bridge, back to where he now stood, and back to releasing savage terror into the lives of those who'd done him no harm. What they'd done didn't matter. It *never* mattered. Who they were, he couldn't have cared less. He just knew he needed someone, *anyone,* to satisfy these primal urges. There was nothing he could've done to alleviate this need, this hunger. He'd tried for so very long, but nothing could ever stop this pressing desire. Nothing but the taste of sweet death.

He saw her then on the other side of the street. Hair as red as the hottest flame. Skin as pure as the freshest milk. A figure too perfect to deny. A backpack dangling over one shoulder, she strode past a university campus, her footsteps the only found echoing in the night. Overjoyed, aroused, and more anxious than words could've ever described, Dimitri hurried across the street and started towards her, staying at least twenty feet behind for fear of being seen. She held an almost childlike bounce in every step, as if she'd walked on air. Her hips swiveled and her hair swayed in the chilling breeze. She didn't see him. Never for one moment did she recognize his mere existence as she continued down the darkened, deserted sidewalks. It was almost as though she were crying out, reaching for death, pulling it towards her, waiting for the moment those determined claws would snatch the life from her. So innocent, and so very vulnerable…

As he watched her, Dimitri licked his lips and felt the beat of his heart multiply. He knew what was coming and he knew how good it was going to feel. He started walking faster, getting closer. Each inch brought him nearer, leaving her closer to the inevitable agony. So close now, he could hear her breathing. This excited him more and more and he could no longer control those urges. Close enough now to inhale the honey scent of her freshly shampooed hair, he held no choice. He *had* to give in to this twisted temptation. He had to taste another's fear once again. Addicted to the rotting stench of death and the cold, heartless grip of unprecedented mayhem, there was nothing that could have stopped him.

He reached out, gripping her hair by its long, curling strands, stopping her from going an inch further. Dimitri dragged her into an alley, listening as her cries rang out. The sounds of her startled shrieks rocketed him into a world of indecipherable bliss. A world only he could understand.

Placing a hand to her mouth, he flattened her against the alley's brick wall, pressing his body against hers so tight she could feel his erection. He leaned in so close, so tight, the tips of their noses grazed one another.

"Don't even breathe," he whispered, keeping his right hand pressed against her quivering mouth.

In an instant, her eyes welled up with tears and he could see the begging and pleading behind them. He could feel her shake and twitch underneath him and only then did he realize, really *realize,* how much pleasure he derived from causing so much pain.

Her hands clasped his wrist as she tried to pry the force pinning her to the wall away. He wouldn't budge. Nothing or no one could've freed her of this grip. He couldn't risk her making another sound. He held tighter, her head pressing against the frozen brick. A mound of soft, curling hair in-hand, he jerked her head forward and then slammed it back against the cold bricks once more. Hard enough to inflict pain, but not hard enough to kill. Her eyes rolled as she moaned in agony, watching the stars surround her and hearing that incessant ringing.

"Don't fight it," he whispered maliciously, leaning in close enough for her to taste his hot breath. "You can't."

The tears began to fall. Streams ran down her face as she fought so hard to release a desperate sob. Dimitri's grip, so hard and firm, allowed no more than a few soft whimpers.

She prayed someone heard. She prayed someone would help. But no one could hear those muffled cries. *No one* could help…

He reached into the front pocket of his wool coat and pulled forth a readied buck knife.

"What are ya gonna use that for, son?" the old man at the hardware store had asked when Dimitri bought it, examining him through thick, wire-rimmed glasses.

"Hunting," Dimitri had stated proudly.

The woman's eyes widened at the sight of that blade. Now, she fought harder than before. With every ounce of strength she had in her, she fought to scream and she fought for freedom.

He laughed, teasing her with the blade, allowing its serrated edge to slide back and forth across her neck. Her tear-filled eyes watched him grip the handle, watched him move the blade.

More terrified than ever before, she could feel the pounding of her heart inside her heaving chest. She would've given anything not to have gone out tonight. The comfort of her own bed felt more like paradise than anything ever had before. She feared it would be a comfort she'd never experience again.

"God, I wish I could hear your voice," Dimitri said. "But I can't allow that. You'll scream, won't you?"

She shook her head vigorously, almost breaking through his grasp. Almost, but not quite.

"Yes, you will." He shook his head. "You'll scream like a stuck pig. So, I guess I'll just have to savor the look in your eyes. The look that tells me you know death is near. The look that tells me you'd give anything to face another day. But you won't. And I'm not going to apologize, if that's what you're expecting. I feel no remorse. I feel no regret. I feel alive in a way you'll never understand. You'll *never* understand, so I won't even begin to describe the thousands of lights burning within me and the surge of empowerment that soothes my very soul. The unmistakable sensation that satisfies my tainted core. So goodnight, my beautiful. Goodnight and goodbye."

He raised the knife, then jabbed it forward into her face, puncturing her left eye socket. He shoved the knife deeper, digging in, hearing the shattering of bone and the rushing fluids. It sprayed and oozed, spilling her skull and all its contents onto the concrete. He released the grip on her mouth, wanting to hear her scream once more. He knew he couldn't return home that night without hearing once last cry. This was the sound that would rock him to sleep. This was the vision he'd see when he closed his eyes.

He retracted the blade and she slumped to the ground. Tearing through the night, he ran from the darkened alley, fleeing through the streets in a maniacal frenzy. Dimitri's breath caught in his throat; he wheezed and panted as he ran.

Far off in the distance, he heard sirens. They were coming. Someone had heard her screams.Someone knew what had happened. Faster and faster. He *had* to get away. He would've stopped at nothing to hold onto his freedom. It was freedom that allowed him to experience this indescribable thrill. Through the streets, he continued until his legs felt drained and weak. When he reached the subway station, he felt alive and vibrant, brimming with a surge of adrenaline. There was nothing else that could've ever made him feel this way.

Down the stairs and into the terminal he disappeared, struggling to catch his breath but unable to hide a smile of blissful content. Dimitri paid the fare, staring the booth attendant straight in the eyes, wondering if she knew what he'd done. It was almost as if he *wanted* her to know. He wanted the whole world to know of his conquests and his savage ability to take lives without remorse or consequence.

Down another flight of stairs, he stood and waited, watching the tracks alongside of him. Silent, he was a lone patron waiting for the evening's final train. The long, stretching tunnels seemed to go on for an eternity. For a split second, he considered venturing down into the darkness, just to see what might await him far beyond.

The screeching of tires and once again, the shrill bellow of a police siren trickled down to him from up above on solid ground. Beyond that, the church bells. Even beneath the surface of the earth, he could hear their joyous call. Twelve distinct chimes.

He turned and there it stood—the train that seemed to have glided across the tracks in midair. Silent, it awaited him. He approached the open doors. This was not the train he'd ridden night after night. Its windows were fogged a pitch black and though he struggled, he couldn't see beyond them. A shell of steel that normally appeared so strong and invincible now seemed frail and tattered.

It all seemed… decayed, withered in the hands of time.

He climbed aboard and regarded the few passengers inhabiting the rows of paired seating. Four miserable souls stared off, not moving, not speaking. The doors closed and the ride began. Dimitri crossed toward an empty seat and sat, nearly toppling over from the force of the train's progress. Barreling down the tracks, it didn't make a sound.

As the train continued on, picking up speed with every yard, the four men began to weep. Burying their sullen faces in quivering hands, they sobbed and moaned like bruised children. As each moment passed, their cries grew louder, their unspeakable agony more and more apparent. Dimitri watched them, confused.

Minutes passed and still, they ventured on, the train pushing onward down a track that seemed to have no end. Further and further, deeper and deeper, faster and faster. Dimitri stood, brushing past the weeping men, starting toward the doors, waiting the moment of full stop. They should've been there by now.

Each minute seemed to last a lifetime. It seemed that no mattered how far they ventured, the end was nowhere near. Panic overcame him and Dimitri reached for the buck knife caked in dried blood. He held on tight, the cold steel comforting him. He charged down the aisles and back again, feeling caged, feeling captured. He wanted out. He needed air. He needed light. He needed to feel the ground beneath his feet again.

Suddenly, he fell to his knees, the knife slipping from his fingertips and sliding down the aisles. The train had stopped. The doors opened. He looked up as the four men stood and made their way out, still sobbing and whimpering.

"Oh, God," one of them moaned. "Oh, sweet Jesus…"

And then they were gone.

Dimitri remained still. Finally, he brought himself to his feet. He started toward the door and stared out. Beyond him stood a cave of bright red, a cavern of burning flames and infinite torture. He saw the four men marching forward, their heads low, their footsteps listless. Each then disappeared, lost in the moans echoing against the jagged rock.

Dimitri stepped out into the dirt. The scalding ground singed his feet. Even through the soles of his thickest hunting boots, he felt the heat and cried out. He turned once again.

The train was gone.

The Lancelot Effect

BY

Mark Finnemore

"I can trace all of our problems back to that one day. Back to that one second actually—the moment Penny saw her kiss me."

Doctor Marshall nodded and scratched some notes into his digital notepad. "This other woman, why did you kiss her?"

Jack Paladin frowned at the doctor's image on his computer screen. He considered breaking the connection, but this guy was his last chance to keep Penny from leaving him.

"I didn't kiss her," Paladin said. "She kissed me. On the cheek. Not even a real kiss."

Marshall looked up from his notepad. "And why did you and Penny get married with this problem unresolved?"

Paladin hadn't noticed before, but Marshall had a vague accent—British, maybe, or Austrian. It sounded fake; probably digitally-enhanced in a failed attempt to make his voice sound more soothing.

"I thought it was resolved," Paladin said. "She hadn't brought it up lately. I figured getting married meant she agreed it was nothing."

Marshall nodded. "Why were you with this other woman?"

Paladin sighed. Marshall seemed slow to grasp the point here. What did he expect from a guy Roxanne had found online at PsychiatryConnection.com? Rumor was some guy in Florida had licensed his iguana as a therapist just by paying the state fifty bucks. These days, who knew what was what?

"She's not 'this other woman'," Paladin retorted. "She's my ex-wife."

"Oh?" Marshall pushed up his glasses. "Tell me more."

Paladin shook his head. "It was nothing. She just needed my help."

"What do you suppose came first, Mr. Paladin, the damsel-in-distress or the knight in shining armor?"

Paladin stared at the doctor on his screen. "What the hell, Doc? I got serious problems here and you give me riddles?"

"Did she really need your help?" Marshall asked. "Or did you need to help her?"

Outside Paladin's window a lawnmower revved loudly. He pushed the curtain aside. As Marshall waited silently, Paladin watched his neighbor's new maintenance bot push the mower across the lawn. He shook his head. Damned waxers weren't even reliable yet; the SPCA already had a flood of reports about accidentally-minced cats.

Paladin dropped the curtain and turned back to his computer. "Listen, Doc, I don't mean to be rude, but that's not the problem here. The problem is Penny thinks we were kissing and I can't convince her she's wrong. What I need you to do is erase the event from her mind so everyone can move forward and live happily ever after."

Marshall frowned. "Erasing memories isn't safe, Mr. Paladin. There are just too many other memories built around the offending memory to make it feasible, not without damaging the subject's underlying personality."

"But she's gonna leave me, Doc!"

"I am sorry to hear that. Maybe I should refer you to my partner for relationship counseling?"

Paladin wasn't a psychologist, but he'd learned plenty about reading people. Clearly Marshall and his partner didn't want to lose a sale here. "I would love that, Doc, but unfortunately I don't have the time right now with my business picking up. I'm sure you and your partner can understand that?"

Marshall nodded.

Paladin smiled. "And since delegation is the key to successful time management, I'm delegating this to you. I know you can do it."

Marshall waved his hand. "But I'm not—"

"You're a pharma-psychologist, so you are the right man for the job. And money isn't a problem. I'll double your fee. I'll triple it! And as a consultant for some top firms, I know lots of other busy people who don't have the time to spend months talking about their feelings and their childhood and all that. If you do a good job here, it'll mean big business for you and your partner, Doc—huge business!"

Marshall's expression softened. "Well, maybe a synth-ox regimen would work."

Paladin frowned.

"Synthetic oxytocin," Marshall explained. "Oxytocin is a hormone that creates the attachment between infant and mother and vice-versa. Synth-ox harnesses that maternal instinct to make people more trusting and attached to others. It's used mainly in adoption cases, but it might work here."

Paladin leaned forward. "This'll make Penny trust me again?"

Marshall shook his head. "It won't make her trust you; it enhances the natural trust between people. To quantify it, let's say that after this kissing incident Penny trusts you sixty-five percent. Ideally, synth-ox therapy can increase that to ninety-five percent when combined with—"

"A thirty-percent boost in trust!"

"Up to thirty percent," Marshall corrected. "If properly administered you should be able to count on a twenty-percent, um, 'boost', at the very least."

Paladin leaned back. "This is great, Doc! Perfect! Let's do it!"

Marshall pushed up his glasses. "Synth-ox is administered via scent, so I can transmit a program for your computer's scent-emitters, but I recommend incense, or, even better, candles combined with a romantic dinner to add some organic feelings to the equation."

Paladin held up a hand. "Just go ahead and send me the scent program."

* * *

The smell of brewing coffee and toasting bread drifted into Jack Paladin's office via his computer's scent-emitters. Doctor Marshall probably meant the smells to be soothing, but it just reminded Paladin that he hadn't eaten.

"Good morning, Mr. Paladin."

Paladin shook his head. "No, Doc, unfortunately it's not. That ox-stuff didn't work. Penny still doesn't trust me."

Marshall looked over the top of his steel-rimmed glasses. "As we discussed before, this isn't a magic potion. Oxytocin only gives you up to a thirty percent trust 'boost', to use your term. You still have to earn Penny's trust and build on it."

Paladin sighed and ran his fingers through his hair. "I guess we need to try something else then."

"Have you considered trying this the old fashioned way—you know, with love and caring and communication?" It might be Paladin's imagination, but it seemed Marshall kicked the fake accent up a notch when it suited him. Definitely digitally-enhanced. "Have I mentioned that my partner is a fully-qualified relationship counselor?"

Paladin held up a hand. "I don't have time for that right now, Doc. I wish I did, but I don't."

Marshall leaned forward and tented his fingers. "Maybe we should give you the synth-ox as well. Maybe that would help you develop more loving feelings toward Penny."

"You're not giving me that stuff!" Paladin pushed back his chair. "And anyway, I already do love Penny."

"If you love Penny so much, who's she?" Marshall's finger thrust out of the screen to point behind Paladin.

Paladin turned. Behind him stood a buxom brunette in a tight black skirt and a white blouse that showed more cleavage than was, strictly speaking, professional. Paladin laughed. "That's not a who, Doc, that's a what. That's just Roxanne, my Holographic Personal Assistant. I couldn't run my business without her. Delegation's the key to successful time management, you know."

Marshall nodded. "So you've said. But why settle for a

holograph? They make remarkably natural-looking android bodies these days. You can hardly tell the difference."

Paladin shook his head. "From what I hear the programming's still wonky. Guy down in Atlanta last month, his waxer went berserk and—"

"Nonsense!" Marshall waved a dismissive hand. "Horror stories propagated by ignorance. And must you use the term *waxer*? It's very offensive."

Roxanne's image faded away with a scowl and a mumbled curse, but Paladin didn't notice.

"Let's just get back to the issue here," Paladin said. "What're we gonna do about Penny?"

Marshall shrugged. "Well, I suppose in addition to continuing the synth-ox regimen—and I suggest you try the dinner and the candles this time—we could also try implanted memories."

"You said erasing memories was too dangerous. Adding them isn't?"

"It's complicated." Marshall pushed up his glasses. "The brain still isn't fully understood. But think of a computer. You've added software programs onto your computer, right? It's easy. The program knows what to do and installs itself where it needs to go. But try to take one out and it's spread itself into everything and it's a big mess. Sometimes the computer never works the same after."

Paladin nodded. He'd had to re-boot Roxanne just last month after he tried to make some alterations to her new upgrades.

"Implanted memories are mostly used for eating disorders," Marshall continued. "We introduce two types of memories: unpleasant ones about unhealthy foods, and pleasant ones about healthy foods like fruits and vegetables. In your case I thought we'd implant Penny with more pleasant memories about you."

"Sounds good," Paladin said. "So, how do we do it?"

"We can't do this over the Hypernet," Marshall said. "Penny will have to come to my office."

"She'll never agree."

"Tell her I'm your relationship counselor. She'll think you're making an attempt at change."

* * *

Doctor Marshall looked at Paladin over the rims of his glasses, as if reluctant to view him in focus. “How are things going with Penny?”

Paladin frowned. “Not good, Doc. And now she hates my HPA for some reason.”

“Ah, yes, Roxanne,” Marshall said. “I wonder why Penny would hate her.”

“Exactly. I mean it’s just lights and electronics for Pete’s sake!” Paladin shook his head and snorted. “She did speak highly of you though.”

“Did she?” Marshall raised an eyebrow. “Well, you know you can program your HPA as a man, or at very least a more appropriately-dressed woman. Mine’s set up as a talking rabbit.”

“This isn’t a joke, Doc, this is my life. Be serious.”

“I am serious,” Marshall said. “I’ve met Penny several times during our memory implant sessions and she’s a remarkable woman—beautiful, intelligent, funny. I can’t believe she’s the cause of all your relationship problems. And she doesn’t deserve to be treated like she is. Maybe you need to look at yourself.”

Paladin shook his head. “I tell you, Doc, she’s being the unreasonable one here. She’s like an unforgiving computer—she remembers everything! Every time some little thing comes up, she drags up every other little thing that ever happened!”

“Like the kiss you didn’t participate in.”

“Exactly!” Paladin said. “It’s like it’ll never go away no matter what I do. You see I’m trying here, right?”

“Have you tried apologizing?”

Paladin coughed out a humorless laugh. “Of course! Hundreds of times. But she still won’t let it go. Me, I’m over it; it’s in the past. But she can’t move forward.”

Marshall sighed. “What do you think you should do?”

“Well, how about that thing you mentioned the first day,” Paladin said, “the thing about erasing memories?”

Marshall shook his head. “I told you that was extremely dangerous.”

Paladin nodded. "But you could do it?"

Marshall pushed up his glasses. "You'd risk damaging Penny's personality?"

Paladin shrugged. "Her current one isn't helping."

Sunlight coming through Doctor Marshall's window lanced through Paladin's monitor and into his eyes, increasing an already-pounding headache. "You little sneak!"

"What do you mean, Mr. Paladin?"

Paladin stabbed his finger at Marshall's image. "You know what I mean. You stole my wife with all your oxy-what's-it and memory implants!"

Marshall shook his head. "That's not it at all. You were willing to sacrifice Penny's well-being for your own selfish needs. I couldn't let that happen."

Paladin threw up his hands. "You stole my wife and you're blaming me?"

"You've got a lot of personal issues to work on," Marshall said in his infuriatingly-soothing accent. "I urge you to see my partner. You'll be a happier man. Trust me."

"Trust you?" Paladin cocked his head toward the scent-emitters on his computer. "You used your synth-ox on me! You drugged me, made me screw it up with Penny so you could steal her away! That was your plan all along!"

Marshall spread his hands in appeal. "Mr. Paladin, you know your problems with Penny started long before you hired me. That's why you hired me. Now listen. Please. I'm trying to help you. You should talk to my partner, Doctor Chevalier."

Doctor Chevalier scratched some notes into his digital notepad and then looked over the rims of his glasses. "Tell me what happened. Start from the beginning."

"I thought I was rescuing her. At least that's what I told myself. I convinced myself I was her knight in shining armor, but maybe I was just a selfish thief."

Chevalier pushed up his glasses. "You realize how ridiculous this is, don't you?"

"Yes." Marshall pushed up his own glasses and nodded. "Not only did I fall victim to the Lancelot Effect, but with a client's wife for Pete's sake!"

"That's not what I'm talking about." Chevalier shook his head. "I'm talking about the fact that you're just my android personal assistant. You're just a machine."

Chevalier terminated the program and Marshall's synthetic body slumped over. What a terrible mess this all was. Obviously some of the program's settings were out of whack. Maybe the financial-incentive priority was set too high? Maybe the ethical priorities were too low? But he wasn't a computer programmer. He couldn't have known.

He should sue the software company, that's what he should do! Better yet, he should sue the consultant who'd convinced him that delegation was the key to successful time management. He dug through his wallet and pulled out a business card: Paladin Consulting. A good attorney should be able to come up with some sort of transfer of liability theory to pass on at least some of the responsibility here to Jack Paladin.

But he hoped this wouldn't reflect badly on Mr. Paladin's assistant, Roxanne. She'd seemed like a bright young girl with plenty of potential. Sure, she obviously had some self-esteem and body-image confusion, but maybe he could offer her a job, help her find herself?

Chevalier's secretary buzzed him on the intercom. "Excuse me sir, but there's a Penny here to see Dr. Marshall. She says it's extremely urgent."

"Penny?" The name sounded vaguely familiar. Whoever she was, he couldn't just ignore a woman in need. "All right; send her in."

Mister Checkers
by
Murphy Edwards

Edwards has appeared in over fifty professional magazines and journals including "Dimensions Magazine," "The East Side Edition," "Horizons," "MidAtlantic Monthly," "Walking Bones," and most recently in "Escaping Elsewhere," Hardboiled Magazine," and "Samsara, The Magazine of Suffering."

Packs of sugar were always available at the Burger Hut. White granules, glistening and sweet. Tony used them to bait the ants. He sprinkled the sidewalk and waited patiently. Two, eight, a dozen. Soon there were too many to count. He pulled a magnifying glass from his pocket, aimed its glare at the largest swarm, and let the sun do its work. It was Saturday and Tony had all day to play. By afternoon the sidewalk looked like a tiny battlefield. Dead ants littered the hot concrete. The undead quivered for relief. Tony slipped the magnifying glass back in his shirt pocket and sat back on the front lawn admiring his work.

"Tony, lunch is ready!"

Tony waved at his mother standing on the front porch. "Okay, Ma. I'm coming."

He scuffed his foot across the charred ant carcasses and ran to the house, whacking his dog Jax on the head as he napped in the porch swing. Jax let out a painful yelp and scurried off the porch.

"Tony, you need to stop being mean to Jax."

Tony wrinkled his freckled nose and stuck his tongue out at his sister Katie. "I didn't do anything. Besides, he likes it."

"He doesn't like it! You tease him, you scare him, and you're being mean!"

Tony smacked his sister on the ear and sat down to his bologna sandwich.

"Mom, he's doing it again!" She brushed her long red hair out of her face and rubbed the back of her ear.

"Am not! Katie started it!"

"Now, you two. I've had a busy morning and I still have to clean the living room. Stop bickering and eat your lunch!"

Tony swung his feet wildly under the table, landing a toe squarely on Katie's shin.

"Ouch! Mom!"

"Tony! You stop kicking, and Katie, you stop yelling!"

Tony munched his sandwich and smirked at Katie. Bits of lettuce and globs of mayo dropped from the corners of his mouth.

Katie stirred her tomato soup, waiting for it to cool. "Mom, I need two dollars for my school project Monday, remember?"

"Yes, dear, I put it in an envelope and taped it to the side of the fridge."

Tony gulped down milk while watching a fly crawl across the table. He snatched it up in his hand, plucked the wings off, and dropped them in Katie's bowl.

"Mom, Tony put fly wings in my soup!"

"Honestly, Katie. Why would he do a thing like that?"

"Because, he's mean."

"She's making it up. She always makes stuff up. She does it to get attention."

"Tony! Katie! Eat your lunch and hush!"

"But Mom, he..."

"Enough! Eat your soup or it will be there for your supper!"

Katie gagged down a spoonful of soup and desperately searched through the broth for the fly wings.

Tony belched and wiped his mouth on his sleeve. "Well, I

gotta go."

"Sit back down, young man. Aren't you forgetting something?"

"Sorry Mom. May I be excused?"

"Yes, you may."

He jumped up and smacked Katie on the other ear, snatching the envelope off the side of the fridge on his way out. Jumping on his bike, he rode the two blocks to Johnny's Grocery and headed straight for the candy rack.

"Hey, big spender," Johnny grunted from behind the counter.

"Hi, Mister Gaston."

"More baseball cards, huh? Got some new ones in yesterday."

Tony picked out four packs and tossed them up on the counter.

"Okay. That'll be four twenty with tax."

Tony pulled Katie's school money from the envelope and added it to the stash he had pinched from his mother's change purse. "Here ya go."

Outside, Tony unwrapped the cards and tossed the wrappers to the curb. He waited until he was around the corner to eat the candy bars he'd pocketed from the rack at Johnny's.

Sunday. Tony wanted to sleep late. He pulled the covers over his head, hoping his Mom would forget about him. No such luck.

"Tony! Church starts in forty-five minutes and I don't want to be late!"

He knew not to argue. It always ended badly. He ground his fists into his eyes and rolled out of bed with a yawn, red hair jutting out in all directions. He crept down the hall and snuck into Katie's room, crouching next to her bed. "He was here last night. I saw him."

"Was not, Tony! You're making it up."

" 'Fraid not. It's true, and he asked to see you! Mister Checkers! Looking for you!"

"It's a lie! He didn't!"

"Don't worry. I didn't tell him you were here. But, I might, next time."

"Stop it, Tony! It's a lie!"

"Oh no. It's true. He carries a big ol' machete too! Just like I said. All cold, and black, and bloody. I woulda' been scared too, except he didn't want me. He wanted you."

"I know. Not funny at all. His broad bulky hand with big hairy knuckles; the one not holding the machete that is, had someone's hair in it."

"Did not!"

"It did. And at the end of the hair was a little girls' head, all bloody, and hacked around the neck."

"You two better be getting dressed! We've got thirty minutes till church!"

Tony flashed a wicked grin and grabbed Katie's cheeks, pinching them hard between his fingers. "I'll tell you more later."

Tony dressed quickly and went to sit on the porch. Jax dozed in the porch swing. Tony plucked a straw from a broom leaning in the corner and began running it up and down the dog's paw pads. Jax twitched his leg—slowly at first—and then so violently he fell off the swing and hit the porch with a squealing thump.

"You keep teasing that dog, something bad's going to happen to you."

Tony turned and glared at Katie, who was standing on the porch in her Sunday dress. "No. Something bad is going to happen to you. Right now." He grabbed Katie's arm and popped her with his knuckles, raising a big knot. "Frog!"

Katie sat on the porch steps crying into her hands. Jax curled up by her feet whimpering into her shiny shoes.

The Sunday school lesson was "All God's Creatures Great and Small." As the teacher read from the book of Ecclesiastes, Tony drew pictures of a huge dark creature on the front of his church bulletin. Its huge hands were swinging a large blade into the side of a little girls head. Above the girl's head he scrawled the name KATIE in bold block letters. When the teacher had everyone stand to sing a closing song, Tony placed thumb tacks on the chair in front of his.

After church, Katie met Tony in the hallway. There was a big smile on her face and a cardboard box in her hands.

"What's in the box?"

"It's a surprise. I made it for Mom."

Tony grabbed the box and ran out the church doors into the parking lot. "I'm going to give it to Mister Checkers when he comes for you tonight. He'll stomp it with his big, bloody steel-toed boots."

"Tony, please! I've been working on that for a month. Give it back!"

"No way. This belongs to Mister Checkers. He loves surprises!"

"Tony, what's that you have?" Mom brushed the hair out of his eyes while standing behind him.

"It's a surprise for you, Mom! I made it in Sunday school."

"Did you, now?"

"He didn't, Mom. It's from me."

"I see. Well let's sort this out at home. I've got supper to cook."

While supper was cooking, Tony snatched a rubber band from the kitchen drawer and crept out onto the porch. Jax snored loudly, paws and muzzle draped over the edge of the swing. Tony edged forward and inched the rubber band over Jaxs' muzzle, letting it close around his mouth with a snap. Jax clambered out of the swing, down the steps, and disappeared around the house, bawling like a calf. Tony laughed until tears ran down his cheeks.

Katie appeared at the front door and eased out onto the porch. "If you keep it up, Jax is going to get mean. I'll tell Mom you've been teasing him."

Tony pounced on Katie and grabbed her around the neck while clamping a hand over her mouth. "You'll tell Mom nothing!"

Katie stomped down hard on Tony's toe with her heel. She

wriggled free and ran off the porch in search of Jax. She found him under a shrub in the back yard. He was whimpering and scratching at the rubber band with both front paws. Clumps of bloody hair began shedding from his muzzle. Katie coaxed him out and pulled him up on her lap, rocking him gently. When he was calmed down, Katie slipped her fingers under the rubber band and eased it off his muzzle.

On Monday, Tony stuffed his backpack with baseball cards and a notebook and ran to the kitchen. Katie was crying into her cereal and trying to defend herself from her Mother's lecture.

"Katie, how could you be so irresponsible? There's no excuse for losing money like that! I specifically put it in an envelope and taped it to the fridge so something like this wouldn't happen!"

"But Mom, I didn't move it! I didn't even think about it till this morning."

"You need to *start* thinking young lady. I work too hard for my money to have it lost so easily."

"You're right, Mom," Tony said. "She is so careless. I think she does it to get attention."

"Tony, eat your breakfast. This is a matter for Katie and me."

"She knows where that money is, Ma. You may have to beat it out of her."

"Anthony Michael Brownway! Honestly! Where on earth do you come up with such nonsense?"

"Sorry, Ma. Just tryin' to help." He gulped down his orange juice and headed out the door.

Katie caught up with him on the front sidewalk just as he plopped a big wad of bubble gum on Jax's tail and pushed it in with his thumb. "Tony, you just keep that up and he's going to get even with you. He doesn't like that."

"Pretty big talk for a little thief. What did Mom do to you for stealing the money?"

"I have to pay it out of my allowance. But it's not fair. I didn't steal it!"

"Hey, I know nothing! But, Mister Checkers knows. He knows it was you and he's coming for you! Coming with his big ol' machete and those big bloody steel toed boots."

"I *didn't* take the money, and I *don't* believe Mister Checkers is coming for me!"

"We shall see, won't we?" Tony stomped the back of Katie's heel, stripping her shoe and sock completely off her foot.

Jax crouched down and let out a low menacing growl. The hair on his back stuck straight up and his teeth gleamed white and frothy. Tony took a step back. Jax inched towards him. His muzzle began to twitch and the pupils in his eyes turned solid black . Tony took another step back, then swung his foot, hitting Jax in the ribs. Jax lunged, coming up with a mouth full of denim and skin.

"That son-of-a-bitch mutt bit me!"

Jax placed his body between Tony and Katie. His jaws were still clamped tightly around a piece of pant leg. The corners of his mouth dripped Tony's blood.

"If it's the last thing I do, I'll get him." He stared at his blood collecting in a small puddle under Jaxs' muzzle. "And you," Tony sneered, pointing a shaky finger at Katie, "I'll let Mister Checkers take care of you." He turned and ran, Jax hot on his heels.

By the time Katie had her sock and shoe back on, Jax had returned. The bloody piece of denim still hung from his mouth. She pulled him close and rubbed his ribs as he whimpered softly into her cheek.

After school Tony hurried home, trying his best not to limp. The antiseptic and bandage he had swiped from the school nurse's office covered the gash in his leg, but it was starting to throb. He couldn't wait to get home, prop it up, and watch some T.V. As he eased his aching leg up the last porch step Mom appeared in the doorway.

"Tomorrow is trash day. I need you to take the trash to the curb, please."

"But, Ma..."

"No buts, just do it or no allowance this week."

Tony dragged the trash can down the driveway to the curb. The ants were back, and this time without the sugar bait. Even with a sore leg he couldn't resist. He unzipped his backpack and pulled out the magnifying glass. The swarm was thicker this time. Tony focused the glass and narrowed in on the rolling mass. Ten minutes passed; then twenty. Nothing. The ants weren't dying as easy. They actually seemed to enjoy the heat, gravitating to the center of the beam. Tony stuffed the magnifying glass in his pocket and stomped at the rolling ant pile with his good leg. They felt like marbles under his shoe. More ants began pouring out of the cracks in the sidewalk like water from a spring.

"This sucks. I'll be back, you bastards, with a can of gas and some matches!"

After supper and an hour of channel surfing between MTV and some R-rated flick with all the juicy parts cut out, Tony became bored. He went to his room to play video games, but stopped in the hall when he spotted Katie stretched out on her bed reading her science book. He belly-crawled into her room and slid under the bed unnoticed. After a few minutes he grabbed the bed frame and shook it so violently it scared Katie out of bed and into the hallway.

"That's how the floor will shake when Mister Checkers comes for you, stomping down the hall in those bloody boots. By the time you hear it he'll have you! Chop! Swish! You're gone!"

"Tony, that's not one bit funny!"

"Tell me about it. He'll keep your head, but he eats the body so no one will ever know what happened to you. I sure wouldn't want to be you when he shows up!"

Katie ran to the bathroom and locked the door behind her. Tony turned to go to his room and ran straight into Mom coming down the hall.

"What in the world is wrong with Katie now?"

"I don't think she's feeling well. Probably feeling guilty about that money she lost." He slipped into his room, flopped on the bed and turned on his console. He fidgeted to get comfortable but it was no use. His leg was pounding from Jax's bite. He switched the game off and stuffed a pillow under his leg. Tomorrow he would get even.

* * *

Tony was late for school. It was a Tuesday, warm and pleasant. He took a shortcut through the open field, a couple of lawns, and over the back fence. He would be on the school grounds with five minutes to spare, but he would have to hurry. At the corner, Tony ditched Katie by knocking her books to the ground. As she scrambled to pick them up, he disappeared between some hedges.

His backpack tugged heavily at his shoulders. He was halfway across the field when he noticed the first pinching; light at first, then more intense. He reached back to adjust his shoulder straps. The backpack suddenly felt like an anvil around his neck. He let it slip from his shoulders just as his foot hit a fresh pile of dog droppings.

Tony knelt to untie his shoe and clean it off. The grass around him rumbled and came to life.

The ants moved in and covered his legs, rushing up his thighs and digging into his groin. Others attacked his dog-bitten leg, eating their way to the bone. His eyes swelled shut and he tumbled to the ground, struggling to catch his breath as he landed face down in a bloody boot print speckled with white granules. Sweet. Glistening. Ants burrowed up his nose and inched toward his brain. His ant-clogged voice box refused to let out a scream as something cold and sharp pierced the back of his neck.

At home, on the porch, Jax let out a soft sigh of relief and settled in for a long peaceful nap on the swing. Between his paws, resting near his muzzle, was a machete. Cold. Black. Bloody. A broad bulky hand gently rubbed hairy knuckles over the dog's aching rib cage. Jax wagged his tail approvingly.

Katie stuffed empty sugar packets through a crack in the wooden porch planks. She smiled up at the gently rocking swing, casting heavy shadows over big, bloody steel-toed boots. "You like Mister Checkers, don't you, boy?"

Jax thumped his tail wildly.

In the distance, the school bell rang.

Devonshire
by
M.D. Maurice

First featured in "Bareback Magazine," M.D. Maurice has been writing since junior high. Considering writing a gift, Maurice writes mostly fiction but inputs truth and values into every character and story.

The morning greeted Martin with bright sunshine. He listened to the chirping of spring birds and the staccato burst of battling squirrels above his head. After loading his fishing rods and tackle into the back seat of his battered sedan, he lowered his considerable bulk down into the driver's seat. His feet crunched down on the collection of old drink cups, candy wrappers and empty Newport boxes scattered around the floor.

Martin eased the sedan out onto highway 701, which ran directly past the front door of the ramshackle little house he had inherited from his grandmother.

The scenery, still shaking off the clutches of a hard New England winter, flashed past him as he motored steadily along the rural highway. He fished a fresh box of smokes from the front pocket of his flannel shirt, kicked the car's cigarette lighter in with one knuckle and hummed contentedly while he waited for it to heat up. Following an audible "pop" he lifted the orange coils to the tip of his Newport and inhaled. Martin grinned; escaping smoke snaked through his yellowing teeth.

He wiggled the letter opener he'd wedged into the car's radio to make it work and tuned in to the only rock station he could get. The radio lost reception in the middle of Martin's favorite CCR song when he turned off route 701 and onto the thickly wooded, narrow road that led into the state forest and down to the Devonshire reservoir toward his favorite fishing spot. Martin coasted up onto the embankment where the road was the broadest. He stuffed the smoking remains of his Newport into the half empty can of Mountain Dew perched precariously in his cup holder.

He parked the car and heaved himself up and out the door. Collecting his rods and tackle, he slogged off down toward the chain link fence that ran along the water's edge. The laces of his worn-out work boots trailed along behind him as he looked for the place where the fence had been partially cut.

Finding it, Martin tugged the metal as far apart as he could and forced his large body through the hole. He leaned back to retrieve his gear, careful not to damage the tips of his rods as he pulled them through.

Martin picked his way down to the reservoir's edge. He parked himself on large tree root that had burst through the ground and begin to work on setting up his fishing rods.

His big fingers were surprisingly nimble as he re-lined the poles with test line and tied on the delicate lures. He baited his favorite rod with a shiny, flashing silver lure that caught what little light filtered down through the leafy canopy. Martin outfitted the other rod with a lure that was made to look like a fat, juicy tadpole then added a standard red and white bobber.

He took off, navigating along the shoreline, the water gently lapping against his work boots until he found a place where the vegetation thinned enough for him to cast. Drawing his arm back over his shoulder, he sent the lure and bobber sailing out over the water's rippling surface in a smooth, graceful arc. The bobber hit the surface about 200 yards out with a pleasant "plop."

He set the rod down, wedging the end of the pole between an exposed root and the heel of his boot. He picked up the other rod baited with the silver lure and began the process of casting it out and reeling it back in. It looked like a bait fish, sparkling just below the reservoir's rippling surface.

He passed the better part of an hour in this steady rhythm, pausing only once to check the other line when the bobber suddenly bounced on the surface. It was "only just nibbles," he decided, after having reeled it in to find the tadpole still intact.

Martin was just about to call it quits when the rod with the lure quivered. Martin jerked it back sharply. There it was, the insistent tug of a hooked fish. He began to reel the line in. It whistled down the rod throwing droplets of water off as it collected on the spool.

At last the fish broke the surface about forty yards off, a decently sized small mouth bass. Martin whooped and continued to bring the fish in at a steady pace. Finally it was below him, slapping about in the shallow water at his feet. He set the rod on the ground and reached down, grasping the fish with both hands. He gently pried the hook free with his pliers and held the bass up, inspecting it.

It was thick-bodied and beautifully colored; Martin rotated it, examining the lines of its body, the pulsating gills. It was a beautiful fish. Sighing, he planted a big, noisy kiss on the fish's head and released it back into its watery world. He watched it make off toward safer depths.

He bent down again to pick up his rod when the hairs at the base of his neck all stood straight up. The world had gone eerily silent; even the swarm of black gnats, his constant companions, suddenly vanished. No more than twenty feet directly in front of him, something else had broken the surface of the water and was looking right at him.

No sooner had the thing registered in his mind than it was gone, leaving nothing more than silent ripples on the surface. Martin, sweating and feeling a little sick, grabbed his gear and dashed up the bank. He fought the urge to look back, terrified it would slow his escape.

He stumbled back through the fence, tearing both his shirt and the flesh beneath on the jagged metal. Back in his car, breathing in painful gasps, he dared to look out at the reservoir. With the exception of some low flying gulls, it was devoid of any activity or movement. Even the air had a tranquil smell about it, as if nothing out of the ordinary had just happened.

Still feeling the prickling of panic, Martin pulled back out onto the road. When he was safely out of the forest and back on 701, he rummaged in his pockets for his cigarettes and lit one with shaking hands.

It had been watching him.

"What the hell?" Martin involuntarily stomped on the accelerator.

The car raged forward as he let loose a stream of obscenities. He didn't dare think about it, but he was thinking about it.

"A river otter..." he thought, "that's what it was."

Martin felt the flood of relief. River otters were rare and elusive creatures but the occasional sighting was reported in this area. He shook off some of his fright and began to feel a little silly.

Later that night, tucked into bed, the vision of those bright, wet eyes hovering above the water crept up on him. They had been so round, so bright, unlike any eyes he'd ever seen before. Two turquoise pools, heavy-lidded and rimmed with the most brilliant shade of green.

"No, not a river otter at all," Martin decided as he drifted off to sleep.

It took him the better part of a week to drum up enough courage to go back to the reservoir. This time he brought only his old Olympic camera, fully loaded.

He sat down on the bank near the same spot as the last time and guzzled a Mountain Dew with trembling hands, watching the water.

After two hours, his neck and shoulders were sore with tension. Martin stood to relieve his aching bladder. Suddenly there was a splash so close by that his entire body jerked in fright. He looked out over the water, scanning for movement on the surface. Nothing.

Then there was a sudden flash of color. There was something moving through the reeds on the far side of the reservoir, something long and slick looking.

Martin raced up the bank, crashing noisily through the vegetation toward a place where he could gain a better vantage point. He finally broke out farther down the shore. The thing had slipped under water again, only to surface about thirty feet from where he now stood.

A smooth head that looked to be covered in thick, brown ropes rose up out of the reeds. Gill-like slits on either side of its head flared as it surfaced, and a thick bullfrog struggled feebly in its jaws. Martin held his breath as the creature slid effortlessly out of the water and onto a partially submerged log.

"Definitely not a river otter," Martin thought again, his bowels trembling.

It had its back to Martin now, the long rope-like things trailing down its back, the lower half of its body still below the waterline. There was a crunching noise as it chewed on the frog and a low mewling that made Martin's stomach ache with a new fear.

He took a step back, lost his footing and went crashing down to the ground in a heap, dropping his camera into the brush. The thing's head snapped around, seeking the source of the threat. Martin got a good look at it and screamed.

It had long, sinewy arms with talons wrapped around two halves of the large frog. Below the eyes, wide with hostile alarm, was a flat face framed by gills. It had a wide, fish-like mouth filled to the brim with jagged, blood-soaked teeth. It dropped the partially eaten frog and turned its body completely toward Martin. He could make out two beautifully shaped breasts that swung like ripe melons as it raised its arms and hissed. It launched itself into the water, its broad fish-like tail slapping the water violently. Martin screamed again and felt the warm flood of urine coursing down inside his jeans.

Gasping and sobbing with fright, he lumbered to his feet and began to scramble back up the embankment. He tore back through the undergrowth and for one second of pure panic, feared he'd lost the path back to his hole in the fence. Finally he spotted it and charged through. Certain he'd see the creature dragging itself through the woods with its bloody jaws snapping, Martin didn't risk looking back.

Back at home, Martin took a sip from his open beer can while his laptop screen flickered, his latest Google search results were displayed. Frustrated and tired, he cursed the machine. Having searched everything from swamp monsters to mermaids, his results had yielded nothing that would help him. The colorful storybook images did not even remotely resemble the creature he had seen.

Admittedly, his search criteria were limited. The thing he'd seen was definitely aquatic and female. Martin felt an inexplicable stirring in his loins as he remembered its large, eerily perfect breasts. Those breasts had hardly fit in with the rest of it, those beautiful flashing eyes and menacing jaws.

He thought back to the awful sounds it had made as it tore that frog to pieces. There were those unmistakable gills and those bizarre ropes.

"Like hair or…" Martin wracked his brain for the right word, "...dreadlocks."

That's what they had been: thick, wet dreadlocks. He took a long, thoughtful pull on his beer, drained it and tossed the can over his shoulder.

One search result caught his eye. He clicked on the thumbnail picture of something called a Fiji mermaid. The picture opened full screen and he felt a rush of cold dread. This was closer, much closer to the thing he seen. He leaned forward and read the caption below the picture. "A man-made relic from the days of PT Barnum's traveling sideshow."

It was apparently an ugly example of taxidermy genius, pieced together from monkey parts and the tail of some large fish. It looked to be about four feet tall and was black and shriveled. The sharp ragged teeth in its twisted mouth were clearly discernable.

Martin thought of people standing in line, waiting to get a peek at this monstrosity. For the first time since leaving the reservoir, he remembered his camera was lost somewhere in the undergrowth. PT Barnum's monster was man-made; could that creature in the reservoir be some kind of experiment gone wrong?

Martin popped the top on a fresh beer and reluctantly recalled the creature's image again. It had been a long time since he'd been in school, but he remembered Darwin's theory and that thing in the water had looked nothing if not evolved. It struck Martin as having been far more adapted to its environment than the product of any human intelligence, no matter how advanced.

Had the PT Barnum creation been based on reality? Had its creator once seen the same creature that was now occupying Martin's secret fishing spot? Martin found he was both fascinated and repulsed by the possibility.

An hour later, Martin's six-pack was gone. He'd managed to find several more references to the Fiji mermaid but they were too obscure to be helpful. He stumbled to bed with the realization that he had to go back. He had to get a better look, more evidence. He wasn't sure what he'd do with that evidence yet but he was driven by the need to understand.

Armed with a new plan, Martin lugged a fishing rod and a full bait bucket from his car down to the water's edge. The bucket was heavy with two dozen fresh water eels. He'd hatched this new plan two days ago but he hadn't considered how colossally stupid it was until this moment. He stood on the shore, scanning the perimeter of the reservoir.

"What did he think was going to happen? He was going to try to lure it out into the open with live bait, then what? What if it came after him?" Martin thought, looking down and checking that the laces on his boots were securely knotted. If he had to make a run for it, he didn't want to trip and break his neck.

He pried the lid off the bucket and fished out a wriggling black eel. He hooked it through the jaws, and then set it down in the shallows. The eel instinctively began swimming out into the depths. Martin let the line out. The sun caught the filament. The eel was already a good distance from the shore and moving out toward the middle of the reservoir. Almost out of line, Martin snapped the bale shut and waited. Nothing.

He repeated the process three more times, each time moving to a new location on the shore and letting the eel work its way out. When the eel would stop moving, Martin would reel it in and replace it with a fresh one. He was in the middle of retrieving the latest eel, when the line grew taut and the pole jerked in his hands. Something had taken the bait, and it was a big something.

He dug his heels in, backed up the bank and reeled in earnest. His heart pounded and sweat ran down his back, more from fear than from exertion. About ten feet in front of him, the broad, mud-brown back of a large snapping turtle broke the surface. The eel came free with one snap of its powerful jaws and the turtle disappeared. Martin stomped and swore loudly, tossing his pole aside. He waded into to the water and upended the bucket, setting the remaining eels free.

It moved so quickly, so silently, that Martin barely had time to jump out of its way. It had come from somewhere off to his right, and it rushed past him, keening and launching itself after the fleeing eels. He caught a glimpse of the creature's misshapen back and its flat, iridescent tail.

He backed up, away from the shore but stood stock still, watching it feed. The creature disappeared underwater, and then re-emerged, spewing bloody bits of eel and mucus. He stood, transfixed as it casually rolled over onto its back, its breasts bobbing obscenely. It slapped the surface of the water with its tail, the noise sounding like a gunshot in the otherwise quiet morning. It clutched another eel to its mouth and sucked at it. Martin shuddered with revulsion.

The thing finished off the rest of the eel, then turned in Martin's direction. It began, ever so slowly, swimming toward shore, toward him. Martin took several involuntary steps backwards, and then stopped.

"You want more?" he asked aloud, his face flaming with embarrassment.

The thing stopped and hissed. Its jaws hung open and a long black tongue flashed behind hundreds of sharp, pointed teeth. It didn't look like the shriveled thing in the photos he'd seen, like something long dead washed ashore. Instead, this animal, this thing, looked impossibly vibrant, like something that stepped out of his nightmares.

Its head appeared a bit too large for its body. Its skin was the color of tapioca and was covered by fuzzy spots of green discoloration. The shoulders and arms were taught and narrow, the claws looked more like the hands of an old crone. The nails were blackened, chipped and caked with grime. It turned away from him, its dreadlocks making a wet, slapping sound as it disappeared beneath the surface. Feeling both terrified and oddly exhilarated, Martin raced back to his car.

The bait shop owner had looked at him strangely when he returned and bought every freshwater eel and minnow he had in his live wells.

"Fish are really hitting these today." Martin had offered by way of an explanation before paying the man with a handful of crumpled bills.

This time, the creature seemed to be waiting for him. It surfaced as soon as he reached the edge of the reservoir, moving closer as Martin began chucking handfuls of eels and fish out into the water.

It seemed to be insatiable, attacking each new meal with zeal. Amused, Martin saw it jump up and snatch an eel out of midair, tearing it in two and stuffing the parts into its gaping maw before splashing back down.

He checked his bucket. One eel left. Martin bent down and picked it up, then froze. The creature was directly in front of his face. Its body was fully extended, its head partly submerged with only the eyes above the waterline. It dragged itself forward and pushed itself up out of the water, its face pressing into Martin's, its fetid breath making his stomach heave. The gills flared and its jaws opened wider. It locked gazes with Martin with its expressionless, unblinking turquoise eyes.

He counted what had to be hundreds of razor sharp teeth. He slowly extended the hand that held the eel. In utter amazement, he watched as it reached out with one claw and took it from him. Martin stood transfixed as it swam away, his sweat pooling between his shoulder blades and his breath coming in ragged gulps.

The phone was ringing when he stumbled through his front door. Martin snatched it up. He answered in a voice that sounded like he'd been chewing gravel.

"Martin? Martin, is that you? What's wrong?" His only sibling Melissa lived thirty-six minutes from the end of his driveway, but it might as well have been three states away.

"Nothing, Mel. I was just sleeping." He dropped down into a chair.

"You sure everything is okay?" Then, perhaps fearing he'd find some reason to end the call early, she got right to the point. "It's Jason's birthday tomorrow. I'm making dinner and I want you to come."

Martin grimaced. "Mel, you know I don't like parties."

Over the years, he had kept his distance from his sister and her children. He found that he didn't do well with others, especially his own family. There was likely some deep-rooted psychological explanation for it, but Martin had never had any interest in finding out what. He just liked his isolated life.

"Martin, you haven't seen the kids since Christmas. Would it kill you to make it to dinner? Jason loves hanging out with you. What are you going to do, live in Grandma's shack and never get out into the world?" Melissa's voice was ripe with disapproval.

Martin thought his nephews couldn't care less about him. The boys always made him feel like some kind of large bug, something that made them curious but not curious enough to get close to it.

"I didn't get him a present. I've been...busy."

His sister scoffed. "Busy? Martin, doing what? Testing video games? Illegally trespassing on the reservoir to fish? Give me a break! I'm raising two kids on my own and you know that I don't ask you for much." Melissa let that last bit sink in.

Melissa had lost her husband to a freak heart attack several years back. Though he ached for her loss, her grief made Martin desperately uncomfortable. He knew she had suffered but she'd never sought comfort from her sole sibling. He had never once offered his brotherly shoulder in support either, a fact she often used to manipulate him.

"Okay, but I can't stay long."

"Good, come by at 7. I'm making a roast." Melissa hung up without saying goodbye.

The next evening, Martin fumbled around his place looking for something Melissa would deem acceptable to wear. His wardrobe consisted largely of flannels, faded tee shirts and jeans. He finally located an old sweater she and the boys had bought him last Christmas. It was still partially wrapped and had the tags attached. He shaved in the kitchen sink, checking his reflection in his old toaster. He looked a little less like the Unabomber now, he thought.

Martin snagged the set of bright orange walkie-talkies he'd got Jason. It had been a last-minute purchase. After spending two clueless hours in the toy store he'd finally admitted he knew nothing about what his nephew was into. He had finally broken down and asked the perky female salesclerk who'd suggested they were "just the thing boys loved to play with."

Melissa, seeing his freshly shaven face and the sweater, had given him a half-hearted hug and an approving smile. She ushered him into the living room, calling out "Boys, Uncle Martin is here."

Michael, his younger nephew, was watching television. He jumped to his feet. "Hi, Uncle Martin."

He had grown at an alarming rate, his eight-year-old body reminiscent of his late father's wiry frame.

Martin awkwardly patted the boy's head. "How's it going, tough guy?"

Michael shrugged, mumbled something incoherent, and glanced back over his shoulder at the TV.

"Hey, it's okay. Finish your program, Mikey. Where's your brother at?"

"On the computer, again. He's supposed to be doing his homework but he's talking to girls." Michael made a gagging motion.

Martin found Jason in the back room, sitting in front of the computer. The boy was typing into an open chat window.

"Hey there, birthday boy."

"Uncle Martin!" Jason jumped and abruptly closed the window. "Just doing homework."

"Oh yeah? Mikey says you just use that thing to talk to girls." Martin had meant it as a joke but his nephew's eyes flashed with alarm.

Jason had Melissa's soft looks, dark smoky eyes and long lashes. If it weren't for his broad shoulders and large build, he'd look almost feminine. Martin cast about for a way to change the subject. There were textbooks strewn about the desk. Martin absently glanced down at an open one and could not believe his eyes.

"Jason, what is this?" Martin picked up the book and held it out in front of him.

"History. We're studying mythology."

"No. no. What is this?" Martin pointed excitedly at the large picture of a female creature, half obscured by pond lilies. You could clearly see a golden tail and long, black hair that hung in thick chords. It was decidedly less monstrous than the thing in Devonshire, but the similarities were stunning.

"It's a water nymph. Niadmes? No, wait, naiads. It's some stupid mermaid thingy that live in ponds and lakes." Jason gazed back at him curiously. "Why?"

"It doesn't look like a mermaid," Martin insisted. A rush

like ice water coursed down between his shoulder blades and gooseflesh prickled his arms.

Jason took the book from him, flipped back a page and held it up.

"Look, this is how they look normally. When they get pissed off or sick or something, they get to be ugly, like this one here." Jason turned back to the other picture.

Martin took the book from his nephew. He went back and forth between the two pictures, his mind burning. "What's that?" Jason gestured toward the hastily wrapped present.

"What? Oh, that's for you. Go ahead, open it." Martin handed over the gift without taking his eyes off the book. He began to read as the boy eagerly tore off the paper.

"Cool, walkie-talkies! Thanks, Uncle Martin." Jason beamed at him. Martin's euphoria was temporary interrupted by an unexpected thrill at having pleased his nephew.

"Glad you like them, Sport. Sorry I forgot the batteries but maybe your Mom has some?"

Jason took off for the kitchen and Martin, thankful to have a few extra minutes, sat down to finish reading about the naiads.

Dinner had gone remarkably well. The kids bickered less than Martin remembered and Melissa seemed relaxed and even a little happy. Still, Martin found himself rushing through his cake, eager to get back home in front of his computer and pursue a new direction of research.

Before leaving, he'd asked to borrow his sister's digital camera. Melissa handed it over, without a single question. Martin felt a sudden flood of gratitude and affection for her, almost enough to make him initiate a hug.

"When did you quit smoking?" Melissa had asked.

Martin had been surprised to admit that over the last few strange days he had not had a single smoke. The realization startled and unnerved him. He had suddenly wished that he and his sister had been closer; he might have been tempted to share his discovery with her

"You should take the boys fishing sometimes." Melissa suggested.

Martin shrugged. "Yeah, Mel, maybe I will do that sometime."

The two shared an awkward hug before Martin made off for home.

Martin had stayed up all night reading everything he could find out about fantastic creatures of myths and legends. He wasn't sure if the thing in the Devonshire reservoir was a water nymph or mermaid or some combination of those things. He had no idea where it had come from but the images he'd seen in Jason's textbook had got him thinking about another possibility—what if it had been something else before?

Martin had lived alone for a very long time. His reclusive lifestyle had not afforded him many opportunities to meet women. Martin had to wonder if that's perhaps why there was this fixation on the idea that this creature could have once been something magical and alluring.

Martin could admit his isolation had heightened his sensitivity of the female form. He thought again of those beautiful breasts and of all the lovely water creatures floating amid the pond lilies in Jason's textbook. His throat grew thick. It wasn't hard to see why so many lonely men had met their demise at the hands of such beguiling visions. Thinking of those poor lost souls, Martin was suddenly grateful to feel the tug of sleep. He stumbled off to bed to catch a few hours rest.

The water of the reservoir was cold and clear. Martin's feet sunk to his ankles in the soft silt. The afternoon sun felt warm on his back and he stripped down to his sleeveless tee shirt.

She was close. He could feel her moving through the water, sending ripples of excitement through him. She surfaced, just a few feet from him. Her eyes were sparkling pools and her skin, nearly translucent in the light, shimmered like a million cut diamonds.

She edged closer and Martin felt his groin stir. She was almost upon him now, the points of her breasts with their hardened, carmine-colored nipples rising out of the water. He ran his eyes over her, feasting. He reached out, cupping one breast in his shaking palm, stroking the warm flesh.

She drew him back out into the depths, until the water rose up over his waist. She pressed up against him, pressing her body to his, impossibly warm and achingly beautiful. Martin felt her powerful tail ease up, between his legs. He ran his hand down over the shining orange scales, the foreignness of it, inspiring an almost painful lust. She moved against him with it and he felt himself grow hard and erect beneath the water's surface.

Her lips moved over his stomach, light and moist. Martin made a sound that began as a moan of ecstasy but became a scream of anguish as a hundred snapping teeth tore apart his flesh.

Martin sat up, still screaming and covered with cold sweat.

"What the hell was that?" He leapt from bed, pulling up his sweatshirt, examining his stomach for damage.

He rummaged around under his bed until he found a half empty bottle of vodka, and stood, taking several deep swigs from it. He got dressed and sat on the edge of his bed, waiting for sunrise, too frightened to fall back to sleep.

The morning was quiet out on the Devonshire reservoir. Certain she was close by, Martin emptied the first bucket of eels into the shallows. He saw the flash of her tail as she gave chase to her prey. He marveled at how different this creature was from the erotic beauty of his nightmare.

He started off, picking his way around the shoreline, not entirely certain what he was looking for. Jason had said that these creatures could transform when they got sick or upset. Martin thought that perhaps there was something wrong with the reservoir that could be affecting it.

The reservoir spanned roughly eight acres and Martin intended to search its entire circumference. He felt certain his secret entrance was the only access apart from a locked gated fence that crossed the service road, used only by the town's officials. In all the time he'd been fishing down here, he'd never come across another soul, nor seen evidence that the authorities made excursions with any regularity.

As the morning gave way to the bright afternoon sun, Martin continued his trek around the body of water. His process was slowed in many places by thick undergrowth. Out of shape and in no condition to have undertaken such an ambitious hike, he had to stop frequently to catch his breath and wipe the sweat out of his eyes. There seemed to be no other breaches in the fence and by mid-afternoon, he'd worked his way almost three quarters of the way around.

The creature, having long finished her meal, had been steadily keeping up with him. Martin stopped every once and a while, and found her eyes watching him from above the water's still surface. Unnerved but determined, Martin continued trudging along. At last, he came to a point where he could make out his fishing spot beyond a rocky outcropping. He'd come nearly full circle.

Martin made his way up over the rocks, and his nostrils suddenly picked up the heavy scent of stale cigarettes and beer. Dropping down off the top of the rocks, Martin might as well have touched down in a landfill.

The shoreline here was littered with empty bottles and cigarette butts. The water that ran up over the little beach was heavy with sludge-like mucus. Martin counted nearly fifty pieces of fast food debris, countless crushed and crumpled cigarette cartons and booze bottles. Martin noted several dozen used condoms with disgust and even the charred remains of a small fire pit. Apparently someone had been sneaking down here at night, using the reservoir as a private partying spot and dumping ground.

Several trees had been covered with graffiti and hundreds of broken branches covered the ground. With horror and guilt, he realized that this damage was his fault. His was the only hole in the fence. The vandals had gained access the same way Martin trespassed. Instead of using the Devonshire to fish and appreciate nature, they used it to exploit the privacy of its acres. He looked down at the fire pit. They could have set the entire place on fire. Martin stood, taking in the refuse, burning with guilt and shame.

A sudden inspiration hit Martin as he remembered the camera. He fished it out from his pocket and began snapping pictures of the filth. He heard a familiar hissing and turned around. The mermaid or naiad, whatever she was, had pulled herself halfway up the beach, the long fins at the end of her tail trailing in the scummy water. Her jaws opened and closed, her claws raked the mud.

She made a low sniffing sound and looked up at Martin. For an instant, the beastly features of her face seemed to soften and swirl into something else entirely. For an instant, the lovely apparition of his nightmare seemed to surface before his eyes, and then it was gone.

"I'm sorry," Martin said. "This is all my fault. I'll fix this. I can fix this."

The creature slipped back down the beach and out into the water. She fixed her eyes on Martin one last time before disappearing. Those eyes had reflected such a deep sorrow that it made him ache inside. Martin waited, but she never surfaced again.

Two days later, a plain manila envelope arrived at the Office of Public Works. There was no return address. It was filled with pictures printed on low-grade photo paper showing an area of Devonshire reservoir that had been trashed as well as pictures of the broken fence, the apparent access point for the vandals.

A crew was dispatched to clean the area and the fence was

fixed. The inspector also arranged to have an officer make regular passes during the night in an effort to catch the trespassers. So far, they'd managed to nab a few stoned teenagers during the nightly patrols—thanks to what the papers referred to as "a mysterious, concerned Samaritan."

Martin had scanned the newspapers for weeks after but the cleanup efforts seemed to have gone through without any type of creature sighting. He felt both relieved and strangely disappointed.

The walkie-talkie in Martin's coat pocket buzzed. "Big Bass, its tadpole. What's your location? Over."

He smiled. He set down his pole and retrieved the walkie-talkie. "Tadpole, Big Bass is at bridge. Over."

Jason's voice crackled with excitement. "Michael just caught a fish, Uncle Martin. He's bringing it in now. It's a big one!"

Martin grinned. He'd begun taking his nephews on afternoon fishing outings shortly after the authorities re-secured the Devonshire reservoir. Mount Misery Lake lacked the quiet serenity and exclusivity his old spot had afforded him, but it was stocked with plenty of fish and the boys seemed to enjoy it.

"Okay, guys, I'm on my way. Over." Martin packed up his rod and tackle and headed off to meet the boys.

It was a perfect day. The sun was high and bright, the water was cool and refreshing and the fish were biting. Martin sighed and gazed up at the blue sky. He hoped the Devonshire was passing the same kind of idyllic afternoon and that somewhere in its cool, clean depths, its lone resident was at peace. Fully restored to her former beauty, he imagined her swimming in lazy, unmolested circles.

Martin wondered if she missed the taste of eels.

Skull Face Returns
by
Terry W. Ervin II

Ervin II is an English teacher who enjoys writing Science Fiction and Fantasy. His short fiction appears in markets including "The Sword Review," "Fear and Trembling," and "MindFlights," and is debuting his novel, Flank Hawk, *in 2009.*

The campfire's flame sent shadows dancing across the camp director's clean-shaven face, casting a sinister view, one perfect for the story he told.

"And poor Hobo Bob never saw the bus filled with campers coming around the curve. Didn't hear it as he bent over to pick up a Pepsi bottle along the road for the nickel refund."

This was Shawn's second year as a camp counselor, and the ninth time he'd heard the tale. He stood behind the group of nine-year-olds as they leaned closer. Shawn smiled, knowing that more than half of his campers would have trouble getting to sleep tonight. And more than a few of those would wake from nightmares.

Shawn began to wonder if they told the "Skull Face Tale" during the girls' weeks at camp, but returned his focus to Mr. Glinka's narrative as it neared the climax.

"A big *thump* told Old Bus Driver Agnes she'd hit Hobo Bob. No second bump or bounce indicated she'd run him over, so she peered through her thick glasses into the rearview mirror to see if Hobo Bob was just knocked aside and okay."

With a nod, Mr. Glinka inserted authoritatively: "She was running behind schedule, you know."

His vision panned across the wide-eyed boys. "'Be quiet!' Old Agnes yelled at the laughing bus-riding campers. But to no avail. Because of the noisy campers, she couldn't hear Hobo Bob's scream. Trapped in the wheel well, his face dragged across the pavement. Scraped to the bone.

"By the time the Old Agnes stepped on the brakes, there wasn't anything left. No cheeks, no lips, no eyebrows. Only blood and bone.

"Finally, the bus stopped. Mad with pain, Hobo Bob rolled from the bus into the ditch, pressing what shreds of skin still clung to the bone against his face with his blood-soaked hands. He half stood and staggered into the weeds, toward the woods and was hidden from sight before Old Agnes hobbled out of the bus to look around.

"Now, as Hobo Bob crawled up the hill, his ears still worked fine. See, he never cared for campers. Always making fun of him and throwing things out the bus windows at him."

A deadly serious look fell across Mr. Glinka's face. "The only sound he heard was campers laughing and cheering. See, the camp was within sight. But Hobo Bob didn't know that. Poor injured Bob. Loathing and hate grew in him. Bob thought the campers were laughing at *him*. Cheering for the bus driver who had caused his misfortune. Only on her deathbed a year later did Old Agnes ever mention that she'd seen blood on the road, leading into the woods."

Mr. Glinka let his words sink in before finishing. "Of course, by then it was too late. Hobo Bob had gone mad. And his scarred face never healed. Only a few have seen him wandering the hills hereabouts. His bone-white face. Some say his hatred has kept him alive. Others say he really isn't alive—but he's still around, haunting the woods. Searching the night for campers. Noisy, laughing ones. Ones outside their cabin. To steal their face!"

The fire was dying down. The campers were torn between moving closer to hear the end, and running to hide beneath their bed sheets until morning.

Mr. Glinka held up his thumb. "They say he's grown a long, sharp nail to cut away the face of any camper he can get a hold of." The director dragged his thumb in a circle around his face. "The face of a hated camper. A fresh face to replace his own—the one that he lost all those years ago."

As Mr. Glinka stepped out of the flickering firelight, the campers, wide-eyed and slack-jawed, turned to one another for support before looking back to their cabin counselors.

"Roosevelt Cabin," Shawn said, motioning for his twelve campers to gather around. "Come on, guys." He took a head count like the other counselors before heading back up the dirt trail toward the cluster of cabins.

Shawn smiled inwardly. Experience told him that the Skull Face story might keep the kids awake and worried, but they'd be quiet and wouldn't dare leave the cabin.

Shawn chuckled. "Give me some room, guys."

The nine-year-olds reluctantly complied.

Shawn shook his head. "Jordan, here. You take my flashlight and lead the way."

Eisenhower Cabin merged with Roosevelt. Vernon fell into pace with Shawn. "That story was kind of intense, don't ya think?" the first year counselor asked Shawn in a quiet voice. "Glinka told it last week and it really disturbed my kids. Looks like a repeat for this week."

Shawn shrugged but didn't voice his opinion, *Whatever makes my job easier.*

It wasn't that Shawn hated kids. Sometimes he even enjoyed his job. But that's what it was—a summer job. One that offered room and board. Since it was a camp for the underprivileged, working there retired a sizeable chunk of the student loan debt he'd racked up during the past two years of college. It was a good deal, he reminded himself, even if the kids didn't listen half the time.

"It'll help keep them in line," he finally replied. "You'll see."

"I wonder if there's any truth to the story."

Shawn frowned. "What do you mean, 'truth'?"

Vernon scratched his neck. "The best stories, just like the most convincing lies, have some truth in them."

"If you say so."

It was Vernon's turn to shrug. "Eisenhower, follow me."

As they neared the cabins, the porch lights gleamed brightly and steadily in comparison to the erratic flashlight beams. Shawn watched the group of ten-year-olds and their counselor peel off from his group. Jordan and the rest of the cabin members slowed down until Shawn caught up.

Shawn expected this. Roosevelt, twenty yards ahead, was the cabin nearest to the hill that ran along the camp's western edge. Two sets of clotheslines laden with swim towels on a ten-foot ribbon of crabgrass were all that stood between the cabin's bank of west-facing windows and the steep, tree-covered hillside.

"Is there really poison ivy on that hill, like you said?" Jordan asked his counselor.

"Yeah," Shawn replied. "Why? You thinking of climbing around up there?"

"Then why doesn't Skull Face—I mean Hobo Bob get it?"

Shawn let the question hang in the air for a second before taking back his flashlight, whose dimming light told him the batteries were getting weak. "Why do you think?" He shined it on the boys' faces as they huddled under a midsized oak.

The echoing smack of Tyrone swatting a mosquito emphasized the silence. Finally Mitchie, the smallest of the group but also the most intelligent, spoke up. "He wears long sleeves and pants and boots and you can only get poison ivy if it touches your skin." He paused before the rest of his answer squeaked out. "And he ain't got any skin on his face."

Shawn knew that allowing the campers' imaginations to run wild and fill in the blanks increased their terror. "Makes sense. Bone doesn't catch it then."

Jordan added, "He prolly knows the hills and places around here so well, any patch of ivy he'd know where it is."

"Good observations, gentlemen." Shawn ushered his campers toward the cabin.

Moths fluttered around the yellow porch light set above the wooden sign with faded white letters spelling out "Roosevelt." Shawn pulled the screen door open and waved his arm in a tight circle. "In-in-in before the bugs get in." Why they'd mounted a light above the door, Shawn could only guess. Probably an architect who'd never been to camp. He remembered two guys in his calculus class that planned to be architects. Nerds. So the light's placement made perfect sense.

Really, the cabin was pretty basic and didn't take much thought to lay out. Rectangular cinderblock. A door at each end. The south wall held a fireplace to the left of the door, used every Thursday evening. The counselor's room, barely big enough for a bed, dresser and desk, was on the right. To the left of the north door was the lavatory with three toilet stalls, three shower heads, and three sinks. To the right was a small room for the water heater, fuse box, and a bit of storage. Brown tile floor, except in the lavatory, which had cement. The main room ran forty-five feet, holding brown-painted metal bunk beds with stained, cotton-stuffed mattresses on metal links held by aging springs. Five bunks lined the east wall and six the west, each aligned with a window. It had served as Shawn's summer home for going on two summers. Sometimes that depressed him.

He thought about flicking on his boom box to play his new cassette's lead song, "Eye of the Tiger," but figured it'd only rev his cabin up.

It was his night for "hill duty." To hang out and patrol around the cabins until eleven-thirty. He was partnered with Vernon, while the other counselors, director, assistant director, nurse, head cook and her kitchen help, watched TV and played cards and ping-pong down in the boat house.

"Crank the windows closed," Shawn told the campers. "It's gonna cool down tonight. Wash up, do your business and get in your bunks."

Yep, Shawn consoled himself. *Responsibility. That's why you're earning the big bucks.*

* * *

Shawn and Vernon sat on a pair of old stumps next to the woodpile centrally located among the cabins. Everything had been quiet. No fireworks or loud boating down on the lake. No cabin lights flicking on and off. No ruckus or shouts. No campers dared to venture out.

Vernon angled his watch's face to capture some of Washington cabin's porch light. "Eleven-twenty. They'll be shutting things up in the boathouse."

"Time sure flies, doesn't it?"

Vernon ignored Shawn's sarcasm. "Think we should make one last round?"

It wasn't really a question. Shawn knew his hill duty partner was right. "Sure," he said, getting up. Movement on the hillside beyond Roosevelt caught his attention.

"What is it?" Vernon asked, trying to follow his partner's focused gaze.

"Thought I saw something up on the hill."

"A camper?"

Shawn shook his head. "Probably a deer. Maybe a big raccoon."

"Where? How far up?"

"Ahh, forget it." Shawn stretched. "I hate taking a shower just before bed."

"I know," Vernon said, shaking his head. "But better than having bug-spray-smellin' sheets. I'll start at Grant and circle back to Eisenhower."

"I'll start with Hoover and work back to Roosevelt."

"Watch out for Skull Face up there on the hill," Vernon teased.

"Watch out for the wet dream you'll have fantasizing about him," Shawn retorted, grabbing his flashlight and trying to remember if he had any fresh D-cell batteries in his room.

Shawn had just finished showering and was drying off with one of the camp's cheap white towels when he heard a brief, piercing shriek. He started to smile to himself, until it was followed by a crashing thump, and chorus of screams and cries of terror. Something more than a nightmare and a camper falling out of bed was going on.

Shawn whipped on his boxer shorts and ran to see what was happening. As he flipped on the lights the south screen door slammed shut, adding to the din.

Shawn shouted, "What's going on?"

His boys were sitting up in their bunks, screaming, or hiding under the covers, whimpering. Jordan had crawled underneath his bunk and was pulling himself up against the frame and mattress.

Shawn ran over to little Mitchie's toppled bunk. The camper wasn't there.

As the counselor, Shawn realized he had to get control of the situation. In his Orders-of-the-Day voice, he boomed, "Attention, gentlemen!" That startled a few from their frightened panic. "Anyone know where Mitchie is?"

After a few seconds, Jordan peeked out from under his bunk. "S-Sk-Skull Face took him."

"Who? What?"

Tyrone, perched atop his bunk pointed out the nearest window, up the hill. "There he goes," he said to his counselor. "He's got Mitchie too!"

Shawn ran to the window and cupped his eyes to block the reflection from the cabin's lights. At first he thought he saw something dark moving—maybe a trick of his imagination, shadows in the darkness. Then again, maybe not.

"Tyrone," Shawn ordered. "Right now. Run over to Eisenhower. Tell Vernon to ring the Emergency Bell and to get over here."

"But Skull—"

Shawn didn't have time to debate. "He's up the hill. Not at Eisenhower." The counselor pointed. "Go, *now*!"

The door had slammed, so it might have been Mitchie, Shawn thought while counting heads of campers as Tyrone sprinted out the door, toward Eisenhower cabin. Shawn ran to make sure Mitchie wasn't in the storage room. He wasn't. Shawn marched across the cabin to his room, checking it while slipping into his boots. He grabbed his flashlight and windbreaker and shook his head, thinking about putting on a shirt and pants. "No time," Shawn muttered. His jacket would have to do. He put it on and stepped out the south door.

Tyrone was standing next to Vernon outside of Eisenhower. "What's up?" Vernon shouted.

"Either Mitchie McCormic took off or some pervert came and snatched him," Shawn replied, suddenly putting together a scenario that scared him. "Tyrone saw someone on the hill. Ring the bell and get Glinka. I'm going up to see—"

Shawn didn't finish the sentence. He didn't really know what he was going to see—if there *was* anything to see or find. A sense of responsibility galvanized him. He ran for the hill. Some other kid might run off or screw around and hide. Not Mitchie.

Shawn heard Vernon yelling for him to wait, but a sense of desperate urgency drowned everything else out.

His flashlight's beam landed on a white towel torn off the line and lying between a pair of trees about a dozen steps up the hill.

It wasn't hard for him to find a path with branches bent aside and a few stomped down. Keeping a steady stride and watching ahead, Shawn tried to guess what was beyond the hill. Cottages, mostly lining the lake, with a few gravel access roads leading to them from the main road that ran past the camp's entrance. He guessed the gravel ones would be as long as the camp's length, maybe a half mile. On the main road going west almost a mile down was Courtright's Tavern. He and a few of the other counselors had visited it last year to celebrate the end of camp. He'd call the camp from there if he hadn't found Mitchie.

Shawn worried that he'd lose the trail once he reached one of the gravel roads. Whoever had taken Mitchie had a good head start, and Shawn's passage was severely impeded by thorns and brambles. He flicked the flashlight's beam on his scratched and bleeding legs, and sighed.

The bell sounded in the camp below. But that wasn't what caught Shawn's attention. It was a dog's barking. It reminded him of his Aunt Violet's German shepherd and he followed it across lightly wooded ground, now level and sporting less undergrowth.

He shut off the flashlight to save the dying batteries, and trotted west, toward the lake and the barking. He crossed one gravel road and found a narrow dirt path, probably made by the locals, that angled toward the still barking dog. It was hard to see, but his eyes began adjusting to the dim light of several scattered, distant floodlights near the vacation cottages.

No lights on the insides, Shawn noted. Probably because it was a weeknight.

He could see the lake through the thinning trees; a few boats with lanterns dotted it. He passed two dark cottages with small chain-link fences around them.

The German shepherd was still barking, but with less urgency. Shawn spotted the canine at the end of a chain, facing southwest, until it sensed the counselor approaching. For a second it hesitated, then ran along the chain's length, barking at Shawn.

"Damn dog," Shawn muttered, turning on the flashlight again. The smack of a door slamming shut to the southwest drew Shawn's flashlight and the German shepherd's attention.

A dilapidated wooden structure that looked more like a long shed than a cottage had to be the source. Shawn flicked off his flashlight again and made his way to it. He crossed a gravel road and onto a rutted car path circling up to the shack. It looked long abandoned, grass and small trees growing in it, but recently trodden grass revealed it was still in use. Shawn positioned himself between two tall oaks and hunched down about thirty feet from the tin-roofed shack. One tree blocked the dog's view of him, giving Shawn hope it'd stop barking. The other shielded him from observation through the shack's door.

Shawn crept closer. He couldn't hear the camp's bell anymore and wondered if someone was following after him. It'd probably take the sheriff forever to respond.

Crouched under a window to the left of the shack's rickety screen door, Shawn tried to peer in. Three of the four panes of glass were broken out, but a grating backed by a dark curtain blocked any light which might've been in the shack. He listened and inched closer to the door.

He heard Mitchie whimpering somewhere inside and a harsh,

half-whispered threat, "Shut yer trap err ya's gonna regret it."

The crying lessened, but was followed by a thump that reminded Shawn of a brick hitting flesh.

Shawn couldn't see in the door, as the thick fabric had been tacked behind the torn and rusted screening. He didn't think it was locked.

Shawn ran through his possible courses of action. He could try the windows, and risk giving up any chance of surprise. He could bolt in and just try to get the upper hand. He'd placed fourth in the state wrestling tournament his senior year. He could yell, and try to bluff and scare the kidnapper into inaction. Or he could go for help now that he knew where Mitchie'd been taken. Not back to camp—too far. One of the cottages. They might have a phone.

The last plan sounded best to Shawn, especially since the kidnapper probably had a weapon, a knife at least. All he had was a twelve-inch plastic flashlight.

Then Shawn heard, "Welp, guess nobody's out there. Time ta gets to business."

Mitchie's halting sobs recommenced, accented by a frightened, "Noooo."

Although adrenaline had been pumping through Shawn's veins since starting up the hill, it spiked. Mitchie was his responsibility. He couldn't leave him to be raped and maybe even left for dead after that. No choice. Fight, not flight.

Shawn flicked on his flashlight, smothering the beam against his jacket. He dismissed a fleeting thought of tossing a stone onto the backside of the roof as a distraction, and instead yanked the door open and leapt in.

An oil lantern hung from a hook and chain screwed to a board supporting the roof. Mitchie sat huddled in the southwest corner on scattered rags covering the dirt floor, tears, snot and blood smeared across his face. In the center sat a lopsided picnic table. Behind it stood a hunched old man with frizzled gray hair and a stringy beard, wearing a black trench coat. He'd tied a blue bandana across his face, folded to stretch over his nose. The old man's eyes were wide and wild as he stared over the muzzle of his double-barreled shotgun at an equally wide-eyed Shawn.

Survival instinct kicked in. Charging a crazed-looking guy standing behind a table with a ready shotgun was a losing proposition. And backing out the door would give the old man too much time. Out of options, Shawn flung his flashlight at the man's face and dove right, hoping the coming blast would miss.

The shotgun blast filled the shack. And the lead pellets found Shawn's naked left calf.

Half of the tight pattern had missed high, striking the wall, and a few pellets had imbedded themselves in Shawn's leather boot. But enough of the small-game sized shot struck, sending searing pain up Shawn's leg. Even so, he crawled, seeking cover from the expected second barrel's blast.

There was nowhere to hide or take cover. Shawn saw the old man's dusty boots moving around the table toward him. The old man said something, but Shawn's ears were still ringing from the first gunshot.

Shawn hobbled to his feet, steadying his weight on his good leg while trying to formulate a plan. Blood trickled from the old man's forehead. *My flashlight must've hit him*, Shawn thought. The crazed old man didn't even duck, ensuring his shot's accuracy. And that scared Shawn even more.

Shawn's eyes locked with the old man's. They were narrow, with a hint of mirth that matched his menacing, yellow-toothed grin. "Run, Mitchie!" Shawn yelled. It wasn't an altruistic tactic. Sure, the camper might escape,but he might draw the old man's attention for a fraction of a second. Maybe even the second barrel's load.

Mitchie didn't move. The old man didn't flinch. And Shawn wasn't fast enough in his off-balanced lunge at the old man, hoping to grab hold of the shotgun. The old man stepped aside and slammed the shotgun's hardwood butt against the base of Shawn's skull.

Pain, radiating from his skull and leg, was the first thing Shawn noticed as he regained consciousness. The second thing he noticed was that he was lying on his back at a downward angle, tipping slightly to his left with gravity forcing blood into his already throbbing head. The sound of duct tape being torn from its roll was the third, quickly followed by the realization that he couldn't move, or speak.

That he was still alive surprised Shawn. He opened his eyes. The oil lamp dangled above him. He couldn't lift or turn his head, or even shrug his shoulders. His arms and hands were secured along the edge of a thick, rough board. He listened to duct tape being pulled and torn, and felt it stretched down across his right ankle. Shawn determined the gray tape was pinning him to the lopsided picnic table he'd seen the old man standing behind when he foolishly burst into the shack.

How long had he been out? Shawn wondered. Did anybody hear the shotgun blast? Or did they mistake it for fireworks? Was Mitchie still around?

"I see you's awake," the old man's gruff said. He stepped into Shawn's view and pointed with his thumb. "Yer little friend over there said you'd come fer him. Said you was brave an' tough." The old man sloughed off his trench coat and rolled up the sleeves of his tattered flannel shirt. "We'll see soon nuff."

The old man adjusted the straps of his bib overalls and spat on the floor before grabbing Shawn's taped chin, mouth and forehead, seeing if the counselor could move. The old man nodded in satisfaction.

Something didn't appear right about the old man's face, partially covered by the folded bandana. It was hard for Shawn to tell. The man's face was shrouded in shadow, but it seemed too flat.

"Ta tell ya's the truth, I'm glad ya decided to folla yer friend, Counselir Shawn." The old man shook his head. "I busted him in the face to git'm ta shut up. Mighta busted his nose." He looked over his shoulder. "Kinda small anyway."

Shawn tried to talk, anything to stall whatever the crazy old guy had in mind, but the tape over his mouth allowed only a mumble. Someone at the camp had to have heard the shotgun blast.

"Yer friend there calls me some sorta Skull Face." The old man looked over his shoulder and stared back into the corner before laughing and checking to see if Shawn's arms and legs were secure. "Heard tell of that ol' story. Some truth to it, specially Agnes bein' a lousy damn driver. Near blind ya know.

"Anyhow," the old man continued, reaching up to adjust the lantern, shedding more light across the room. "Let's get down ta business." He untied the bandana from his face and began unfolding it.

Shawn's eyes went wide half in shock, half in horror. The center of the old man's face was nothing more than two holes surrounded by a mass of mottled scar tissue.

The old man spit on the bandana and then wiped down Shawn's face, especially his nose. "See yer seein' the purpose of our meetin'. My name's Robert and I'll be yer surgeon today." He pulled a gleaming scalpel from the front pocket of his overalls, the lone pristine object in the shack. "Thank ya's kindly fer volunteering fer our organ donation program."

Shawn bucked and tried to scream. He nearly knocked the table over, but the old man caught it with his hip.

The old man shook his head and grinned and clamped his right hand over Shawn's taped-down forehead and drove the scalpel into Shawn's face with his left hand, just above the bridge of Shawn's nose.

From his corner, Mitchie screamed.

Pain lanced through Shawn's face and blood poured into his eyes, blinding him. He moaned, straining to break free while the old man calmly spoke as he worked. "Just like carvin' jack-o-lanterns."

Shock started to set in. Shawn couldn't breathe. He began snorting and gagging as blood filled his nasal cavity and made its way into his throat. He heard a man shout, "Freeze!" Three crisp shots from a revolver followed.

Shawn's hospital room probably exuded the typical antiseptic odor but he doubted he'd smell that, or anything else, ever again. Making things worse, the doctors insisted on keeping him strapped down. Nightmares. Thrashing and clawing and yanking on the bandages covering his face only complicated the delicate situation, where the surgeons had attempted to reattach his nose.

Beeping equipment, paging of doctors, dim lights and a white ceiling filled with square tiles, each holding exactly 576 pin-prick sized holes, comprised Shawn's world. His mother, Rose, along with the occasional nurse and doctor provided minor distractions to the itchy, burn-filled pain beneath the gauze and bandages.

The IV-delivered morphine, Shawn guessed, dulled most of the pain in his face, and the dull ache in his leg. Shawn told himself the pain meds also helped him endure the droning soap operas his mother watched religiously along with the wife of the comatose heart attack victim in the bed next to him.

Shawn spent most of his time with the powder blue curtain drawn, pretending to be asleep whenever his mother arrived. While the ploy blocked his view of the wall-mounted TV and the ticking clock underneath, it was the only way he got information. She'd talk to the doctors and he'd overhear things. The graft wasn't taking.

He heard someone knock gently on his door, and his mother get up from the TV. She slid the curtain aside a foot or two to check on her son.

"How is he?"

Shawn recognized the whispered voice of his aunt Violet, his mother's identical twin sister.

"He's asleep, Vi."

A commercial was airing, so Shawn figured they'd talk some.

Aunt Violet's heels clicked on the tiled floor as she stepped into the room. "Is he still tied down?"

Shawn's mom sighed. "He's still having bad dreams."

Shawn pictured them standing on the other side of the curtain, hugging and leaning close.

"It'll be okay, Rose. What about Rexford? He hasn't made it back yet?"

Right, Shawn thought. *Work first. Family second. It's Dad's fault for my face as much as anybody. He's socked more than enough money in his three the bank accounts to pay for my college.*

The response his dad gave everyone who asked about the cost of college ran through Shawn's head. *"The boy will appreciate his education if he works and pays for it himself."*

Shawn refrained from clenching his fists. *That's why I ended up working at that crappy camp.*

"Rex?" Shawn's mom said. "You know what his over-the-road schedule's like. He made his drop in San Diego yesterday. He'll make it to Kansas tonight, drop his freight tomorrow in Indianapolis and then be here tomorrow night."

"What about the lawsuit?" Aunt Violet whispered.

"Well," his mother said timidly, "the camp's lawyer left a message. He wants to interview Shawn when he's feeling better. Some more of the parents are filing a suit against camp, maybe one even against Shawn." She took a deep breath. "I was told they don't have a case."

"They should sue that mental hospital that let that lunatic loose."

"I know, Vi. They're suing them too. Everybody and anybody."

Shawn gritted his teeth. Mitchie's parents were blaming him and the camp in general for what happened. Their traumatized little darling. *Ungrateful ingrates*, Shawn fumed. *The whole damn lot of them! What about me?* He tried to keep calm as the throbbing in his face intensified. He didn't want to trip the monitors into sounding warning beeps.

"Rose, how is Shawn's nose healing?"

Shawn heard his mother slide the curtain open a few inches to check on him and then slide it closed again. "The doctors…they're not sure. Not confident."

"Not sure about what? How long it's going to take?"

"What to do next." His mom sniffled and the two women shuffled over to the visitor chair. The vinyl creaked as his mother sat down. "I wish Rex were here."

"More surgery, of course," Aunt Violet said.

More sniffling followed.

Finally, his mother spoke, sounding as if she'd regained her composure. "They're talking plastic surgery. The camp's insurance will cover it. They're suing the mental hospital. Rex talked to one of their lawyers and we will be taking them to court too."

Damn right, Shawn thought. If it meant money, his dad wouldn't hire any cut-rate attorney.

"But," his mother said, "the surgeons keep lowering expectations. Telling us more what they can't do than what they can." Her sobbing renewed. "All the damage that crazy old man did. And now they're recommending a psychiatrist for Shawn."

"It's okay, Rose. That crazy old lunatic got what he deserved."

Right, Shawn thought.. *A hole in his face and decades in a mental ward. Because of that camp. And I'll end up just like him. Any settlement will go to trying to fix the hole in my face—which won't work. I'll look just like him. And once those parents get done in court with the hospital and the camp, they'll have tons of money, and their precious babies will get over* their *trauma.*

I saved their *sorry asses.*

Thoughts of despair intensified, finally breaking through his defenses. "And what for?" he silently mouthed. "I was an idiot to give a rat's ass about them!"

He tugged at his restraints. His face grew hot, throbbing. He didn't care. It didn't matter. He was going to be a disfigured freak, locked up like Hobo Bob. Probably in his padded cell. But, Shawn knew, he'd get out some day. And then…Yeah.

And then *they'd* pay.

A Functional Man
BY
MARTIN ZEIGLER

Zeigler is a retired software developer, and dabbles in piano, song composition, and comic book illustration. He enjoys writing primarily mystery and science fiction, as he finds thes often maligned genres thought-provoking and entertaining.

He appeared to be in one piece. No broken bones, no blood. From head to toe, however, he was spattered with what seemed to be chunks of yellow, pink, and brown clay. What a pretty mess.

Loraine watched her husband nudge his wire rims back up his nose and wondered what good that did. His glasses were flecked with the same stuff, which, as she thought about it, didn't look that much like clay after all.

"Carl, look at you. What happened?"

Carl held up a speckled hand. "Do you have sixty-five dollars?"

"Not on me. Why do you need—"

"He's out in the driveway. He needs sixty-five dollars."

Loraine stepped out onto the front porch and peered over the camellia bush. A tow truck sat in the gravel driveway. Their Echo, its windows, like orange cellophane, reflecting the setting sun, hung from its winch.

"Oh, Honey," she said. "Already?"

Yesterday, pride had coursed through Loraine like adrenaline. After twenty-three years of ferrying her husband to and from the lab, she had finally got to witness the impossible: Carl's brandishing a driver's license bearing his photo. And not just a photo. It was more than the stand-behind-the-yellow-line picture they usually click at licensing stations; this one captured the Essence of Carl: his middle-aged face, smooth with inexperience; his knowing and unknowing smile; those lone strands of hair poking out of his head as if sheer intellect had burned off all the rest.

This morning, though, as she had stood in her robe and seen Carl drive off to work for the very first time, a sort of buyer's remorse had taken hold. She had begun to wonder if it might be better for all concerned if Carl relinquished his license to the DMV, explaining that his passing the test had to have been a fluke. She could well imagine how Carl would take to the road. If a stop sign came up, he would think not about stopping but about the symmetries of octagons. If a light turned red, he would sail right through it while pondering the nature of the entire spectrum.

And now, this evening, after taking in Carl's spattered clothes and the Echo hanging from the hook like a big scarlet fish, she brushed by him, stepped off the porch, and strode along the flagstones toward the driveway, where the tow truck driver was leaning against the cab, tapping an unlit cigarette on his palm.

"What happened to the car?"

"That's a real good question." The driver stopped tapping the cigarette and began rolling it slowly back and forth between his hands. "Ma'am, I need to tell you something. I don't mean to sound out of place. Your husband seems like a nice guy. But I don't think he should be out there on the street driving."

Loraine nodded a little too quickly. She tried to cover up with, "What makes you say that?"

"This afternoon I get a call from him down at the garage. He says his car's in error. I say, 'In air? You mean your tire needs air?' No, he says, his automobile's got a serious error. Well, I never heard car troubles called that before, but in this business, you meet all walks, you know? So he gives me directions, and I take my truck out there to the Patterson Laboratories. That's where he works, I take it?"

"Yes, that's right."

"Man, something weird was going on there. But that's another story."

"What do you mean—weird?"

"Probably nothing. Egghead stuff."

Loraine nodded. Maybe, at long last, there was something to talk about over dinner.

"So anyway," the driver continued, "the first thing your husband says to me when I hop out of my truck is how afraid he is to drive the Echo as long as it's in error. There's that word again. So I ask him, what makes him think the car's in error, and he says because the needle is pointing to E."

Loraine shook her head. "Oh, no."

The driver nodded. "I tell him, look, the E stands for empty, not error. It means out of gas. Either that, or—say, is that your phone?"

"Why, yes, it is." Figuring Carl was still on the porch, Loraine called up to him. "Oh, Honey, be so kind and see who that is."

From behind the camellia, Carl said, "You mean the telephone?"

"Yes. Could you go answer it?"

"Are you sure that's what's ringing?"

"What else would it be? Carl, please answer the phone."

Loraine heard the screen door squeak open and slap shut, then turned back to the driver. "So the car's out of gas. Is that the problem?"

"Well...no," the truck driver said, "the engine was turned off. That's why the needle was pointing to E. So I ask your husband to start the car. After grinding it a few times, he fires it up. Needle shoots to midway on the gauge. I pat him on the back and tell him the car's doing just fine."

"So then why are you here with it?"

"He won't believe me. Honest Abe, Ma'am. He's sitting in the driver's seat looking up at me, and he says the car still has something wrong with it. Lookit, I tell him, the needle's smack dab in the middle. It's not anywhere close to the E. Then he comes back with, well, the car's not fully functional either, because if it was, the needle would be all the way to the top, pointing at the F."

"Oh, Carl."

The driver stuck the cigarette in his mouth, then took it out again and resumed tapping it. "He wanted me to tow him home so he could *investigate it further.* That's how he put it. And what else could I do? The customer's *always*, you know? So here I am lugging a car that's half-gassed-up and running like a top."

Loraine, weary of reacting with words, let out an exasperated sigh.

"But I still got to charge you sixty-five bucks."

Through the years, Loraine had mastered the art of contesting unjustified costs. Now, facing a bill for something that wasn't even broken, she asked simply, "Will you accept a check?"

The driver patted the logo on the cab door. "Just make it out to these guys."

"I'll get my checkbook."

Loraine turned around and almost bumped into her husband. "Carl," she said, recovering. "What are...when did you—who was on the phone?"

"I don't know. I can't figure those darn things out."

"Honey, they work just like any other...never mind. Maybe they left a message. Meantime, would you be a dear and get my checkbook? It's on the kitchen counter."

"I won't have to listen to any messages, will I?"

"No," Loraine sighed. "I'll do it later. Just get the checkbook."

After Carl disappeared once again into the house, Loraine found herself staring at the camellia, consciously ignoring the truck driver. She wasn't trying to be rude, but business had been agreed to and there was nothing more to discuss. Yet she felt she had better chat about something, if only to show him she had no hard feelings about the tow charge.

"So," she began, "this weird thing that happened at the lab. What was that all about?"

"Oh, that. A real weirdfest, let me tell you."

"Yes, I understand it was weird. But in what way?"

The driver gave the cigarette a disgusted look and slipped it under the flap of his shirt pocket. "The lab's got a chain-linked fence around it, but I still got a good look at what was going on. And maybe it wasn't weird. Just a typical day in the life, you know?"

"Weird or not," Loraine said, "what happened?"

"Okay. I'm driving to where your husband's parked, when I see four or five guys in white coats come busting out of the lab, waving their arms and shouting. One of these guys gets to the fence and starts rattling it and yelling at me."

This was not shaping up to be the filler talk Loraine had expected. "Yelling about what?"

"Beats me. My window was closed. The yelling comes through but not the words. But get this." The driver edged away from the cab and slunk toward Loraine speaking in a low whisper. "Armed security guards show up."

"What?" Loraine found herself whispering, too.

"There must have been a dozen of them. In no time they start herding the white coats back into the lab. All except for the guy at the fence. He's clinging for dear life and looking right at me like he's begging me to save him. Two guards grab hold of him and pull. Then a third guard sees this guy's giving them a run for their money and he...well..."

"And he what?"

"He pulls out his gun."

"My God! He drew his gun?"

"Sure as shoot—well, there wasn't any shooting. There didn't need to be. The egghead takes one look at the muzzle and heads back inside, all nice and polite. And I continue on my merry way to rescue your hubby."

"Did you ask *him* what was going on?

"I was thinking of it. But after the business with the gas gauge, I decided to let it go."

The driver went back to his truck and leaned against it exactly as before. Was this a required stance for tow truck drivers awaiting payment? "Genius is a funny thing," he concluded.

Loraine was about to agree when she heard a call from the porch. "What do I do here?"

She walked over to the bottom of the stairs and looked up.

Carl showed her the open checkbook, his pen poised. "Who do I make this out to?"

Loraine looked over at the truck. The driver gave her a polite salute. "Merrill's Towing," she said, as she climbed the stairs to look over her husband's shoulder.

"Yes, I know, but is this where I write it?" Carl pointed to a line on the check.

"No, that's where you sign it."

"You sure about that? I don't sign it here where it says, *Pay to the order of*?"

"No, that's where you put Merrill's Towing. Carl, did something happen at the lab today?"

"This doesn't make any sense to me at all," Carl said. "I ordered the tow truck to come pick me up. So I should put my name by 'Pay to the order of.'"

She took the pen from Carl and tapped different areas on the check. "Watch, Carl. You put Merrill's Towing here. You put the date up here in the corner. You sign it down here. And you put the amount here." She looked back to see if the driver was catching any of this. Thank goodness he was unhooking the Echo, apparently satisfied he would get paid.

"What about here?" Carl said.

"You put the amount there, too."

"Really?"

"Yes, really. Now, Carl, what happened at the lab? The tow truck driver says there was a panic. And that a guard pulled a gun."

"Nothing happened," Carl said, scrutinizing the check. "But why do I have to put the amount of money down twice?"

"My God, haven't you ever...come to think of it, I don't think I've ever seen...this is unbelievable."

Carl's hangdog look, on the other hand, was something she had seen before, many times in their years together. And now, spattered with stuff that looked nothing at all like clay, he seemed more helpless than ever. Patiently, she explained that on this line, the amount is written as a number, and on this line the number is spelled out.

As she slowly wrote out *sixty-five and no/100 dollars*, the driver materialized on the steps. “How are you two coming along with that there check?”

Carl looked up from his wife’s writing. “Almost done.”

“Don’t forget, it’s sixty-five dollars.”

“Oh, don’t worry,” Carl said. “We’re even putting it down twice.”

After Loraine switched off her phone, a wave of nausea ran through her. With both hands she gripped the receiver as if to squeeze the illness out of the message she had heard. Her stomach tightened when Carl appeared in the doorway waving a yellow receipt.

“Look what the driver gave me, Loraine.”

“Carl, tell me something. How did things really go at the lab today?”

“Pretty good. I polished up a few things.”

“Oh, is that how you put it?”

“I would have come home earlier, too, if the car hadn’t errored out. But I promise I’ll troubleshoot that later tonight.”

Dropping the phone on the sofa, Loraine stood up. “There’s nothing wrong with the car. And who are you to fix anything? I had to hold your hand so you could write out a simple check.”

“So?” Carl said, his defenses up. “Writing out numbers twice—one up here, one down there—whoever heard of anything so silly? And then spelling them out. Can you imagine what would happen at the lab if we had to spell out all our data? Seventy-two point four would become—S-E-V-E-N-T-Y dash T-W-O point F-O-U—”

“Stop, Carl. Stop.

The silence of the neighborhood invaded the living room. Loraine went over, clicked the front door shut, and took in a deep breath to allay her trembling. With surprising calmness, she managed, “Maybe if you scientists had taken the time to spell out your all-important numbers, the horrible accident wouldn’t have happened.”

“What horrible accident?”

Loraine swung around and looked her husband in the eye, or as best she could through those spotted lenses. "You know full well what I'm talking about."

"No, I don't."

"Gregory Michaelson. Know him?"

"Never heard of him."

"He obviously knows you. He's the one who called up earlier. He wanted you to explain things."

"How did he get hold of a phone?"

Loraine wanted to tear those glasses right off of Carl's face. "What difference does that make?"

"The phones were supposed to have been confiscated."

"Why in the world..." Loraine freed herself from the space between her husband and the front door and escaped into the heart of the living room. "Never mind. I understand. I wouldn't want word of a major disaster to get out either."

"Loraine, it's not that at all."

"It isn't? Not even when everyone in the entire lab was destroyed?"

"Not everyone," Carl pointed out. "And it wasn't the lab, just the annex."

"Carl, it's more than the count. It's what Gregory saw. It's what he saw."

Loraine sank back into the living room sofa and stared at the hallway as if it led into an abyss. "He saw them on the floor. He saw them all over the walls. He saw them seeping through the cracks in the tiles. No longer human beings, just pools of liquid flesh. He said the picture he would never get out of his mind as long as he lived was the lab coat lying on the floor and a face leaking out of the collar. Eyes, nose, mouth, ears. All flowing in a waxy stream. Those were Gregory's words before he was cut off."

"The guards must have spotted his phone and taken it away," Carl surmised.

"You mean the same guards who forced your colleagues back into the lab at gunpoint? Those guards?"

"I don't know. We have several guards."

"My God." Loraine looked up at Carl, her hands pressed

between her knees. "Why didn't you tell me about this when you got home? Wasn't this accident foremost in your mind? How could it not be? But your only concern seemed to be—"

"It wasn't an accident."

"—seemed to be paying that truck driver. And for what? For a gas gauge that...what do you mean, it wasn't an accident?"

"I mean, it wasn't an accident."

"You mean these people were destroyed deliberately?"

"Not destroyed. *Transformed.* I transformed them."

"*You* did this? On purpose?

Carl fell silent. This was good, Loraine thought. It meant he was weighing very carefully the next words out of his mouth. She sat up, her hands in her lap, awaiting his explanation, his remorse, his repentance.

Finally, after clearing his throat, he began, "Honey..."

"Yes?"

"I don't know how to say this..."

"Just do the best you can."

"That watch you gave me for my birthday? I think I lost it."

Loraine glared up at him. "Your watch?"

"I need to know if it's nine o'clock yet."

"Carl, is that all you have to say—you need to know the time?"

"The time is important to me."

Loraine shot up off the couch and stepped in close to him. "It's important to me, too. Do you know how worried I got when you didn't come home this afternoon? Do you know how long I waited to hear from you? Do you know how many times I called your office at the lab, only to get no answer? Or when I held my breath and phoned the State Patrol, dreading their news that you'd become a traffic fatality?"

"True, I was a little late getting home, but as you can see," Carl thrust his arms out, "I'm a-okay."

"I didn't know that, Carl. I was beside myself. I feared the worst had happened to you. But it was the opposite. The worst had happened to others—at your hands."

"That's not true."

"Carl, you destroyed those poor people."

"*Transformed*, Loraine."

She sank her head into her hands. After all these years indulging Carl's charming incompetence, the thing she had been secretly dreading finally came to light: finding out what he was capable of.

She faced the wall in disgust, refusing to turn around, even when she felt Carl's brief touch on her shoulder.

"Loraine, I can explain all this. Please hear me out."

And yet she had to think this through. If Gregory Michaelson's message had claimed that Carl had fixed a leaky faucet or bought a shirt on his own, she instantly would have doubted it; so why should she readily accept his role in such a dreadful holocaust?

Without turning to face him, she let her husband gently coax her to the dining room table.

"Please sit," Carl said. "Please listen."

Loraine held herself rigid, refusing to sit.

Then she sat, refusing to listen.

Then she listened.

With a flourish Carl clicked his pen and thrust it into his grit-speckled shirt pocket. "Here you go, Loraine," he said, sliding the sheet of paper across the table. "This should clear up everything."

She had seen scribbles like this before. Many a night she had climbed out of bed and stepped into the den, only to find her husband in his pajamas huddled over his desk, churning out pages and pages of these rapid-fire hieroglyphics.

Now these symbols were supposed to explain all. But when she looked at them—the arrows; the vertical lines; the double vertical lines; the letters with numbers above; the letters with numbers below; the sideways ems with numbers running along their legs; the croquet wickets; the sideways croquet wickets; the strange words like deg, lim, dim, mod, ker; the pitchfork shapes; the Chinese temple shapes; the tongs and ladles; the bars buckling under the weight of their collective numbers—Loraine felt as if she were staring at the E of an alien gas gauge.

"You're confused," Carl said.

"What does all this have to do with what happened at the lab today?"

"I've been struggling with this transform for over two years. Last week I finally had a breakthrough. Today, for the first time, I successfully demonstrated that it works."

"How? By transforming human beings into puddles?"

"Well, that's not why it's called a transform. Look..." Carl reached over and tapped the symbol-cluttered piece of paper. "See this? This means we're dealing with a structure of identities and inverses. Inverses and identities. Don't you see?"

Loraine shook her head, but not for the reason Carl probably thought.

Carl gave his calculations one final tap and sat back. "Take the identity. The identity is something that remains unchanged. I defined my own set of molecules as the identity, and that's why, when I activated my transform, my physical being remained unaffected."

"Why am I not surprised?" Loraine said.

"What do you mean?"

Loraine turned the sheet of calculations over as if it had had its day. "Nothing affects you. When you promised me you could explain all this, I was hoping to hear you say this Gregory Michaelson fellow was mistaken or there was some illusion in the lab caused by the lighting. Or that, yes, this devastating accident did occur, but it was an accident after all. Or if you truly were responsible that you would show regret or at least have the courage to admit you have no explanation. But I hear nothing. All you've given me is an equation."

"A *transform*," Carl said wearily. "And if you'd been listening to me the same way I listened to you go over the parts of a check, you would have heard me mention not just identities—but what else?"

"What else *what*?"

"Inverses!" Carl pushed back his chair and rose from the table. "What do we mean by inverses? Let's look at the number eight."

"Oh, God."

He offered a hand to the open dining room window as if it were a blackboard. "Now the number eight looks like a person, more or less. Let's transform that person. Let's add five to it. What do we get? Thirteen, obviously. Now thirteen doesn't look anything at all like a person, does it? In fact, it's now two separate entities, a one and a three. What are we to do? That's easy. We perform the inverse operation. Where we once added five, we now subtract five, and what happens? Why, we're back to eight, our original person. Uh, question?"

Realizing she had raised her hand like an eager student, Loraine immediately dropped it to the table. "What are you implying? That you can undo what you've done? That you can walk up to the widows and widowers you created today and guarantee a miracle?"

"Not a miracle," Carl said, his hands resting on the back of the chair. "A transform."

"Carl, human beings aren't figure eights."

"Oh, I know," Carl admitted. "I was just providing a simple—the telephone. Loraine, you better see who it is."

Even before she put the receiver to her ear, the voice on the other end began jabbering. The words fired away non-stop, as if the speaker had mere seconds to spill everything. Loraine recognized right off who it was and put her hand over the mouthpiece.

"Carl," she said, "do you mind stepping outside until I'm through?"

Loraine ran onto the porch as if suddenly cured of the black plague. "Carl, you'll never believe this."

"Believe what?"

"That was Gregory Michaelson."

Carl was sitting on the top stair, his scalp gleaming in the porch light. "Okay."

"And guess what he said. You'll never guess what he said. I still can't believe what he said." Realizing she was talking as rapidly as Michaelson, Loraine tried to slow down. "He—Michaelson—

Gregory Michaelson—returned to the lab to—"

"Everyone's back to normal," Carl said.

"He'd got hold of a camera. He wanted to get proof of what happened in case there was some cover-up down the road. But when he returned to the lab he saw that everyone was...back to... but how did you know?"

"When we were in the dining room, I could see the kitchen clock. I didn't need my watch after all. It was past nine."

"Past nine? Carl, I'm talking about the people. How could this be? How could they be normal now when, seconds before, they were just blobs of flesh?"

"That's what I tried to tell you. My transform contains identities and inverses. Identities keep things the same. Inverses reverse things. I stayed the same. And I reversed things."

"Gregory Michaelson said everyone in the lab seemed confused and disoriented. Some people found themselves lying on the floor or leaning against the wall. He asked a few of them if they knew what had happened. They said they felt as if they had gone through some terrible ordeal but they didn't know what. And that they felt like celebrating, but they didn't know why."

Gripping the railing, Carl eased himself up from the stair and brushed off his rump. "Earlier today I had programmed the transform to reverse itself at precisely nine o'clock. I wanted to be away when this happened so people wouldn't think I was manipulating the data. I knew it would work. That's because *I* calculated it. Those equations I showed you? Those are *my* equations."

"I thought they were called transforms."

Carl smiled at his wife like a master to a sharp-eyed apprentice. "Very good. Very good."

Although she had intended to be sarcastic, Loraine still felt herself blushing at the complement. "And the transform worked?"

"Yes it did. But it might not have if word had got out. People would have come in and mopped everything up, and there's no telling how things would have turned out in that case. That's why I took away everyone's phone."

"But now everyone is fully restored, Carl? Exactly? They're exactly as before? Carl, please tell me these people are exactly as they were before."

"Well, like every experiment, this one had certain discrepancies."

"Discrepancies?" Loraine felt the fear again, rising up in her throat like acid.

"Yes," Carl said, "but they're negligible. They all lay within acceptable tolerances."

She didn't understand, but it sounded reassuring. "All I want to know is...are you sure everyone's okay?

"Positive."

With that one word, all tragedy vanished. It was if Carl's hand had reached out and swooped Loraine from a maelstrom. She went up to him, smiled, and kissed him, deeply and gratefully. Then, resting her face next to his and closing her eyes, Loraine pulled her husband tight to her breasts. "You're my genius."

"It was nothing," Carl said. "But what about the car? I should take a look at it before it gets too late."

"You go ahead," Loraine whispered. "You fix our car."

As soon as Loraine let him go, Carl was off the porch and around the camellia. The night much cooler now, she folded her arms, and in so doing, felt something on her skin. Under the bright porch light, she could see that some of the grit that had been covering Carl had rubbed off on her. She saw it on her arms and hands and on her shirt, and she felt it on an earlobe and in her hair.

Examining the specks on her hand in all their colorful diversity, Loraine was reminded for some reason of the lab picnic last year where, finally, she had got to meet Carl's colleagues. A motley team of great minds from such distant cities as Manila, Bombay, Helsingborg, Sao Domingos, Kenya.

Rubbing a dark clump of material between her thumb and forefinger, she recalled the vice-like grip of one Doctor Wambua Mithaiwala, and hoped his handshake was still just as vigorous.

And now, focusing her attention on the lighted garage, Loraine wanted to shout to her neighbors and to the world how she loved everything about her man: the way he could not write checks or open jars or slice bread or ride a bicycle or paint a shelf. The way he could scribble arrows and ladles and ems with numbers along the sides and croquet wickets. And how he could diagnose errors in automobiles and especially how he could transform living people into flowing shapes and then bring them back again, fully resurrected, except, perhaps, for those tiny and quite acceptable differences.

Deer Illusion

BY

Lesley Conner

First published in Abaculus II, *Conner writes mostly horror stories with strong female protagonists. A mother of two, she lives with her family in Hagerstown, and is currently working on a historial horror novel.*

Jules crouched in the weeds alongside the desolate road, waiting. She hadn't seen a car or truck in the last half hour. The right one would come along soon enough; a lone car with an innocent driver. Gravel crunched under her black, military-style boot as she shifted her weight, trying to find a more comfortable position. She knew that she wouldn't find one. It was cold, raining, and starting to get dark.

Comfort wasn't a part of the deal.

Todd Bibbee hummed along with the old Johnny Cash song crooning from the truck radio. He couldn't get into the stuff that they called "new country" music. It sounded like shit to him. Still, as long as there were men like him in the world he figured he'd be able to find a station that sounded like old honky-tonk, and that suited him just fine. He stretched as well as he could behind the steering wheel of his old, rusty Dodge, and scratched his ever-expanding belly.

A smile settled onto his worn face. His wife of 34 years, Tricia, was always nagging him about his eating habits and his weight. His youngest daughter, who was studying nutrition at WVU, was coming home this weekend from college, and he knew that the two of them would use the opportunity to gang up on him. With a wife and four daughters, it was good thing that Todd had gotten used to all the scolding. He loved it, because he knew it meant they cared enough to pay attention to what he was doing.

"Dammit," Todd muttered. "I wish I could see." His smile turned into a sneer at his own procrastination. The defroster in the truck had stopped working a couple months back, and he hadn't gotten around to fixing it yet.

The rain had started shortly before he had left town, and had gotten steadily worse as he drove the 16 miles home. It was to the point now that he could barely see two feet beyond the windshield, except for the occasional flash of lightning behind the trees. With the rain came a fog that no headlights could penetrate. If it weren't for the old beer cans thrown in the ditch by the young kids driving home on the weekends, Todd never would have been able to see the edge of the road. He swiped at the windshield with his slightly used handkerchief, and pulled himself closer to the steering wheel in an attempt to see the road. After 28 years of driving this stretch of back country West Virginia, he knew that being able to see was a must, especially during hunting season, when animals tended to be more skittish.

His eyes caught a movement on the right side of the road and for a moment he thought he saw a woman with fire red hair. Just as he was wondering what the hell a woman would be doing out in a storm like this, a deer stepped in front of his truck. He slammed on the brakes and waited for the impact. It was too close. There was no way that he was going to miss this one.

The thud never came, but it didn't matter. The old Dodge started to skid on the slippery, wet leaves that lay on the pavement. Todd fought for control of his vehicle. It started to careen to the left, which would have led to a deadly crash into the bottom of a ravine. Jerking the wheel quickly, he sent the truck spinning, but managed to pull it to the right side of the road.

Before he slammed into the embankment and the tree that was keeping the earth from washing away in the rain, Todd saw the woman again; standing in the road where the deer had been. Her red hair was blowing wildly in the wind, electrified in the storm. With her hand on her hip, she looked bored stiff, just waiting for everything to be over so that she could get out of the rain.

The impact of the crash threw Todd face first into the steering wheel that he had, moments before, been crouching so closely to. Pain erupted in his face, and there was a heavy feeling in his chest that he figured was a broken rib or two, but he would walk away. He didn't think his truck would be so lucky. The front end was completely smashed in, and all the windows had broken on impact.

"Shatter-resistant, my ass," he mumbled as he reached down to open the door. The walk home in the rain was going to be an ordeal, but he didn't see any point in delaying it. That's when he noticed that the woman was still standing in the road. For a moment he had thought that he had imagined her during the crash, a fantasy flashing before his eyes instead of his life. There was no denying that she was a remarkably gorgeous woman, and in his younger days, before Tricia, she was exactly the type of girl he would have been chasing. But there was something unnerving about her. Menacing.

Frozen with his hand on the handle of the door, Todd couldn't take his eyes off of her. Lightning flashed behind the woman. It looked as if she were on fire, standing in the pits of Hell. Her eyes, an icy blue , seared his soul. Todd wasn't a man that scared easily, but the strange woman sent a shiver of primal fear through him. As she took her first step in the direction of his truck, he felt the warmth spread through the front of his jeans as his bladder gave way to the panic that the rest of his body was feeling.

Jules quickly closed the space between herself and the wrecked truck, peering into the opening where the driver's side window used to be. She hated this type of weather and couldn't wait for a hot shower and a dry bed. The deer illusion worked every time on roads like these, especially in wet weather like tonight. She couldn't pass up the chance to perform the task that was required of her, no matter how much she didn't want to do it. Not when the situation was so perfect.

Looking in at Todd, Jules could see that his face was a bloody mess, as smashed-up as the front of the Dodge, maybe even worse. With all of his front teeth either missing, broken, or lodged in the steering wheel, it was hard to understand what he was trying to say when he saw her walk up beside him, but she knew it was something about thinking he saw a deer. Shock and fear were setting in and he was beginning to get delusional, mixing up what he thought he had seen, what had truly been there, and the terror that was overloading his system. He knew that his truck never hit anything until it smashed into the tree. He couldn't understand where the deer had gone; he had just seen it.

Jules felt sorry for the man. Almost. But she couldn't let her personal feelings get in the way of what she had come to do. She had learned that a long time ago. He wouldn't let her. She shivered: not from the cold, but from the thought of him; the demon that controlled her every movement, and made her less than human.

Reaching through the broken window, Jules pushed a few stray hairs away from Todd's forehead, looking into his confused, brown eyes. She understood the confusion. She had seen it so many times over the years. Too many times, but she couldn't stop now. She had made her decision a long time ago; this wasn't the time to reconsider.

When her cool fingertips brushed his clammy skin, she saw his life unfold in her mind: his wife, his daughters, and the love that resonated in his home. A tear slid down her cheek, falling from her chin and becoming one with the rain. She steeled herself against the grief that threatened to overwhelm her. Her eyes now as hard and cold as ice, she moved her hand to his chest and stopped his heart with nothing more than a thought.

Jules left Todd's body in his truck, and walked back to the place where she had been hiding in the weeds. There she picked up the backpack that she had left before stepping into the road and causing the accident. She opened the bag and pulled out a small, blue, glowing orb, holding it in front of her face. Blowing gently, she deposited Todd's soul in Hell. That was one more for Lucifer. One more towards the insurmountable amount that would eventually set her own soul free. One more soul that he got that wasn't destined to be his.

Shouldering her bag, Jules walked down the road in the direction that Todd's truck had come. She knew eventually that it would lead to a town. There she would find a motel, take a hot shower and climb into a dry bed. Her version of paradise. She could hear the orbs in her bag tinkling as they bumped into each other. Her bag was getting full and she knew that she would have to meet with the demon before long to drop off the collected souls. She shivered at the thought of it. The demon was lurid and always made a pass at her. She tried to keep things strictly professional, but it was getting harder to push off his advances. Pretty soon he wasn't going to take no for an answer.

The rain splattered on her face and rolled down her leather jacket. Her steps were confident, even in the slippery conditions, and she allowed her mind to roam. She had been trying to think of a way out of her contract for a long time. If she could go back, she would have just entered Hell, and taken her eternity of punishment instead of listening to the demon who had offered her a way to get her soul back and a chance at happiness. But if she could go back that far, then she wouldn't have slashed her wrists in the first place. Suicide hadn't fixed her life and it fucked up her afterlife. It wasn't worth it.

"Help me."

The voice coming from her bag startled Jules. Peering into the darkness, she could see Todd's face pushed against the inside of the orb. Her eyes widened. She had never had a soul talk to her once she had pushed it through the gateway into Hell. She would hear the occasional moans and screams of anguish, but nothing that was directed to her. The orbs were like a personal ticket, a soul's own entrance, but once through she had never had one find its way back to the door. Todd stared at her, his eyes pleading but not hysterical.

"You have to help me get out." His voice was resolute.

"No, I don't," Jules said.

"You don't want to do this. I don't deserve to be here."

"Most people I send over don't." Her voice was quiet. She hated to admit that, even to herself, and here she was telling someone else. It hurt, even if he was dead.

Todd's eyes stayed fixed on hers. He was silent, but occasionally a look of pain would cross his features. Jules didn't want to think about what was happening to him out of her line of sight, and she wondered how long he would be able to hold on.

"Please."

Jules felt her resolve crumble. Reaching into the bag, she plucked the orb from among the others. She raised her hand over her head and then slammed the orb onto the road. It burst open, allowing Todd's soul to flee. Because it was a gateway only for him, his tormentors couldn't pursue. They screamed angrily at his escape. A huge smile covered his face, full of relief. His body was transparent and he hovered near her. Spinning, he looked down at her.

"Thank you."

"You need to get out of here. I've released you from Hell, but I can't bring you back to life. I don't have that type of power."

Todd's smile faltered.

"But what about my family?"

Jules shifted the bag back onto her shoulder, looking down the road and dreaming of the bed she knew was in that direction. Squinting up at Todd with rain water dripping down her face, she sighed.

"They'll find your body in your truck, grieve and then move on. You get to enjoy your afterlife in heaven and eventually you'll all be reunited. End of story." Jules knew that she was being cold, but she was tired and didn't feel like getting into a long conversation with the man she had just murdered. He didn't seem to be happy with her explanation. His face was scrunched into a scowl.

"But it wasn't my time to go. You stole my life from me."

Jules turned and began walking down the road once again. There was no point in denying what Todd said. It was true, but she couldn't change that. She could feel him floating above her, following her.

"What about the others?"

She spun around and glared at him, her patience gone.

"What others?"

"The others that don't deserve to be in Hell." His voice was just as cold as hers had been.

"They're paying for my freedom."

"That isn't right, and you know it." Todd started to float away, his words hanging in the saturated air. He melted into the tree line at the edge of the road. Jules was furious.

"And what would you have me do about it?" she screamed. "You've been there, in Hell. If you were given the opportunity to get your soul back and start over, wouldn't you? No matter what?" Her breath was tearing raggedly from her lungs. She stared at the trees where Todd had disappeared, looking for any sign of him. He didn't reappear but she heard his voice close by.

"Not if it meant turning over others to a place I wasn't willing to go."

"Then what do I do?" Her voice was softer now that her anger had been spent. Todd was telling her things that she had been struggling with herself for a long time. She wanted to go back, make different choice, but she didn't know how to do it. Suddenly, Todd was there. He hovered directly in front of her, giving her a look that she was sure his daughters were very familiar with.

"Set them free." His face was solemn as he gestured to her bag. The words came out husky, soft with emotion. Jules looked into his big, brown eyes and wished that she'd had a father like him when she was growing up. Maybe things would have been different for her.

Grasping the bag tightly in her hand, Jules made a decision that she knew would change everything for her. She raised the bag high above her head, her eyes locked on Todd's, and then brought it down with all of her strength, smashing it into the cracked asphalt. The orbs shattered, releasing all of the souls that she'd collected over the past several months. Transparent figures of men and women, young and old, flew into the air with a sigh of relief. Todd smiled at her, nodding his head in a proud manner, and then slipped into the tree limbs with the other spirits.

Leaving the bag and the broken glass in the road, Jules walked away. She knew that she would pay for what she had done. It would probably set her back a hundred years before she'd be able to make it up to the demon and set herself free, but she couldn't worry about it now.

Depression settled over her as she realized that she wasn't sure that she was willing to make up anything. She didn't want to be a soul collector any more. It made her feel bad and dirty. If she wasn't willing to perform her job, she knew that she would be forced through her own gateway and someone else would collect souls. Someone who was willing. She wondered how much time she had before she had to make the decision.

A loud pop sounded behind her. Jules jumped, goose flesh breaking out on her arms. Whirling, she saw the demon strutting towards her. He had a wicked grin on his face.

"Jules, my girl, what has happened to you?" His voice came out like a hiss, sending a shiver of fear through her. Jules didn't know his name. She knew it wasn't Lucifer, he wasn't that high up, but he did hold a lot of power and that power increased if she did her job well. She was supposed to find the freshest, most innocent souls. He had hinted to her several times that children would be the best, but she couldn't bring herself to do that.

"I slipped. Um, I dropped my bag. The road is wet. The orbs all smashed." Jules stammered over her words, looking for an explanation that would seem the most plausible.

"Tsk, tsk." The demon cocked his head as if he were admonishing a small child. "We both know that isn't true." A moment of clarity passed over his face, dropping his voice an octave when he spoke again. "You haven't the heart for this anymore."

With no other clues as to his action, the demon leaped through air and knocked Jules to the ground, landing squarely on her chest. He reared back. His face contorted to allow rows of dagger like teeth to form and his eyes glowed yellow. Jules tried to break free, but his weight held her still, giving her little more than wiggle room.

Diving forward, he bit deeply into her shoulder. The pain was fierce. Screams poured from her as she thrashed beneath him. He ripped off a hunk of flesh and swallowed it with a gulp. Smiling, he leaned forward for more. Jules screwed her eyes shut, blocking out the sight of her blood running down his face and the loathing burning in his eyes. She tried to imagine that she was anywhere but where she was, but instead could only replay all of the events that had led her to this place. Regret flooded her as she felt the demon lap at the wound he had created.

Suddenly, the weight was removed from her chest. The demon's screams mixed with her own. Opening her eyes, Jules saw the freed souls circling her attacker. They spun around him furiously. She could feel heat building and saw the demon's skin writhing along his arms and torso. He looked her in the eye, pain and rage etched onto his face. The heat kept building and building until he exploded, showering the road with hissing sparks that quickly cooled in the pelting rain.

Jules was stunned, staring at the charred remains of the demon. Silence filled the forest. Slowly, souls began leaking from his remains. They poured into the night sky, gaining speed until they whipped past her in wide ribbon of transparent flesh. Todd rushed towards her, his face beaming with glee.

"We did it. We set them all free."

As he raced into the dark sky, joining the other spirits and whooping with happiness, horror flooded Jules. She backed off the road and into the forest, trying to find some sort of cover. Blood poured from her shoulder, but she ignored it. She huddled down and watched as more and more spirits escaped from Hell. The flow was immense, and it didn't look like it was ever going to stop. A sad keening sound seeped from her as she rocked back and forth. The only thought that made it through her despair was that she should slice her wrists all over again, but she wasn't sure that it would help. The doorway was open.

Jules had just released all the souls in Hell onto earth, and she knew that not all of them were innocents who weren't meant to be there. Most of them were evil, and now they were free.

By Maggots be Driven
By
Robert Essig

Essig sees stories in just about everything, and has had his fiction features in markets that include "Tales of the Talisman," "Cemetary Moon," "Sinister Tales," and "The Nocturnal Lyric." Forthcoming shorts include placements in "It Was a Dark and Stormy Halloween," and "The Etheral Gazette."

It was on a dreary day in of April that Kelly discovered the first maggot gently inching its way up her thigh.

Kelly sat in her living room, staring through the picture window at the rain, each drop like a soldier in a war to turn the earth into a muddy pool. Her thoughts were elsewhere, not admiring the rain so much as wondering how she would be able to go on.

At first the maggot was undetected, the itch nothing more than a minor irritation, possible a stray thread from the inner hem of her pants.

The past year had been rough after Gary died, leaving Kelly a widow and their daughter fatherless, but Little Erica seemed to be taking it rather well. Kelly told her that her father had gone on a very long vacation, one he may not return from. How was she supposed to break the news of Gary's death to her seven-year-old daughter? After all, Kelly was having a hell of a time dealing with the devastation herself.

That was six months ago and here she was staring out the picture window at the empty street, a metaphor for the way she felt inside.

She noticed the itch on her thigh, the crawling. Realizing it was something alive, something moving, she reached her hand up the cuff of her sweatpants and grabbed the little bugger, pulling it free from the cave of her pant sleeve.

She wasn't one to become squeamish at the sight of a bug, but a maggot was different. When she opened her cupped hand and saw the little white globule in her palm she screeched, dropping it on the floor.

As devourers of the dead maggots are harmless to the living, but that mattered little to Kelly. To her, a maggot was disgusting, something that lives on the undersides of road kill, in the muck at the bottom of a garbage can or in a rotting corpse.

Where did that come from? Kelley wondered.

She looked down. *Oh god, it's on the floor!*

She was on her knees in a matter of seconds, her hands searching franticly for the little white nasty concealed so well on her white carpet.

As she searched, she felt things crawling on her arms. Shivers ran down her spine as she made childish noises, brushing invisible bugs from her goose-pimpled flesh.

"Mommy, what are you doing?" Erica asked as she stepped into the living room.

Kelly looked up at her daughter as if she had been caught in a sex act. "Uh..."

"Are you looking for something?"

"Um...yes, I found it," Kelly lied. "My earring fell on the floor."

"Oh," Erica walked by her mother and into the kitchen.

Kelly looked back to the carpet, thinking about what just transpired. She must have looked like a lunatic, frantically brushing away unseen bugs.

She found the maggot inching its way through the carpet fibers, invisible save for its miniscule black eyes. The fear of it had subsided a bit from her initial discovery. She used a tissue to kill it.

The thought of how out of place the maggot was seemed to elude her.

The two ate dinner at the little round table in the dining alcove next to the kitchen. After Gary died there was no need for a large dinner table. It would be Kelly and Erica until the end.

The end! What does that mean?

Not the end, Kelly thought, but until Erica goes to college.

Kelly looked at her daughter, watched the little girl shovel macaroni and cheese into her mouth as if it were the last box of the stuff on earth. The kid had an appetite, that was for sure. Kelly couldn't say the same for herself. Since Gary's death she had lost twenty pounds, leaving her at an emaciated one-hundred ten.

How could she get over her father's death so easily? Kelly wondered, a bit resentful of her daughter ability to forget. Maybe I should have been convinced he went on a long vacation.

She watched her daughter eating, unable to find her own appetite, when she saw something moving on the little girl's forehead at her hairline.

Oh no! Another one.

"Hold still, honey," Kelly said reaching across the table to pluck the filthy little maggot from her daughter's head. She didn't want to touch it, but had to be strong for fear of frightening her daughter.

"What is it, Mommy?"

"Just..."

Kelly pulled the maggot away between her thumb and pointer finger.

"Ewwww, is it a bug?"

"Just a little one." Kelly placed the maggot in a paper towel, smashed it and threw it into the garbage.

"There's no more on me, are there?" said Erica, frantically running her hands through her hair. "Mommy, check and see, there's no more, are there?"

"Honey, calm down, there's no more."

"What was it?"

Erica was nearly in tears at this point. Kelly thought it wise to take a piece of advice from her fib about Gary's death. "It was lice, that's all. You remember what lice are, right? What Jessica had."

"Ewwwww, liiice."

"It's not a big deal, Erica, all kids get it. We'll wash your hair real well tonight and make them go away."

Erica lost her ravenous appetite and joined her mother in a sort of melancholy. Their house often had this sort of desperate atmosphere, and the rain outside did nothing more than further dampen the mood.

Kelly lay in bed that night thinking about what had happened. It made no sense. Fortunately she was able to keep it from her daughter, but for a moment there she thought the urge to scream would win.

It was during Erica's bath, as she sat in the tub playing with bubbles, her mother washing her hair acting as if she was looking for lice. Only instead she found maggots.

The first one startled her.

It can't be!

But it was. She popped it in her fingers, wiping the residue on a towel. One was the limit, right? No, there was more than that, a lot more.

They seemed to sprout from her daughter's head. She couldn't get all of them, some sliding down the little girl's body into the bubbly bath water.

At one point Kelly couldn't do it any longer. The crawling feeling on her arms and legs intensified. Her hands tingled with movement, as if the maggots were coming out of Erica's head and on to her flesh. It was difficult to stifle the urge to vomit.

Erica was completely oblivious to the phenomenon. It was as if maggots sprouted from her head on a regular basis.

Soon the bubbles would dissipate and the death devourers

would be floating in the water. If her daughter were to see bugs floating in the tub with her she would scream and possibly slip and injure herself trying to escape the bath.

"Okay, I think we're done here," said Kelly.

She succeeded in getting Erica out of the tub before the little girl saw anything and wiped her down, inspecting her head as she did so. It was clean and maggot free.

Now, as Kelly lay in bed, she wondered what happened today. Even under the safety of her covers she could feel things crawling about, tingling and writhing. It was everything she could do not to throw the sheets onto the floor and examine her body. She knew they weren't there, but then again...

It was one of those sleepless nights of tossing and turning in attempt to be comfortable, glancing at the clock radio every five minutes. How she finally fell asleep, she didn't know.

The following morning Kelly would wake up to an unpleasant surprise.

Kelly woke with a dull throb in her head and a crawling on her body and in her hair. Her eyes opened wide, brushing away the sluggishness of sleep immediately.

She drew the sheets away in revelation, a scream escaping her lips as she did so for what was crawling amongst her body was an army of little white soldiers: maggots!

She began trembling like a junkie in need of a fix, her hands franticly shaking her hair to liberate her scalp of the retched creatures, her breathing quick and panicked, small sounds escaping her mouth, sounds of fear and disgust.

Jumping out of bed, she pounced, hoping the maggots would lose their grip and fall to the floor. Most of them did, and as she jumped she began to grind them into the carpet.

From there, she jumped in the shower, washing every maggot down the drain.

Reluctantly, she reentered her bedroom. Everything was still, not an inch of a little white larva to be seen. It was as if it had all been a dream, but it wasn't. They were hiding somewhere, perhaps under the bed. They were sneaky like that.

She decided on the vacuum cleaner, the hose attachment. They wouldn't get away from her, wouldn't get into the corners and crevices to breed like roaches.

Removing the sheets from her bed she found some of them, caught them probably in the act of mating.

The smile on her face was that of sweet revenge with a twist of madness. She flicked the ON switch and began sucking up every maggot she could. She worked at them for a half an hour until her daughter came in the room, driving her away from her half-baked daze.

Kelly looked at Erica wide-eyed, examining her body for signs of larvae. She was clean.

They ate breakfast without a maggoty interruption. Erica enjoyed her Cream of Wheat, mostly because of the amount of brown sugar and butter she put in it. Kelly, on the other hand, couldn't help but wonder why hers was crawling.

Kelly left her daughter at the table, left her slopping breakfast into her gullet greedily, left because she couldn't bare to witness someone so jolly so soon after her own father's death. Erica made her sick that way. Seven years old or not, she was taking the loss with a grain of salt.

That little bitch!

At times, it was all Kelly could do not to slap her snot-nosed brat of a daughter across the face open handed. Teach the kid a lesson in respect for the dead.

Good-for-nothing little brat!

Kelly stewed in her anger, pacing her bedroom back and forth. The maggots were an issue that made no sense, one that, previous to Kelly's newfound frustration with her daughter, gave her the creeps. The other issue *was* her daughter.

She's not the problem, the better half of Kelly's mind chimed in. *You told her he went on a long vacation, didn't you? What reason does she have to feel the way you do?*

Her subconscious made sense. The poor little girl didn't even know the truth.

Maybe she needs to know the truth. Maybe it's time I fill her in.

Kelly felt it was the right thing to do. She couldn't go around feeling sorry for herself over the loss of her husband when they *both* could feel so sad. It was selfish, but she felt it needed to be done. If she was going to get through this thing she wanted her daughter right there with her, crying with the falling rain.

"Erica." Kelly addressed her daughter in a voice that said: listen up kiddo, there's something we need to talk about.

There was no response.

"Erica, I have something very important I need to tell you."

"Yes, Mommy," the little girl's voice reverberated drearily from the kitchen table, her head cocked down as if praying or perhaps doodling on a piece of paper.

Kelly took the seat opposite her daughter as to face her.

"There's something we need to talk about, something very serious." Erica nodded. "It's about your father."

Where only a month ago Kelly was distressed and confused about what to say to her daughter about Gary's death, she now had no trouble at all. In fact, what she said might have come out a bit too blunt for a seven-year-old.

"You remember what I told you about Daddy going away for a while, don't you? Well, the truth is, he's going to be gone forever. He died in an accident at work." Erica was speechless. "You may not understand death, you may be too young, but it means your Daddy isn't going to be coming home. Ever."

Kelly looked into her daughter's glassy eyes, watching her child-brain register the weight of what she had just explained to her. As she watched, Kelly noticed a movement on Erica's scalp, a little white maggot—well, not so little anymore—inching its way through her hair like a piece of bloated rice.

Kelly reached out, but drew her hand back instead. She figured if Erica was going to have to deal with her father's death then she could learn to deal with the maggots as well.

Think I'll let her stew in it for a while.

Kelly was in her bedroom for the rest of the day, moving furniture in search for the maggot nest. At first she thought they were like roaches, breeding in the walls and scurrying around at night, but when she woke with them crowding her bed, she considered other possibilities.

She found nothing in her bedroom, not a solitary maggot, which should have been a good thing. She had brought out a can of Raid ready to wipe their nest out. She figured it would be a sort of cocoon-looking thing like a wasp's nest. Why: she really didn't know.

The idea that maggots fed and lived off of dead things was no longer in Kelly's mind. Somehow she had convinced herself that they weren't quite as nasty as she thought, that they were nothing more than, say, an ant or beetle.

At this point she was beginning to realize that she may have to get used to them, and if she was going to have to get used to them, damn it, so was Erica.

I never did hear her scream.

Kelly had assumed her daughter would shriek when she discovered the maggot that had been crawling around her scalp.

Don't know how she could have missed it.

Dinner that night was a simple stir-fry (hold the rice) of beef and veggies. It wasn't Erica's favorite (yesterday's Mac N' Cheese taking that high honor) but Kelly decided she was going to cater less to her ungrateful daughter.

Isn't saying much, though, Kelly observed as Erica hardly touched her food. *Maybe she's finally feeling my pain.*

Whether she was feeling her mother's pain or not, she sure didn't seem to feel the fat maggots adorning her face. Once again, her mother ignored them, insisting to herself that Erica would have to grow up and take care of them herself.

She must like them.

After dinner Kelly returned to her bedroom for one last maggot search party before bed. She was surprised to find nothing there.

As she looked around her room she felt a pang of fear at the general disarray. For a moment there she couldn't figure out how her room became so thrashed; for a moment there she thought she had been robbed.

You haven't been robbed, you oaf, you were exterminating the maggots, remember?

"Oh...yes, I was," she said to herself.

How did that saying go? If you talk to yourself, you're not crazy until you respond. Kelly had never heard that humorous little anecdote, and if she had, it was already forgotten.

Lately many things seemed to be forgotten. Take the maggots. The idea that they were like roaches or that they made a hive was preposterous. Everyone knew they were fly larvae that feasted on decomposing matter. That was why they were so disgusting, so unsavory. But something was wrong with Kelly, her sense of logic having become skewed.

Kelly slid into her bed, her face smiling for the first time since her husband died three months ago...or was it a year? Her smile faltered for a second as she tried to remember exactly when Gary died. It was most certainly three months, not a year, or...

Her smile returned. When didn't matter as much as the fact that he was indeed gone, and now that she had told her daughter the truth, she could cry herself to sleep the same way Kelly had so many nights since Gary's passing. The thought of her daughter's sadness was enough to rouse a deeper, wider grin, one like that of a clown or jester, or perhaps a lunatic.

The following morning was not unlike the former. Her bed was once again crawling with maggoty life, though she wasn't quite so frightened by their intrusion. Hell, she half-expected it.

Peeling the sheets away they tumbled onto the floor, plump and fat from feeding. The morbid thought occurred to her that she might already be dead, the maggots feasting on her rotting flesh. That thought brought her into the bathroom for an inspection of her body. She certainly didn't appear dead.

Back in her bedroom they were writhing over the sheets even bigger than before, their color a creamy yellow, causing them to stand out on the white carpet as they crept in a sort of line out the door and into the hallway. As if leading Kelly to something.

She didn't much fear them. As a matter of fact she had begun to remember that they were eaters of the dead, not living, but there was something wholly wrong with their manner. And there were a goddamned lot of them.

Oh god, they're taking over.

Follow them!

Images were surfacing in Kelly's mind, dire images of her family. She could see the way Erica was brooding over her dinner the night before, how sad she was. Images of her husband came to her as she walked down the hallway, careful not to smash the creeping line of inflated maggots, images of...

...Him falling down the basement stairs...no, that's not how it happened, he died at work...no...

The maggots led her to the kitchen. Her hands went to her mouth as a scream echoed through the empty house. She bit her knuckles, trembling in the wake of finding Erica's body sitting at the dinner table just as Kelly left her the night before. Her body now looked spoiled, rotten and infested with a constant movement beneath her flesh.

Oh my god, they killed my daughter, Kelly thought frantically.

Her first instinct was to stomp on the trail of maggots that led her to this macabre scene, but they were gone, a figment of her imagination.

Her daughter was still there, though, writhing with the fattened larva.

Kelly dashed across the kitchen for the telephone, her madness reaching a level of incomprehension. She dialed 911 in a sort of panicked reflex. They asked her what the problem was and all she could do was whimper into the phone, mumbling the word "maggots" over and over.

The police traced the call and held it as a high priority case of possible domestic disturbance. They were prepared to find a disturbing scene, but nothing could have readied them for what they were to discover in Kelly's house.

After no one answered the pounding on the door, they busted it in. The living room appeared very normal. However, there was the unmistakable perfume of rot in the air. One cop retched while others covered their faces with one hand while pointing their guns with the other.

In the kitchen Kelly was crouched in a corner, sobbing and mumbling incoherently, her mental state obviously frayed. At the table was a child's rotting body, bloated with death gasses and crawling with maggots.

On further investigation, after unable to get anything from Kelly, another discovery was made in the basement, one that would seem to make this an open and closed case. It wouldn't be that easy of course, things weren't always as they seemed, but the evidence was pretty telling.

A man, presumed to be Kelly's husband, was lying on the floor of the basement, his body almost unrecognizable from the state of decomposition. Scattered around and in the soup of his body were cell phone records and love letters with big red kisses on them.

To this day, from the mental health institution where Kelly resides, she insists it was the maggots that did it.

FLOWERS OF THE SKY: DISCOVERIES
BY
R.S. HUNTER

The soon to be graduate of the University of Redlands was first published in Abaculus II, and has just completed co-authoring his first optioned screenplay. Hunter writes science fiction because he can bend the rules of reality in his created worlds.

Alec Cole had never seen a real dead man before. This one didn't look like the ones he'd seen in daguerreotypes. They were always dressed in their finest clothes, resting peacefully, hands clasped over their stomach as they awaited their final rites. The body in front of him certainly didn't look the way he'd imagined. He stared at it with a detached sense of incomprehension.

This body, lumpy and bloated, looked like a monster from a nightmare. Yellow and purple bruises covered its face, a line of dried blood and spit crusting its chin. Underneath the bruises, blue veins branched out underneath pale skin. A putrid scent coming off the body mingled with the smells of urine and garbage in the alley, coating the back of Alec's throat.

The dead man wore a brown wool coat over his waistcoat and shirt, which were stained with red-brown blood. These blood stains blossomed from singular points almost like the petals on the flowers he'd seen in lavish gardens in Thyronos's Cathedral District.

It was the dead man's eyes that scared him the most. Open. His eyes, a clear icy blue, stared off into eternity, as if trying to find answers in the brick wall that lined the puddle-filled alley. The ever-present wind that gusted through the alley ruffled the corpse's hair, black, wispy strands fluttering about his head before falling in front of his face. They obscured the corpse's eyes, blocking his dead stare.

Alec turned to leave the alley and the rotting corpse, but another strong gust of wind shifted its coat. It fell open, away from its chest to reveal a small pink flower in a clay pot nestled against the body.

"By the Relicks!" he repeated an oath he had heard his stepfather use.

Alec stared at the flower as the wind tugged at his hair. That small plant fascinated him far more than the bloodstained body next to it ever could. What was he doing with a flower? Only the wealthy could afford such useless plants.

He couldn't tear his eyes away from the tiny plant. Its stem was covered in small, brown thorns. A few leaves sprouted from the stem. But those paled in comparison to the main flower. The petals opened outward in a spiral pattern, the innermost ones being far smaller than the ones on the outer edges.

How long he stood entranced by the flower, he would never know exactly. He blinked and knew he had to touch it. Alec walked over to the body and stretched his arm out toward the flower. His fingers hovered over the petals as if they would burn him. He inched his hand forward, afraid that by touching the flower he might ruin it forever, and stroked the delicate, satin-like petals. To his horror, one of them fell away and dropped to the stone street underfoot just as the breeze picked up. Within seconds it was gone. A piece of this priceless of flower, gone.

Careful not to dislodge any more petals, Alec picked up the clay pot and held it close to his chest. He spared the dead man one last look, turned and walked out of the alley onto a deserted street. People rarely used these streets; they were too close to the railings that created a barrier between the city and the endless sky. Although the wood and metal fences were well over waist-high, accidents still happened.

The wind tugged at his prize, threatening to strip away more petals. He had to get away from the railings and deeper into the city proper, out of the wind. Still trying to shield the flower as best he could, Alec made his way through the narrow stone streets of Thyronos. He weaved through crowds of men wearing long overcoats over brightly colored waistcoats. He stumbled for a second as he tried to avoid stepping on a young woman's long skirt that swished barely above her ankles.

The plant in his arms was so small that he was able to keep it mostly hidden from view. If it became known what he was carrying, he would be mugged in seconds by citizens eager to claim a bit of greenery from themselves. Plants were a luxury only a few could afford on the floating Isles.

He glanced up at the sky and saw a group of airships sail by, like a school of fish swimming downstream. Wooden hulls, harvested from protected forests that were coveted by the Church, hung beneath inflated canvas bags. Three giant propellers located in the stern drove each ship through the air, gray exhaust trailing behind. Each airship in the formation flew Church colors from the twin masts that rose through the canvas. Judging by their route, Alec guessed they were headed for the Cathedral of the Holy Relicks. For some reason the strange events of the afternoon and the sight of their flags brought back memories of being taught the history of the Thirteen Isles in religious-history class when he was six.

Hundreds of years ago, a terrible war between the Gods ravaged the Lands Below, humanity's ancestral home. Explosions hundreds of feet tall killed millions and scattered poisonous rain around the world. It transformed all that it touched, creating abominations that should never have existed. Church writings explained that the Gods' wrath left the world scarred and barren, but they did not forget their children. The Gods created the Isles and the Relicks that held them aloft to save the remnants of humanity. Priests maintained the holy machines so that mankind might one day atone for their sins that caused the war between the Gods in the first place. Each Isle had its own set of Relicks, including a Divine Reclamator that took organic matter and converted it into food and other substances for the faithful.

He grimaced at the thought of the food produced by the Reclamator. There were only so many ways a person could prepare Manna, as the Church called it. Only wealthy city dwellers and the Farm Barons, who cultivated the land outside the cities, were able to afford naturally grown food. But upon further reflection, Alec concluded that eating Manna everyday was far better than attempting to venture to the Lands Below. His fellow classmates spread rumors and tall tales of air pirate captains who claimed to have seen the surface. Each story always had to mention the scarred landscape, hideously mutated beasts, and terrible lightning storms.

Alec watched the airships descend and disappear into Thyronos's heart. Another group sailed by, these ones flying trade guild colors on a voyage to the nearby sister of Isle of Utorcas. Deciding he had wasted enough time watching the airships and musing about the history of the Gods, Alec continued his own voyage. He carried his prize down small serpentine side streets and alleys toward his house. As he got closer to home, the sounds and smells grew more familiar. The wind died down the further he got from the railings. It was replaced by the smells of multiple dinners being cooked, the sweet scent of fuel, provided by the Reclamators, being burned to warm homes. The buildings grew closer together, stone bridges connecting the upper stories of adjacent structures. The sun had nearly set by the time he reached home, a squat, boxy construction made of stone set on top of another house with another on top of that.

The rickety stairs creaked as he ascended to his front door. Voices shouting at one another drifted out an open window. His stepfather, Danos, must have hit the bottle earlier than usual this evening. Alec glanced down at his arms, but this time he wasn't looking at the flower cradled in them. Instead, he saw the purple bruises that dotted his arms, byproducts of the last time he had tried to intervene when his parents fought.

He pushed open the front door and moved quietly through the house toward his room. The flower had to stay hidden. His mother, Lene, would be curious about where he had found it; his stepfather would be furious and then, having beaten him, would take the flower and try to find a way to use it for his own personal gain.

Alec shut the door to his bedroom behind him and set the flower down on his nightstand as gently as if it were made out of delicate crystal. Weary from the long trek back from the railings, he fell on his bed and stared at the cracks in his ceiling. Before long, he dozed off to the sound of his parents exchanging parting shots before one of them stormed out of the house and slammed the door.

Nothing changed when he woke up a few hours later except that it was night outside. Whichever parent that left before was back and their fight had resumed with greater volume. Alec looked at his nightstand to see if the flower was still there, to make sure he hadn't imagined the entire thing. It was still there, perfect in every way. He smiled at his fortune, but it quickly faded when he heard exactly what his mother and stepfather were saying.

"They're dangerous and you know it!" Danos barked. "The Lost are an illegal organization. Now we both know that I am a pious man and if I didn't love this family so much I'd report you to the Inquisition!"

"You would report me? For what? Going to a pub?" Lene retorted.

Alec hadn't heard this particular fight before. Most of them always centered on money and how Danos spent most of it on alcohol. This one was different. Against his better judgment, he crept closer to his door to hear better.

"No respectable lady should be going to a place called the Thunderhead Pub unescorted--robably not at all! It's a Godsforsaken hole infested with scum and possible insurrectionists. But then again, we both know you're not a respectable lady."

"A pious man? You?" Lene's scorn-filled laugh rang out. "By the Gods that's a pack of lies. A pious man who loves his family wouldn't drink so much and abuse them! I don't even know why I stay here anymore!"

"You know why you do. I'm the only one who'd take a slut like you in. You're a whore who's been gallivanting with other men behind my back. That's probably why you spend so much time at the Thunderhead; it's probably all spent on your back."

Alec's face burned with shame at his stepfather's accusations. He knew that his father ran off while his mother was still pregnant. When she felt wistful, his mother would sometimes tell him little snippets about how wonderful his father had been, until he had run away without so much as a goodbye. The fact that Alec never knew his real father haunted him constantly.

The fighting continued in the other room when Lene laughed again, this time laced with even more contempt. "I not only pass time with possible insurrectionists and members of the Lost, I am one! It's time that we reclaim our ancient home. We belong on the Lands Below, not on these floating Isles. The Gods *want* us to go back down!"

Alec scrunched his face up into a frown as he leaned his head against his door. His mother had never expressed such radical political and theological perspectives before. From what he had heard, the Lost were insurrectionists that opposed the Church's rule. They were labeled as terrorists for their radical views because they claimed that the Church was an instrument of oppression that kept humanity on the Isles in order to stay in power. The Church of the Holy Relicks and its heretic offshoot, the Church of the Eternal Sky, kept humanity trapped among the clouds. He almost ventured out of his room to ask her if it was all true, but his stepfather's wordless howl of fury stopped him.

Crockery shattered against the wall and Danos stormed across the kitchen. The sounds of heavy blows and Lene's cries of pain mixed in the air. Normally when this happened, Alec would hide in his room, close his eyes, and try to block it out. It never did him any good to intervene. This time the beating sounded worse. Instead of stopping after a few hits, the blows continued and his mother's voice fell away into tiny whimpers.

"Your bastard boy is next! I raised him as if he was my own and this is the thanks I get?"

The sound of more glass shattering in the kitchen sealed the deal for Alec. He shrugged on a threadbare coat and grabbed the flower from his desk, this time not caring whether or not more petals fell off. He padded over to his room's small window and threw it open. With practiced ease, he swung out the window and onto the building's fire escape. The metal stairs rattled underfoot as he ran down. With the flower still tucked under his arm, he dropped to the street below and started to run.

The gas lamps combined with the moon overhead provided enough light for him to navigate Thryonos's stone streets. The wind pulled at his hair as he drew closer to the districts built next to the railings. He paused for a second to get his bearings. During his wanderings around the city, he had seen the particular pub before so he had a fairly clear idea where it was. He only hoped that he reached it in time, even though he had no idea what exactly he was going to do when he got there.

"Out awfully late aren't you, boy?" a stern voice called out to him from the corner of an intersection.

Alec slowed down, turned his head, and swore under his breath when he saw the figure that was approaching him. Even under the gas lamp's weak light, the double row of brass buttons gleamed on the man's long, dark blue coat. He saw the distinctive tall, peaked helmet emblazoned with a seven-sided star on the front, the emblem of the Constabulary. Alec couldn't pretend he hadn't heard the constable's hail; instead he stopped and watched the man draw closer. His hair was grey and he carried a more than comfortable amount of weight around his middle.

"Yes, sir," he replied.

"Why in such a hurry?" the constable asked. "You're likely to slip on these wet streets and fall over the railings."

"It's important, sir."

"What's that in your hands?"

Having somebody, especially a constable, see the flower was the last thing in all the Isles that Alec wanted. The constable would either arrest him for being in possession of something so valuable or he would just steal it from him outright.

"A flower, sir."

The constable took a step forward. His hand dropped closer

to the truncheon he wore on his left hip, dangling from his belt. The other one hovered a few inches away from the butt of the revolver he wore on the opposite hip.

"A flower? And how'd a Godsforsaken urchin like you get a hold of a flower like that?"

Alec shrugged, "I'm delivering it, sir. A certain young gentleman paid me five scarlets to take it to a certain young lady that lives near the Lyari District. This way was the fastest."

He breathed a silent sight of relief when the constable's hand moved away from his weapons and onto his stomach as he laughed. "Oh ho! Intrigue and romance. I remember what it was like to be young. Be careful, boy. Try not to let anyone else see what you got there."

"Yes, sir. I'll try, sir."

The constable continued on his rounds and disappeared around another corner. As soon as he was gone, Alec broke into a sprint. The conversation with the constable had wasted valuable time. For all he knew, his mother could be dead by now; there was no telling if Danos would have stopped hitting her after a point. The image of her lying battered and bleeding on their kitchen floor rose unbidden into his mind. Her eyes, though brown, stared in the same fashion as the dead man's in the alley. He squeezed his eyes shut to banish the thought and turned another corner.

Raucous music and laughter spilled out into the street from a grungy-looking building at the end of a cul-de-sac. Orange light shone from its dirty windows, and the smell of greasy food mixed with smoke floated through the air. The faded words painted over the door proclaimed it to be the Thunderhead Pub.

Alec stared at the pub's closed metal door. He was alone in the cul-de-sac, nothing but the pink flower in his arms and the swirling winds for company. He should open that door, he had to, but something held him back. Would anyone inside even help him? His fingers stroked the flower and one of the thorns drew blood. The flower was the key. If nobody would help him, Alec decided he would use it as a bargaining chip. It was the find of a lifetime, but his mother's life was worth more. Emboldened, he tried the door, but it was locked. Not knowing what else to do, he knocked. A view slot opened and a pair of suspicious eyes stared at him.

"What do you want, kid?"

"Please, I need to speak to a member of the Lost!"

"Where'd a little bastard like you hear about them? You better watch your tongue or someone might cut it out."

A knife flashed in front of the glaring eyes and the door started to open. Panicking, Alec tried one more time. "Wait! I'm Lene's son! Lene Cole! She's in trouble. I need help!"

The door opened all the way and a man with long greasy hair squinted at him from the doorway. Alec held his breath. Slowly the greasy-haired man lowered his knife.

"Get inside," he growled. He called over his shoulder. "Zarre, this one says he's Lene's son!"

The man sheathed his knife and dragged him into the pub. Alec stumbled and tried not to drop the flower pot in his arms. He felt dozens of eyes staring at him, staring through him. Conversation at the bar died away as he took a few steps further into the middle of the room. Heavy footfalls drew closer and the biggest man Alec ever saw stepped out from a back room. Nearly seven feet tall, he crossed the pub in just a few strides and stopped in front of the trembling youth.

The tall man leaned down and studied him. Up close, the man's face was covered in a network of scars, some hidden by a black goatee. His clothes, though stylish, were well-worn and a pistol with a barrel almost as big as Alec's wrist hung from his belt.

"I see the resemblance," Zarre rumbled. His scars stretched and moved when he spoke, "What's the matter? You said you needed help. Anything for Lene."

"My stepfather, Danos, and she got into a fight about the Lost. He's drunk and normally he stops before he hurts her too badly, but this time it was worse. He's going to kill her. Please you have to stop him."

Zarre straightened and pointed at three men standing at the bar. "Go take care of it."

"Thank you," Alec sighed with relief. He didn't want to know what exactly the three men were going to do, but it didn't trouble him too greatly.

"Like I said, anything for Lene. What's that you got in your arms?"

Alec took the flower away from his chest where it had been half hidden by his coat and showed it to him. Even in the smoky air of the pub, it was beautiful. Delicate petals curled over one another. Tiny thorns grew out of its green stem, enhancing the plant's magnificence instead of detracting from it.

Conversation, which had started up again after Zarre dispatched the three men, died once more. Alec wondered if he had made a giant mistake by bringing the plant here. If his mother trusted these people enough to proudly proclaim her allegiance to their cause, then he figured he could too.

"I found it lying next to a dead man I found in an alley near the railings." He shuddered as once more the corpse's face this time overlaid with his mother's stared at him in his mind's eye. "I don't know who the man was or why he had it, but it's beautiful and obviously priceless. I've never seen anything like it either in books or in the gardens near the Cathedral."

"Let me see that," Zarre whispered, his voice strangely reverent.

He raised the pink blossom to his face and inhaled its fragrant aroma. His fingers traced patterns over the petals, softly, as if he was touching the skin of a baby. He tested the sharpness of the thorns and his dark eyes danced when one of them drew a bead of blood.

Tears ran down his face as he addressed Alec and the rest of the people in the pub. "Thank the Gods. Now we can finally change things around here. We can show them the truth and end the oppression. We can show them that we can all go home. The Lands Below are ready for us.

"This flower is not found on any of the Isles. Not on those controlled by the Church of the Holy Relicks, not on those dominated by the Church of the Eternal Sky. You won't find it on Ozawa or any of the other Unincorporated Isles. But there are pictures of it still…in the right books if one knows how to look. It's called a rose."

IN DARKNESS LINGERING
BY
LARRY IVKOVICH

An Applications Analyst at the Children's Hospital of Pittsburg, Ivkovich started writing after a creative writing class sparked his interest. Since then, he has sold work to "Noctober Magazine," "Another Realm," "Tower of Light Fantasy," Storyteller, and Triangulations. He has also won two honorable mentions in the L. Ron Hubbard Writer's for the Future contest.

A gray half-light enveloped Mikael Seralen like a shroud as he entered the darkened holding cell of the Bandan-Ai. Immediately, he activated his night lens implant, his desire to enter the cell in the murky darkness without augmentation vanishing in a heartbeat.

Despite the protective force-webbing interwoven into his medical fatigues and the Keep's security electronics monitoring every move he made, the skin at the nape of his neck began to prickle.

He had wanted to meet the Bandan-Ai on more-or-less equal ground—both of them would be at a disadvantage in the darkness, surely. But prudence (or fear perhaps?) decided otherwise. He banished those feelings to another part of his mind, irritated at his momentary weakness. *Fool,* he thought. *I, at least, have to make this look good.*

The meager furnishings of the cell—a sleeping mat, small table and chair, bath and waste niches—resolved into clearer focus. Small, and not entirely uncomfortable, the cell was fit for human needs, not for something outside the realm of familiarity.

Something seemed to float in midair near the bath niche, something white and ghost-like. Seralen stepped back, startled. The Bandan-Ai stared out at him from the even deeper darkness of the niche's recessed space. Dressed in the thin, black, floor-length tunic it had been captured in, the creature seemed to want to remain in the thickest gloom possible, almost invisible except for its pale face and hands.

Not seeking any light, Seralen knew, would be completely against the alien's nature if the morphology analysis was correct. Even if the creature wanted to remain in darkness, it would be impossible for it to do so for any length of time—it simply needed the light for part of its life cycle. But then again, it had not been treated well since being brought to the Eastern Hold's main Keep. Perhaps it was justified in hiding.

Seralen tapped the translator patch at his throat and took a step toward the Bandan-Ai, hands held out in front of him, palms open. His throat oddly dry, he addressed the alien.

"I am Prime Arbiter Mikael Seralen of the Galactic Nexia of New Earth," he said, the words faintly echoing with the overlapping translation. "Please. I only wish to talk. You won't be harmed." *Any further*, he wanted to say. Lord Emar was not the kindest of hosts. Some of the galactic rim outreach settlements were barely above primitive designation, despite their level of technology. If not for one of the Nexia's imbedded agents discovering the Bandan-Ai's imprisonment, who knew what the Eastern Hold's warlord would have done to the creature?

The Bandan-Ai seemed to smile. Or was it a trick of the muted light? Or perhaps Seralen's mind anthropomorphizing the alien being? With his sight so enhanced, the creature almost looked human. Almost.

It took a step out of the niche. It was a female, Seralen knew from the briefing and vids—at least it seemed female in the human sense. Still, he was struck by the thin, graceful form beneath the sashed tunic, the long black cilia-like strands that sprouted and hung from the Bandan-Ai's head like a crown of lush hair, the eerily humanoid features set in a pale, thin face crisscrossed with spidery green veins, the three long, nailess fingers on each hand.

Its eyes though—those were what set the Bandan-Ai apart as truly alien—slanted, with no whites or lids or pupils—just a bright full green that stared unblinkingly at the Prime Arbiter.

For a moment, Seralen felt true fear, not the childish, unreasoning fear of the unseen. His profession took him to many worlds of the Galactic Nexia to meet with a variety of alien species. He had arbitrated, negotiated, and helped mediate a number of political, religious, economic, and social disputes; his talent in seeing past impasses and formulating solutions had once been a prized one.

But this...creature standing in front of him was unlike any he had ever encountered.

He had wondered initially why he had been called in for such a seemingly minor issue as this—a local rebellion on a backwater planet. Now he knew—this was like something out of a *nidium* dream—this species he must deal with was unprecedented and would require a more subtle interrogative touch.

A subtlety he hadn't utilized in a long time. Too many years of twisting his precepts to the Galactic Nexia's ends, too much taking from primitive cultures to further his own career, had dulled the sharp insight and idealism he had once possessed.

Seralen was old and tired and he just didn't care anymore. That was the real reason he had been assigned here—to officially fail so he could be "relieved" of his duty. He knew his days as Prime Arbiter had been numbered for some time.

Well, so be it. *Let's just get this over with,* he thought tiredly.

The Bandan-Ai bowed slightly—an oddly human gesture—as if acknowledging Seralen's presence and took another step toward the Prime Arbiter.

That was when Seralen noticed the smell—vaguely familiar—of something burning, somewhere a very long time ago...

He had been only ten years old then, but he remembered it as vividly as if it had been yesterday—standing on one of the elevated, artificial esplanades that crisscrossed and overlooked the talic orchards. The yellow-green sun of Ketch shone brightly in a cloudless sky; twenty-foot-high fruit trees seemed to stretch in rows forever in every direction toward the flat horizon of the western midlands; a transport shuttle cruised low overhead, bringing in a new crop of off-world laborers.

Mikael smiled and waved at the snub-nosed craft, hoping someone would see him. This was the biggest and the loudest of his father's farms, the one he liked the best. His father always brought him to the talic fields during the harvest times. He felt important then, not just a small child but a participant in his family's rich and powerful world.

Hover-combines floated within the orchard just yards away, looking like huge, silver insects. Their operators seemed a part of the machinery, harvesting the tall red trees. He gripped the railing hard, fascinated as always by how the hover-combine's servitor arms and hands rapidly and efficiently stripped the fruit from the talic trees and dropped them into the utility craft's large side bins.

How he wished he could drive one of the combines! How he wished he could steer it to the processing tuns where juice, meal, and feed were made for the outreach worlds. If only his father would let him. If only he wasn't so little!

He smiled and waved at Mendus, the closest of the combine operators. The older man waved back and made one of the servitor arm's triple-digit hands simulate a wave also. Mikael laughed at the sight. Maybe he could ask Mendus to take him for a ride later.

Then something happened, something his young, immature mind didn't understand at first. Mendus cried out as a dark man-shaped thing suddenly reared upwards from the base of one of the talic trees, stretched out, and pulled itself up onto the side of the hover-combine. It was hairy, gangly, and powerful looking, yet it had remained hidden. Until now.

The combine rocked violently from side to side as the large beast scrabbled in the bins, its long-fingered hands grasping and flinging great bunches of talic fruit to the ground. He stared at the huge creature, frozen, unable to move.

The creature dropped to the ground as Mendus tried to regain control of the tilting combine. The operator yelled something into his head-comm as the creature gathered up the loose fruit, stuffing most into a pouch at its belly with blinding speed and picking up the rest in its long, ropy arms.

It rose up and loped in Mikael's direction, suddenly pausing under the esplanade to look up at him. He returned that monstrous gaze, transfixed as two wide eyes set in a furry, broad-nosed, almost-human face stared back at him. And then it was gone, running deep into the orchard faster than anything he had ever seen.

Klaxons went off from somewhere, shattering the relative quiet of the morning.

When his father found him, Mikael was still clinging to the railing of the esplanade, hearing the sounds of lase-rifles, an animal cry of pain.

"But it just wanted to eat!" he had protested later, after he had stopped crying. "It didn't hurt anyone."

His father knelt by his side, his dark eyes flashing, his stern, bearded face set in a frozen scowl. "Mikael, the andu are dangerous animals," he said tiredly. "And nuisances as well. Allowed to roam, they'd decimate the talic groves. We've had problems with them before."

"But you didn't have to kill it!" Tears welled in his eyes again as he remembered the look on the andu's face. It hadn't been a "dangerous" look. It had only wanted to survive. He knew that, even then. "You didn't..."

"Enough!" His father stood, frowning down on him. "It was just an animal."

The Bandan-Ai stood as if waiting. Seralen realized he had been holding his breath.

"You...you have been ill treated," he said, coming out of his momentary reverie, surprised by the clarity and intensity of the unexpected old memory. "I am here to rectify that."

A pause and then a nod. The creature spoke then, its voice soft, yet clear. It was more a series of whistles and sighs than words, and the phrasing would have been completely foreign to Seralen had he not had the translator. The mouth, a slit really, barely moved.

"This entity has no data to impart," the translator communicated to Seralen, its AI core having built the Bandan-Ai speech mode from Emar's security vids. "Such has been conveyed to the other flesh-eaters—this entity does not know where the insurgents' leader is."

It refers to itself in an impersonal third person. Interesting. "And yet you were found at one of the rebels' camps," Seralen replied, deciding to get right to it. The quicker the better. "Why was that?"

Silence. And then an approximation of a shrug. The creature turned away, whispering softly, "This entity was a prisoner there as well as here."

Perhaps, Seralen thought. But reports from Emar's forces had stated there had been more than one Bandan-Ai at the rebel camp, indicating a possible alliance. The elusive indigenes rarely made an appearance outside the northern wilderness areas and most sightings over the last century and a half were the stuff of myth and legend.

Although, according to recent reports, there had been an upsurge of such sightings. Parties of two or more Bandan-Ai had been encountered recently approaching the Eastern Holding's perimeters. Most had been driven off. Some had been killed.

Unfortunately, some of the human rebels and most of the Bandan-Ai found at the rebel camp had been killed in the ensuing firefight with Emar's troops. One of the recovered alien corpses had been brought to the Keep where the imbedded Nexia agents had supervised its autopsy scan and morphology analysis.

The unexpected capture of this live one was special—indeed, historic—more so than just for some backwater planet's political problems. The autopsy scan had discovered the Bandan-Ai were a race of cloranoids—photosynthetic hominids. No species like this had ever been found in the Galactic Nexia's sphere of influence, until now.

The Nexia may be throwing away an opportunity here, Seralen thought, suddenly interested despite himself. *We might learn much from this species.* Yet gaining new knowledge wasn't why he was here, he knew. "Absolute power corrupts absolutely," the old adage went. The wielder of that power became jaded, uncaring of anything other than its own self-interests. The Galactic Nexia was proof of that—an empire coasting in its prime with Seralen merely along for the ride.

And yet...

"I regret what has happened," Seralen said carefully. "I represent the Nexia in this matter and have been empowered to compensate you and your people in whatever form you require for this tragedy. Perhaps, as a start, more suitable quarters for you."

"Why not just release this entity?" The Bandan-Ai leveled its piercing gaze directly at him.

Curious, Seralen thought. *This one is not in the least intimidated by what it's gone through.* "In due time," he replied cautiously. "There are some matters we must resolve first."

There had been no time to prepare a livable interior environment for the alien. Its unique morphology required the absence of light to keep it docile and compliant. Or so Lord Emar had thought.

Yet compliant it had not been, revealing nothing despite torture and deprivation. Emar's nobility and middle citizenry were at war, struggling against the rebellion of their worker class, and all was fair, etc. A glimmer of hope blossomed within Seralen. If he could get this being to talk, it would be quite an accomplishment for him and might help reclaim his previous status. He could, as the ancient Earthans used to say, "Write his own ticket."

"What is your name?" Seralen asked. "Your...sentient designation."

"This entity is designated..." The translator paused for a heartbeat, as if struggling to form the right words. "Dreams-of-Water."

Seralen nodded. "A beautiful name," he replied.

That smile again, thin and twisted. "Please—subterfuge is not necessary," Dreams-of-Water said. "This entity knows why The Seralen is here and will tell The Seralen what was told the other flesh-eaters: this entity does not know where the insurgents' leader is."

Seralen studied his unusual subject. The normal criteria he used for his work would not apply here, he knew, because of the Bandan-Ai's uniqueness. How could he tell if this being was telling the truth? Or lying? Or anything for that matter?

"Tell me of your people," Seralen said finally. "You are a legend here, a myth. It is said that you and your kind can become invisible; that you can cause visions and can bend others to your will with just a word."

"Stories to frighten young flesh-eaters." That smile again. "The Bandan-Ai are a simple race, wanting to live in peace as has been since the Beginning. Nothing more." Dreams-of-Water moved again, walking toward Seralen. Its gait was smooth and fluid, like leaves swirling in the wind.

Seralen involuntarily backed up a step. This creature was not what he had expected. It was sentient, intelligent, even charismatic to a degree. The Bandan-Ai stopped and once more fixed its lidless gaze on the Prime Arbiter.

"Very well," Dreams-of-Water said. "This entity will tell The Seralen of the Bandan-Ai. No flesh-eater has ever asked that question before."

Seralen blinked. Another odor had abruptly manifested itself, again familiar—a musky odor of sweat and...and...

Their naked bodies clung together desperately. In the grip of a passion and lust so intense, he cried out at each thrust of his hips. I'm on fire! he thought. On fire...

Beneath his grinding body, Marinella moaned and arched her back, bringing her knees upward to allow him to plunge deeper and deeper within her.

All too soon, he finished with a blinding eruption of pleasure and pain so strong he nearly screamed. Though spent and covered in sweat, he continued to move with Marinella in their carnal dance, still throbbing, his mouth hungrily finding her dark lips and breasts. She responded eagerly as if just beginning, whispering something in his ear as she dug her fingers into his back and squeezed her thighs tightly against his heaving ribs.

"Marinella, Marinella," he gasped as he finally sank on top of her, exhausted. "That was...that was..."

"Yes," Marinella murmured back in a faint, breathless accent. "Yes, my young, insatiable Earthan. The nidium does enhance the pleasure, yes?"

Oh yes. He rolled over on his side, facing his older Senitte lover. He ran his hand through the long, dark-as-night ringlets that tumbled about her sky-blue face, lost in her alien eyes. Still hard, he groaned and shuddered as she stroked him, wringing the last bit of sensation from his wonderfully aching body.

"You're going to kill me," he said with a tortured smile.

She gazed back at him thoughtfully. "No," she said in remarkably good Galactic Basic. "But that could be my fate."

"Ah, I'm that good, am I?"

She nodded. "For an Earthan," she teased and then became serious again. "But I meant something else."

He and Marinella lay on an air mat covered in blankets in one of the talic farm's many supply domes. Surrounded by cases of tools and implements and shelves of fertilizer and plant-regen, they embraced in checkered dashes of sunlight filtering in through the roof vents. Exhaust fans tried in vain to drown out their still-heavy breathing.

Marinella rolled over on top of him, straddling his body, her hands pressing against his chest. He marveled again at her exotic beauty—the thin, supple bone structure, small breasts, features reminiscent of the ancient Afro-Earthans, dark eyes and hair, and that light blue skin... The Senittes were known for their sexual attraction, men as well as fems. But Marinella...

She bent down and kissed him gently, the faint scent of nidium lingering on her breath. "We cannot do this anymore," she said softly. "We cannot see each other again."

He laughed. "You always say that. Stop toying with me."

She looked away, her eyes closed. "No," she whispered. "This time I mean it. I never should have let it go on for this long." She pushed away from him, got to her feet, and walked to the center of the dome where they had both flung their clothes.

He shook his head as if he hadn't heard her right, turned over, and propped himself up on one elbow. He watched her dress, pulling the simple kamon-lace shift over her lithe body. He had known Marinella almost all of his life. Her father and mother were refugees from Alpha-Seni, fleeing the planet-wide famine that had engulfed their world, arriving on Ketch with practically nothing but the clothes on their backs.

His own father had taken them in, as he had other off-world expatriates over the years, and given them jobs on his farms. Ten years older than he, Marinella worked in the kitchens, always flirting with him as a youngster; until he had reached his nineteenth year, then their relationship had become so much more.

"Your father is the overseer," she said, buckling her sandals on and then tying her luscious hair into a tail. "There is already talk among the other kitchen staff. If he was to find out..."

He rose to his feet then, suddenly alarmed. "We've been over this before. It doesn't matter..."

She stopped him with a heated look, her face etched with pain. "I know, Mikael, my love. It doesn't matter now, but in time it will. You leave for university in less than a moon," she breathed. "Your father has plans for you. A lowly Senitte fem, one who has introduced his son to the pleasures of nidium, no less—a klau—does not figure into them, I would think."

Klau. Alien. "No!" he cried. "I don't care that you're Senitte. You know that! I'll be back often. You can even come with me to New Bonnum!"

Marinella moved closer, shaking her head as she cupped his cheek with her cool palm. "My mother and father may lose their positions if our being together were known. I certainly will, but I am more afraid for them. This just isn't done, my young Earthan. It would never work. It's my fault. I should have known better. I should have..." She smiled a sad smile then, kissed him, and walked out of the dome.

He stood, tears welling in his eyes, his fists clenched at his sides, ashamed of his weakness and inaction—knowing she was right. "She's an alien," his father would say. "You can't jeopardize your future for someone like her."

He left for New Bonnum University later that month and never saw Marinella again.

Seralen came out of his imaginings as if he had been dreaming. A pang of guilt and sorrow gripped his heart. Marinella. It was like he had been with her again! He hadn't thought of her in a long time. Why did he now? At this place? At this time?

"Yes, yes," he muttered, suddenly wary and confused. "Please, I wish to hear and understand. Tell me of your people." He checked the remote security link through his neural interface. Yes, Emar's surveillance and security programs were still functional. They would report any sign of trouble.

The Bandan-Ai nodded and turned then, hands clasped in front of it as it began to pace; another human mannerism. "The Bandan-Ai have lived on the World since the Beginning, sharing, giving, and taking in equal turns. It has been a quiet, peaceful existence in balance with the All." It turned to face Seralen. "And then the flesh-eaters came."

Seralen nodded. Colonization of Ottmahn Minor had been made over four hundred solar years ago by a group of dissident outreach settlers. According to the old flight logs and colony records, no sentient indigenes had been found on the planet at that time. Not that it mattered. Before the Nexia came to power, the ancient outreach settlers took whatever so-called uninhabited rim planets they could and the natives be damned. It had been a wilderness, boomtown mentality at that time in New Earth's spacefaring history. Of course, it was only much later after planetfall on Ottmahn Minor that the first Bandan-Ai sighting had occurred.

Dreams-of-Water continued, "The Bandan-Ai hid and continued their existence, willing to share the World. Why not? There is enough for all."

"But we, the...flesh-eaters, wanted more." *As always,* Seralen thought grimly, surprising himself. *History repeats itself again.*

A nod and then the pacing once more. "The flesh-eaters

continue to expand their holdings and increase their use of..." Dreams-of-Water looked at Seralen as if pondering its next words, "unnatural, sentient-created power." Technology.

"Yes," Seralen said, knowing the scientists of the Eastern Holding were attempting the creation and use of crude nuclear power. "It is a dangerous thing the Lord Emar is doing. I agree with you. But at least there is a modicum of control over such power at present. In the hands of the rebels, the danger of possessing technology of this type of destructive capacity may be magnified."

Dreams-of-Water inclined its head toward Seralen, as if disputing his comment. "This entity's understanding of this matter is that the insurgents rebel to stop the proliferation of such unnatural power."

Seralen pursed his lips as he began to get caught up in the interview, experiencing a professional excitement he hadn't known since he had first become Prime Arbiter.

"We don't really know what their motives are. There was evidence presented that their goal is not so benign. The rebel movement is relatively new, made up of malcontents from all areas of the Eastern Holding's societal groups, although mostly from the worker class."

"Yes." A pause. "That is why this entity was captured. This entity and a small cluster of its fellow Bandan-Ai approached one such rebel group—to commune with them; to see what it was they do and why and how it might affect the Bandan-Ai. But they took the cluster by force instead. That is why this entity was there when the flesh-eater warlord's forces attacked."

Seralen blinked. Dreams-of-Water had not revealed this particular bit of detailed information before, according to Emar's people. Was he making actual progress or was this something else entirely?

"Yes, well, there seems to be no real organization involved within the rebel group."

The Bandan-Ai didn't reply, only looked upward as if listening. It returned its icy, cool gaze to Seralen.

"Ah," it said. "But there is."

The smell of rich earth, heady, fragrant flowers, and freshly cut grass overwhelmed Seralen's senses...

He and his security contingent moved into the ancient, glass-domed pavilion those four standard years ago. He had been ordered to an arts enclave in Xyrius, the capital city of Vometa province on the planet Lasingow II, to resolve an unusual situation. He stood now in the center of the conservatory entrance. Giant palm trees of Old Earth towered above him; the twining bethra creepers of the jungle moon Adius Komon wound their serpentine way over the floor, walls, and ceiling; fronds of a variety of other off-world plants swayed in the artificial breezes; the smells of dark humus and green and blue vegetation surrounded him in a cloying haze.

Beyond the pavilion lay the entrance tunnels to a series of old-style geodesic domes, which contained various artificial environments, still amazingly operational.

Climate-control AIs ran the temperature and humidity variants, the high-pressure fog jets, watering and feeding systems, window-panel operations, fan speeds, and electronic heating and cooling elements that still functioned years after the conservatory, the entire enclave in fact, had been evacuated and presumably abandoned.

"Prime Arbiter," his security chief said, fingers touching his temple. "We have life signs..."

But Seralen was already on the move, rushing through the tunnel to the first dome. His contingent shadowed him expertly, knowing his impatience in this matter and that he might not wait for them. He paused, as the door to the dome irised open, to study the environment within.

Incoming data from his neural interface informed him that this dome contained an Old Earth Tropical Rain Forest system. Lush, broad-leafed vegetation and thick-boled arboreals greeted his eyes. Vines and creepers proliferated, huge fungi sprouted like free-form sculptures, and the floor was thick with clinging foliage. Despite the enviro-suit, gloves, goggles, and headgear he wore, he knew thick, moist air awaited him within.

He walked through the invisible thermal membrane within the doorway that further separated environments and took a few steps into the jungle.

There was movement within the trees and shrubbery. Yes. The In-Dwellers were here.

More movement at ground level. Slowly, figures began to emerge from the surrounding undergrowth—some as small as Earthan dogs and some as big as humans, some walking on four legs with long, whip-like tails, others on two with striped, furry hides and long claws, all watching him with round eyes set in short-snouted animal faces. In the branches overhead, other sinuous forms hung from the trees by tails and long-fingered paws, their attention focused on the gathering below.

Amazing, he thought, not for the first time.

One of the In-Dwellers, possessing a long tail and a mask of dark fur outlining its eyes, stepped forward on two legs and approached him. It stood as tall as a man, but he knew from his data link that it was a genetic clone of an Old Earthan mammal called a lemur.

But now, like the rest of the In-Dwellers, forever changed into something vastly different.

He tapped his translator chip as the In-Dweller chirped confidently in a high, sweet voice. "We greet you and welcome you back, Prime Arbiter Seralen," came the translation. "What we have is yours to share, now and always."

Yes, he thought sadly. *That is the idea.* "I thank you, Mah-Feron," he replied slowly, employing the In-Dweller's ritual response. "May blessings be found under every stone." He paused briefly at the hypocrisy of his words. And then, more to the point, no matter how distasteful, "Have you and your council considered the Nexia's proposal?"

The large eyes of Mah-Feron held his gaze, the In-Dweller's head cocked to one side. "There was nothing to consider, Prime Arbiter," it said in a soft purr. "This is our home. We will not leave."

He sighed, his outward professional demeanor beginning to crumble. "You will be well-cared for," he tried one last time.

"There is so much we can learn from you that may benefit the whole of the Galactic Nexia. The Nanite Infuser unleashed on Xyrius during the insurgent uprising was programmed to attack only living *human* tissue. The populace was nearly destroyed, but non-organic matter and non-human organics survived undamaged."

He felt desperate now, aching for a different ending to this, rambling on. "But you, certain, specific types of animals, not only survived but *evolved* because of unexpected side-effects caused by the Infuser!"

"Yes, Arbiter." Mah-Feron folded its paws in front of its body as if holding court. It seemed calm, almost serene. "We came to live in the conservatory domes after escaping from the sentient-constructed habitats we once called home. Here, we cared for the environments and became part of *this* world. Your scientists are welcome to come here to study and stay as long as they want, but we will not leave."

"A new environment just like this will be constructed," Seralen countered. "One that is safe for humans from residual nanite radiation." *And one that is controlled.* "As Prime Arbiter, I can guarantee that you will want for nothing."

Mah-Feron blinked and nodded. Behind, around, and above it, the rest of the In-Dwellers sat or stood stoically and as quiet as death. In an opposing reaction, Seralen shifted his weight, suddenly unnerved.

"This is your final decision, then?" he asked softly.

Another nod. With that, the In-Dwellers turned as a group and melted back into the jungle.

Seralen turned hastily to exit the rain forest, seeing his security head standing directly behind him. "Prime Arbiter?" the man asked. "Your orders?"

He clasped his gloved hands behind his back so the security head wouldn't see them shaking. "Tranquilize as many as you can find," he answered through clenched teeth. "Try not to cause any injuries and move them into the relocation shuttles. This area will be sealed off until further notice."

Later, outside the conservatory, he ripped his headgear off

and vomited. *What have I done?* he thought, leaning against a decorative obelisk, his legs weak. *You fool. You stupid fool.*

Seralen gasped, stumbling backwards. Another memory, another unpleasant incident in his life, relived—the forced relocation of the In-Dwellers being the final straw that began his own professional and political decline. He had been too weak to refuse that assignment and then, later, too weak to stop its inevitable ending.

"What are you doing to me?" he hissed at the Bandan-Ai, realizing, somehow, that he had been controlled, manipulated. He rechecked the security link. The interface was not responding! "What have you done? What power is this?"

"The power of reflection," the alien answered, its head held high. "To show The Seralen what it once was, what it has become, and what it can still be. But this entity..." Dreams-of-Water moved then, its arms undulating out to its sides, its head arching backwards. "This entity has done nothing."

At that moment, there was something in Dreams-of-Water's tone of voice, in its expression, alien though it was, and in its sudden, strange movements that told Seralen one thing...

...the Bandan-Ai had been lying to him all along.

A white light exploded in the Prime Arbiter's eyes. He screamed, stumbling backwards. He barely kept himself from toppling onto his back before he fell to his knees, struggling to deactivate his night lenses.

His eyes burned and watered, spots of swirling, miniature galaxies dancing within his vision. The lights had come on in the holding cell, almost blinding him because of his augmented night-vision. A shushing noise told him the door was opening. As his vision cleared he saw Dreams-of-Water...

The Bandan-Ai writhed on the floor, its frock torn from its body. Its arms and legs flailed wildly, its naked back arched upwards, and its small-breasted chest seemed to expand as, Seralen reasoned, its body absorbed the sudden light. The cilia around its head danced and wavered like a horde of serpents.

Gasping, Seralen tried to regain his feet. But the Bandan-Ai recovered first, crawling toward him on hands and knees with almost supernatural speed. It knelt in front of him and grasped the sides of his head with both hands.

Seralen felt the power in that grip, the strength that forced him to become immobile for fear of his life. Here, this close, he could see the difference. Dreams-of-Water's face had filled out, the green veins, once so prominent, disappearing under the now-darker skin.

"All the stories are true, flesh-eater Seralen," Dreams-of-Water hissed. "And we of the Bandan-Ai will take our world back. We will not linger in the darkness of fear and uncertainty any longer. The Blight of unnatural technology must be excised. And you have helped us take the first step to regain balance with the All." It leaned in close to Seralen and whispered in his ear. The smell of earth and grass almost overpowered him, mixed with something else...

He fell back as Dreams-of-Water released him, stood up and... vanished. He heard the pattering of running footsteps racing for the open door, saw the flicker of something shiny and mirror-like in the shape of a woman, and then a darkness of his own began to envelop him.

He fought to keep from blacking out as he realized what the plan had been since the beginning. *Dreams-of-Water,* he thought as he lost his fight with unconsciousness, *is the rebel leader.*

Help us.

A delaying tactic. That's all it had been. To give the rest of the Bandan-Ai time to take over the Keep. It had been an insidiously well-organized plan. No one would have suspected. No one had.

Seralen stood within one of the Keep's armory towers, looking through the open window below. The curtains and decorative lambrequins had been removed from every casement in the Keep, letting in as much sunlight as possible. Skylights and balcony doors had been flung wide open. The Bandan-Ai controlled the Keep now, and they had taken over without violence.

Emar and several of his troopers stood outside the Keep's main gate, now also opened wide by the Bandan-Ai. The warlord and his men sat astride their cloned war mounts and motorized vehicles, looking as if they had just awakened from a dream. Many of the Keep's inhabitants milled about the promenades leading up to the gate, whispering and pointing to the uppermost ramparts.

A sighing like a gentle breeze sounded behind Seralen, a smell of dark forest hollows and muddy river banks...

He turned to find Dreams-of-Water standing there, its eyes reflecting the bright, incoming light. No, not *it* any longer—in the light of day, the Bandan-Ai was definitely a *she*, an intelligent and clever being. At the doorway to the tower stood two males of her race, also dressed in the long, black tunics they favored (*To absorb the heat*, Seralen thought absently.), hands folded in front of them.

"What do you want of me?" the Prime Arbiter asked. "Why are my contingent and I still here?"

Help us.

"Because The Seralen wishes it to be," came the answer. "The Bandan-Ai do not coerce any sentient to do what would not be done otherwise."

Seralen looked back outside. "And Lord Emar and his troopers? They aren't fighting because they really don't want to?" He looked back at the Bandan-Ai. "I find that hard to believe."

Dreams-of-Water nodded. "It is so. The flesh-eater warlord and his clusters are afraid, confused, and undecided. The Bandan-Ai have long been monsters to fear and destroy in their mythology. That is why the Bandan-Ai's initial heralds to this Keep were misunderstood and attacked and killed. But we will not resort to such violent means. It is not the way of the All."

"So you fomented the rebellion yourselves?"

"The flesh-eaters approached were already of that inclination. Their own desires precipitated the so-called visions the Bandan-Ai can induce. Further urging was needed. This entity regrets the loss of life incurred as a result, but this deception was needed to divert attention and to gain entry to the Keep."

"So that you could...'coerce' Emar to hand it over. Every time you were interrogated, you worked your coercion on those who questioned you."

"Yes. As cluster leader, it was this entity's duty to perform this service alone and not place more Bandan-Ai in jeopardy."

Seralen shook his head. "But how?" he asked. "How did you know...?"

"This entity did not know," Dreams-of-Water said. "The Bandan-Ai possess a high degree of sensitivity to other organisms and are what the flesh-eaters would call empathic. This entity can sense what other sentients feel and experience and then amplifies those corresponding emotions. The sentients involved provide the rest."

Help us, she had whispered in Seralen's ear. He looked once more out the window. Emar and his men would recover in time and try to take back the Keep, possibly at a cruel cost. Even now, the warlord seemed to be trying to rally his men.

"Now that the Bandan-Ai hold the Keep and its weapons with the possible threat of employing them, this entity wishes to talk with the flesh-eater warlord," Dreams-of-Water continued. "To make the flesh-eaters understand the danger of what they do and to end such power forever, to show that the World can be a haven for all who dwell upon it in peace."

The Blight of unnatural technology must be excised. But not ruthlessly, Seralen realized. There could be another way.

Seralen blinked, beginning to suspect what the Bandan-Ai would say next. He realized he was hoping he would be right, that he *needed* to be right.

"The Bandan-Ai require an entity to negotiate for clusters on both sides in good faith with no illusions or entrapment," Dreams-of-Water said. "Will The Seralen accept the role of Prime Arbiter in this matter?"

Seralen smiled, scarcely believing his ears. Would one decent act atone for all the ones he had turned his back on? Perhaps not. The andu would still have been hunted down and exterminated, Marinella would still have been just an exotic encounter in his younger life to be used and discarded, and the In-Dwellers would still have been taken from their home by force and imprisoned against their will.

But his heart lifted at the thought of another chance, undeserving of it as he was. He, too, had been lingering in a darkness of his own making for far too long. He felt his heart pounding, his body trembling.

"Yes," he said softly. "I accept."

Dreams-of-Water bowed. "The Seralen has this entity's gratitude."

And you have mine. "Then, please," Mikael Seralen said, his spirit soaring. "We have much work to do. Let us begin."

SAVED BY A DAMSEL IN DISTRESS

BY
JOHN X. GREY

Grey writes because of the creative freedom it allows the storyteller. His fiction leans toward fantasy, horror, and science fiction, and he enjoys blurring the distinguishing lines between the genres. He is currently working on a novel.

"Blast!" Lord Dursten Brandt marveled at his drinking companion. Seated at a square wooden table's booth and benches in this cozy tavern, the dark-blonde, green-eyed man rubbed his small trimmed beard, shaking his head in amazement. "You've bested me at this yet again. Are you certain that you learned no dark, secret arts in our student days?"

"I've just had considerable practice in consuming spirits, old friend." Crown Prince Stephan Roderick Eugene of the House of Schweitzen now admired his ornate metal stein, emptied of the aristocrat's favored red sturmbrew. "The result of our misspent youth at Schweitzen Academy's surrounding town establishments."

The twenty-eight-year-old, dark-haired, violet-eyed high nobleman wanted to remain in the Szvord Inn's warm confines, lit by three large fireplaces triangularly positioned in a common room on a chilly winter's eve, filled with five dozen patrons having varied conversations (in continental or other Plaropean regional dialects), the air hazy with odors of food, drink and pipe smoke. The heir to this small mountain kingdom wiped brew foam from his mouth, moustache and small beard, here to forget an impending arranged marriage.

As the Duchess of Aarnd behaves like her family, I shall not drink in such places again.

"Aye," Brandt said, retrieving his green alpine hat and matching fur-lined cloak to cover the brown leather casual attire and patting his former roommate's left shoulder in departing, "and even though the lost twenty crowns were trifling, methinks I will not envy your head tomorrow."

"I feel inebriated enough," Stephan assured him, "not to waste it on more drink."

Knowing his departing companion envied him neither a future crown nor the marriage, Prince Stephan waved at the departing Ranger Lord. The people and leaders of Aarnd practiced temperance since converting to the Universal Church, but its martial religious zeal and military discipline were desirable traits in Schweitzen's alliance quest against the larger, sometimes menacing eastern Holy Serelethian Empire. Stephan was still not "alone" here, noting his two disguised Royal Court bodyguards seated at a nearby table along with the two coachmen that had transported their group here.

The "shadows" Father assigned my protection won't allow straying into the night and having "fun" around the bawdy quarter.

He turned the emptied stein in both hands, its pewter surface decorated with legendary creatures; dragon, oroc and elf. Stephan knew Elves still existed, Orocs once inhabited mountain passes, and Dragons had been extinct for generations across Plaropea. The Szvord Inn in Kronenberg was the extent of his fun tonight, and being good friends with its owner Otho he preferred treatment like other patrons, despite Stephan's fine attire. The beloved young man planned to rule with benevolence like his father..

I'd best be off, to rest this aching head a few hours in my final night of freedom.

Retrieving his own fur-lined gray cloak and matching round hat and leaving two gold Crowns to pay the bill from Dursten's surrendered wager pouch, Stephan was drawn to new music played by two Gensipk men on a balalaika and a pan flute seated near the room's main fireplace, the first middle-aged and the second not old enough to shave. They were accompanied by a Gensipk dancer, her captivating beauty and jingling tambourines appealing to every male patron.

Perhaps I could tarry here a moment longer. This entertainment is promising.

Stephan sat down at Brandt's seat to get a better view of that fireplace. He knew Gensipks by their colorful clothing, never truly at home anywhere in the Wyche-Realms. This misunderstood, shunned trio probably had a festive wagon parked somewhere nearby.

"Aye, girl, dance to chase away this season's gloom!"

From the left eye's corner, the prince glimpsed a brown-bearded heavyset fellow two tables away encouraging that performance. That maid dazzled in her traditional Gensipk costume and Stephan was already captivated. The lady's black curly hair was held under her metal spider's web-style cap, and lobes adorned by disc-shaped bronze earrings. She displayed a simple gold charm across cleavage in the low-cut, long-sleeved, white embroidered blouse, complemented by that red and green pleated ankle-length peasant skirt. The maiden twirled, briefly revealing a glimpse of her legs. Patrons responded with thrown coins or shouted encouragements, but she smiled, seemingly oblivious to that appreciation.

She is a young beauty. Stephan then recalled, *Halle would rebuke my viewing this.*

The dancer's skin was a lovely golden tan. Copper anklets and red slippers adorned her feet. She shook small tambourines in each hand and worked the room. The green-eyed maiden held everyone's attention. Tapping boots to the melody, Stephan nodded as she passed him.

She almost seems one with that music's flow.

At the performance's conclusion, the prince tossed the elder Gensipk Brandt's leather pouch and that man bowed in grateful respect. As the trio departed through a rear exit, Stephan approached Otho Szvord.

"Far as I know, Sire, they're just Gensipks passing through." The short and portly balding redheaded spoke jovially to his important customer. "They needed coins for traveling but I insisted on a partial cut to let them play. I saw you give them the pouch. At least they couldn't pick pockets while performing."

The prince thanked him and rejoined his 'shadows' while putting on his gray hat and cloak, its silver coat of arms the sole badge of rank, for the cold night. Their five-man group crossed a frozen brick road to the parked carriage and its two horses.

Four black-clad figures emerged from the nearest alley opposite them, footsteps crunched snow in this semi-deserted street. The prince's men spun to face them, long swords now drawn. The intruders each opened their cloaks and fired small crossbows. The guards and coachmen fell, killed by poisoned bolts in mere seconds.

Stephan was completely exposed.

From another alley nearer the parked square black carriage, two more black-cloaked, hooded figures emerged. Stephan was surrounded in the street, his silver long sword drawn, ready to fight for his own survival. The four attackers advanced, holding shorter blades now, while their comrades crept closer. Slashing at one man to his right with alcohol-impaired reflexes, Stephan was struck from behind by a blunt blow to the skull and fell face-down.

Blast! There's too many of . . .

The prince was carried away before the dead coachmen or guards were discovered near that deserted carriage.

Hours later, Prince Stephan awoke, still dizzy from those head blows. He was now inside an enclosed wooden structure with four strangers sitting or standing around him, his wrists and ankles shackled in iron manacles bolted to the floor.

"What is the meaning of this? Where in the Realms am I now?"

His haughty tone elicited a hard kick by one seated man into his right ribs, that greasy, scarred, unshaven killer soon holding the short sword at Stephan's throat.

"You're not in charge here, Your Highness, so be silent and enjoy the journey. I guarantee it will be your last."

That foul-breathed man then inspected three human-shaped burlap sacks; two had dried blood upon them, stacked against the far wall's quilt-covered bed behind a red velvet partition. Noting his condition, Stephan realized this was a wagon from traveling vibrations, along with the outside wheel and hoof sounds.

I still have my clothes and boots. Who are they?

The unshaven man opened the unstained sack, revealing the Gensipk dancer from Szvord's Inn. She appeared unconscious, gagged with a red scarf but unharmed. The prince suspected her companions were dead inside the other sacks. This wagon's window curtains were all closed. Two hanging overhead oil lamps and a wood-burning stove situated near an exit door provided the only illumination and heat here. Starting to speak again, Stephen was silenced by another thug's head kick. The first attacker rebuked the thug.

"Don't ruin the face. We'll need to identify him before being paid."

Slowing and stopping some time later, two lean thugs, one sporting thinning salt-and-pepper hair, the other black hair, forced the prince upright and unlocked the floor's chain bolts, then pushed him toward the one exit door. Opening it from outside, two more men appeared, clad in bright Gensipk clothing. One was a burly young blond man, and the second that brown-bearded gent Stephan had noticed cheering on the dancer last night. Gaining his first outdoor glimpse in hours, the captive saw it was late afternoon and overcast, sky hanging heavily above a mountain pass.

Now is my chance to surprise them.

Stepping onto short attached steps below the door, Stephan tackled those men in front, hitting their heads together with a thud, the trio falling into snow. The four other men soon sprang upon the prince with blades drawn before he could recover his stance.

They're too many. I've gained nothing!

Two thugs dragged Stephan off this snow-blanketed dirt road, tossing him onto one flat rocky surface at the wagon's right. His captives from inside there wore warm dark clothing. The man that first spoke to Stephan, acting like a leader, pressed the sword to his throat again.

"Don't act the hero, Your Highness, or I promise you'll only die slower."

The final short bald man with wooden teeth and rancid breath kept his sword on the prince, as the others prepared a campsite. Giggling, he spat at Stephan, taunting before the captive looked away from that whiny-voiced pockmarked killer.

"You'll not be your country's king after all. No one will find the body until spring."

"Who are you men," the prince snapped fearlessly, "to meddle in Schweitzen's future?"

"Let's say," the brown-haired leader answered as all his men dragged their prisoner near to the fire, some laughing at the noble when the brigand made that slicing motion by a left thumb across his own throat, "we've been hired to change your monarchy's destiny."

The short bald man boasted, "All you need know is we're getting the job done."

Stephan had no doubt about their intentions, the Gensipk-disguised duo changing into warmer clothing before preparing the meal. Two others always kept crossbows trained upon him.

"Why did you harm that Gensipk girl? She has no part in this madness!"

"We used the wagon to take you from Kronenberg." The 'leader's' last words were punctuated by his men's knowing laughter. "But she'll serve as tonight's entertainment."

"So, you brought me here at great difficulty, simply for an execution?"

"Not merely killing you," the bandit leader corrected him,

"but securing your severed head, royal cloak and personal weapon as proof for completing our job."

Stephan's eyes widened. "You're from the Assassins Guild of Venetza."

"Save any threats," this tormenter added, "we've protection for this assignment."

Protection—by whom? Is Serelethia's Court behind this?

"Enjoy your last meal, Prince of Schweitzen." The blonde man brought him a bowl.

The prince was staked to the ground near the fire with his chains, eating from the steaming wooden soup bowl by slowly drinking it. Those killers ate with wood spoons the next half-hour, making small talk but never revealing more about their employers as dusk approached.

Prince Stephan was returned to the wagon after eating and chained inside awaiting execution. The assassins left one small oil lantern burning here as it grew colder with nightfall. The captive caught familiar smoked meat or spice odors, mixed with the rotten stench from those sacked Gensipk bodies. During his meal, Stephan was informed he would, as a small mercy, be blindfolded and lashed to a tree, then shot with fast-acting poisoned crossbow bolts, like those that had dispatched his retinue in Kronenberg. The blonde-haired assassin, Serelo the Butcher, a former meat-cutter turned torturer, would sever his undamaged head as their trophy.

The last places I ever see are a Gensipk wagon and some wooded mountain pass.

Stephan then heard moaning as the Gensipk woman wriggled from the burlap sack drawstring closure, her big green eyes pleading. He crawled to the lady and lowered the gag.

She whispered in Plaropea's common tongue.

"Why did they murder my kin, Good Sir? Please, help me."

"I'll try," he offered. *But I die at sundown. I see from the window it's almost here.*

Stephan, still manacled, untied her bound wrists with great

difficulty as she shifted facing away, and glimpsed an odd red mark at the blouse's neckline. The lady spotted the nearby bloodstained burlap sacks and babbled grief-stricken Gensipkian, when the wagon's door burst open and two assassins confronted these captives. Seralo knocked the prince against the floor when lunging for them, as the big bearded man dragged the struggling maiden outside by her still-bound ankles.

"Don't worry." The blond-haired thug pressed his short sword to the prince's throat as the lady was lifted through the door. "She entertains us, then we execute you, Highness."

The assassins secured the carriage door with a strange exterior bolt lock before Stephan charged it. He was held back by his chains, longing to assist the panicked Gensipk. He overheard the men carry their victim toward the campfire, sounds of tearing cloth mixed with boisterous laughter.

"You'll pay for the evils you've caused," the prince vowed, "once I get free!"

Stephen sank onto the floor from exhaustion. He now noticed strange claw marks around the door's sturdy frame and surface, recalling it was locked from the outside.

Why doesn't it lock on this side? Has some sort of animal been kept in these chains?

The lady screamed again.

"Leave her be, vermin!" Stephan shouted.

Less than a minute later, the captive heard loud animal growls drown out the men's comments about their victim. The assassins suddenly yelled, terrified.

"Shoot it!"

"Look out!"

"Run for your liv—!"

"What is that thing?"

"No, she's—!"

Stephan glimpsed one killer hurled past the campfire-lit window to his left. He could not see the source of the assassins' distress, but hoped the girl was unharmed out there. They were being attacked by something that sounded strong and fast.

What in the Realms is going on?

The prince pulled at his chains without any result, until all battle sounds had ended, replaced by a labored breathing as something outside scratched at and sniffed the door, before it fled into the woods.

Was that an animal? What's happened to my would-be killers?

Seeing nothing at either window, Stephan listened at the door as the girl sobbed.

"Please," he cried, "let me out of here!"

The sad, gentle voice replied: "Who are you and why should I help, Stranger?"

"I was a prisoner like you." Stephan hesitated. "Please, unlock the door at least."

After about ten seconds, the bolt slid back and that door opened. The Gensipk stepped away from the wagon into cloud-dimmed moonlight, as Stephan used his lantern to better view that disheveled dancer who had once captivated him at the Szvord Inn. She was bruised and beaten, with blood stains across torn and tattered clothing. Moving toward that exit, the prince briefly forgot his bolted restraining chains.

"Don't be afraid," Stephan reassured her, smiling. "I won't hurt you."

The man was surprised to see two kidnapers sprawled across the bloodstained snow. From all obvious evidence of claw and bite marks, they had been mutilated by some animal.

"There is a key for the chains under my Papa's bed to your left, Stranger," the young woman volunteered, wrapping one dead man's cloak around her body. Stephan located the promised key under the left bed's mattress, freed himself and emerged into the cold night. The Gensipk circled him cautiously, raced inside her wagon and slammed the door. Examining animal tracks in the snow around each body, Stephan thought they seemed from big mountain wolves, sometimes called Worgs. The sound of crying came from inside the wagon.

"Are you all right? Can I help you?"

Receiving no answer, he walked toward the assassins'

campfire and quickly warmed himself, the local temperature having dropped below freezing soon after sundown.

About five minutes later, the Gensipk lady emerged from her wagon, now dressed in the green skirt, white blouse and multicolor shawl, wearing calf-length woolen-lined boots and brandishing a carving knife. Keeping the lantern in his left hand, Stephan approached cautiously, extending a right hand to show peaceful intent. Her green eyes blazed with hatred and mistrust.

"Come no closer," the woman said, "or I'll kill you."

Stephan nodded. "I'm not your enemy."

The prince found personal possessions on deceased assassins—gloves, belt pouches and coins—and discovered his cloak and sword inside one compartment beneath the wagon's driving seat. The Gensipk glared at Stephan as he donned that cloak inside-out, concealing its coat of arms, and hid the ornate sword beneath it.

"I thank you for your aid, good woman," Stephan said, placing small branches on the campfire the killers had gathered from the woods. She approached and sat opposite him there, still clutching the colorful knitted shawl around her body and keeping the knife. "You shall be rewarded, once we return to Kronenberg."

"My name," the Gensipk introduced herself with indifference, "is Mariskka Pechova."

"I am Stephan." He bowed "It might have been the sturmbrew and other liquors I drank," Stephan said, staring at her, "but last night you were the center of attention. That's why I gave your friends coins in appreciation."

Seconds of uncomfortable silence. Then, "My full name is Stephan Lotzek from Kronenberg." He chose his mother's maiden name for an alias. He noted her bruises and bloodstains in the firelight. "Are you seriously hurt, Mariskka? I know some things about tending wounds."

"I'll survive this," she replied. The breath steam punctuated her distant icy tone.

"Did you see," Stephen said as he stirred the fire's charcoal embers, "what killed those men?"

Mariskka shook her head and closed both eyes briefly. "They are dead, and I care not for the reason why. My Papa and brother Vartos are also gone, and your kindness cannot restore their lives."

"I'm sorry." The prince could think of nothing else to say. *My life cost them theirs.*

Adding more firewood, Stephan and Mariskka ate the remaining food taken from the wagon's supplies. Wolves howled in the distance, and Stephan jumped, glancing at Mariskka. She had not moved.

Despite those serious bruises, he thought as he noted her new clothes, *she's still beautiful.*

"Wolves don't come close to campfires unless they're hungry," Mariskka calmly reassured the city dweller. "We're safe."

"Those men planned to kill me, and would have done so by now."

"My father and little brother were all the family I had left in this world!" Mariskka threw her bowl down after one frustrated groan. "Do you understand, Lotzek?" She considered him in the firelight. "Why were they trying to kill you?"

Stephan didn't miss a beat.

"They'd been hired to prevent me inheriting my family's business."

She nodded. "Will you help me bury my kinfolk?"

"We can take their bodies to Kronenberg for proper burial, if you wish."

Mariskka shook her head. "Most folk believe if a Gensipk body is placed in their cemeteries, its soil becomes unhallowed. I will bury them out here."

They placed Mariskka's relatives under wood and rocks, since the ground was too frozen for digging, burlap sacks serving as burial shrouds. The lady uttered an ancient Gensipk death oath and Stephan quoted a few scriptures. They pitched the large tent for her horses, then Mariskka invited him inside. With its stove relit, the wagon's interior was warmer than Szvord's Inn, the odor covering lingering stenches. The Gensipk gave him her brother's bed, across from the father's. They both remained dressed.

Mariskka kept the partition curtain half-open around her bed, watching Stephan intensely.

"So," she said, less harsh now, "you truly enjoyed my dancing?"

Stephan shrugged. "It's more vibrant than that of local mountain folk."

"I know what attacked those men."

The prince sat up in the bed, facing that Gensipk with genuine interest.

"They ambushed Papa and Vartos, stabbing them in an alley. One man grabbed me, placed a sweet-smelling cloth over my face. I woke up in that sack next and saw you." Mariskka paused to break down, sitting up remembering the following near rape. "They dragged me to the fire. I was thrown on the ground. Then, those men tore at..."

Stephan started toward Mariskka, until she shouted: "Stay away!"

"I'm sorry," she added quietly. "I don't know you, Stephan."

He nodded. Mariskka continued, hugging her knees.

"The men held me. I struggled. Then, a shaggy figure emerged from trees, tore all the killers apart. I crawled over and hid under the wagon. It vanished into the woods again."

"What was it?" Stephan's face was an intense, curious mask. "You said you knew."

"I believe my people call any creature like that unnatural beast lunathrope."

Mariskka was completely sincere.

Schweitzen Academy's references said dead men cannot become lycanthropes.

"They're called lycanthropes in continental speech. That's what killed the six men we threw into a ravine?"

"My people believe in such vile creatures," Mariskka retorted, "and not long ago your ancestors also admitted their existence."

The prince had read some of Schweitzen Academy's documented cases from hunts centuries ago, but never believed them as true. Mariskka obviously did.

"I meant no disrespect. If you said that is what killed them,

I'll trust you."

Even if I believe lycanthrope legends, like dragons, Stephan thought to himself, *my instructors only claimed they had become either rare or extinct.*

Stephan offered to keep watch a few hours; Mariskka held the knife against her bosom as she slept. The prince perched closer to the stove, bathed by its glow and lost in thought.

Will I ever learn exactly what slaughtered those Venetzan murderers tonight?

Hours later, Stephan was startled by wolf howls over steadier shrieking winds, and moved to inform Mariskka he would check the horses, then gasped as the Gensipk's eyes opened from a light sleep when he was halfway to her bedside..

"Wolves won't attack us here." She was perfectly calm. "Do they still frighten you?"

"I-I'll check your horses," he stammered. "Animals sometimes fear wild creatures."

Mariskka smiled at his controlled dread, gently shaking her head.

"Gensipk-bred steeds are used to things out here. Sleep now, Stephan. I will keep watch after inspecting my horses."

Climbing exhausted into the borrowed bed, he recalled an odd thing she had mentioned.

"Why did your family travel in one wagon, and not as a caravan like other Gensipks?"

"We were branded Inyio, 'outcast' in your tongue, six cycles ago." Mariskka fed more twigs to the fire. "I am not permitted into any caravan due to a curse upon blood-kin."

I'm glad I wasn't born a Gensipk.

Pulling the blanket tight around himself as Mariskka exited the wagon, Stephan was relieved she said nothing more about her life. He kept his sword close as he drifted off to sleep.

* * *

The wagon was moving. Stumbling from bed in the early morning to seek an explanation, he pounded the ceiling until the vehicle halted. The prince donned that cloak reversed again, meeting Mariskka as she trod through a foot of snow covering this road. His next words irritated in tone, he noticed her bruises seemed faded under sunlight.

"Just exactly where are you taking me?"

"I was returning you to your walled city Kronenberg." The Gensipk met Stephan's glare with confused indignation. "That *was* what you wanted, no?"

Mariskka then clutched his inverted cloak, exposing its hidden coat of arms.

"As I suspected earlier, you've kept secrets from me, *Shopkeeper's Son*."

Stephan remained speechless.

"Would you have ever revealed this to me," she asked, taking a knife from her right boot, "or did you prefer I never know about it? I will have the truth, Nobleman!"

"I planned to tell more only after knowing I could trust you, Mariskka." Stephan replied calmly, "and would have rewarded your help—owing that much. I shielded you from actual and potential perils being in the company of Schweitzen's Crown Prince."

The woman's shrewd gaze revealed a kind of tacit acceptance as she replaced the blade. "I recognized your family's crest."

"I avoid ceremony with friends." He smiled, touching her shoulders. "Be thou friend?"

Stephan released Mariskka as she flinched from pain. He pulled her long white shawl aside to discover fresh blood spots on that blouse and skirt.

"Speaking of secrets, did you intend ever admitting any injuries to me, Mariskka?"

The Gensipk replaced the thick shawl around her body in anger.

"They are nothing worse than I've suffered before. Those men injured me with weapons and blows last night. My wounds are almost healed today."

"I can help with those." Stephan reached for her. "If you'll allow me to—"

Mariskka retreated into the wagon and Stephan belatedly realized that her gaze had meant she would not accept any aid. He scratched his head about the Gensipk's odd claim to be "almost healed."

I think I smelled poison on her. If she was hit by crossbow bolts, how is she still alive?

Stephan took in the snow-covered road bracketed by trees, but had no idea of their location. Wearing a fresh white embroidered dress now, Mariskka tossed him a bundle of bright red and violet Gensipk clothing with tan boots.

"My Papa's old items should fit you better than Vartos' smaller stuff," she said. "Shave with Papa's razor as a final precaution and disguise before we reach Schweitzen."

Miles later through this snow, the prince saw the wisdom in disguise as they drove past one wooden signpost giving Kronenberg's distance as a day's journey away. He guessed they were at the Serelethian Empire's western edge inside the Elepine Mountains. Mariskka drove the wagon as they sat together, looking for all the world the typical Gensipk couple.

"Killers will not recognize you now," she said as she handed the newly clean-shaven man the reins, "and your subjects might have resented seeing their prince in a Gensipk's company."

Considering her with a thoughtful gaze, he dismissed that last prejudicial statement.

"I still want us to remain friends, regardless of how my subjects feel about Gensipks."

"Yes," Mariskka replied with a frown, "but would your parents let you marry one?"

He chuckled. "No, but *I* would never object to it."

They arrived at the Serelethian-Schweitzen border by mid-afternoon, and aside from the usual prejudice toward Gensipks, Stephan and Mariskka passed the frontier without incident. Fighting an urge to tell the Schweitzen customs agent his identity, as the man remarked that they had no "litter"—implying, essentially, that Gensipks bred like rabbits—he continued driving westward past the small hut.

Customs Guard Shickelgrubber might have died of embarrassment if recognizing me.

Running into deep snowfall, the travelers knew they would never reach Kronenberg by nightfall, and soon stopped near an ice-choked stream at dusk. Mariskka prepared diced, dried vegetables and smoked venison in a pot of melted water, after Stephan gathered firewood from under trees. The snow was six inches here, compared to deeper mountain road drifts. He remained disguised for now, enjoying aromas from the lady's small copper kettle hanging over their fire.

"It smells wonderful, but I think fresh fish would've made a better main course."

Stirring their stew, Mariskka responded with dry humor.

"I would still be cleaning their scales and gutting them now, if you had caught any. No, thank you. My liege."

Laughing heartily, Stephan knelt beside her. The Gensipk added salt to the pot, telling him: "Fetch one of the big wicker jugs hanging on the wagon's ceiling. The killers ignored them. My Papa's homemade cider will keep us warm tonight."

He headed into the wagon, noticing her smile and wink at him while stirring.

They ate that simple meal with the late father's "magic" cider, after which they readied the horse shelter tent together. Once inside the wagon, Mariskka changed into a gray wool nightdress behind the front partition, and tied her hair beneath that red silk bandana. Meanwhile, near the door, Stephan was undressing to knee-length, white wool under drawers. The two moved their beds together for sharing body warmth, trusting each other more after that cider. Stephan and Mariskka held hands beneath blankets, enjoying the cozier atmosphere created by the stove's roaring evening fire.

What is that—a bruise those assassins gave her from their

undesired attentions?

Stephan considered Mariskka's strawberry-colored birthmark at the nightdress' right shoulder. He decided to ask about it, but found the cider had affected his speech.

"What —what is that spot, my lovely Gensipk maidenhead? As Clown Prince of Schwietzen, I'll ban-ish you for not telling me any-thing I must know a-bout it, Mar-isk-ka."

Mariskka giggled, both of them affected by the cider now.

"I spoke something about it yesterday, O Clown. My tiny family had been Inyio six seasons. Symbols painted on our wagon warn other Gensipks." She paused, that pretty face darkened by shame. "As a youth I was attacked, bitten and raped by some kindly woodcutter. Our caravan hunted and killed that lunathrope, but my immediate family was shunned after I had been cursed."

Is—is that the spot where... where she was "bitten?"

Confused, Stephan stared toward the ceiling and shook his head. Mariskka pulled the nightdress collar lower to reveal a full wolf's head mark, then pointing there with her left hand when describing its origin. He had trouble focusing on it.

"This mark was made by a silver-topped staff of the Matron Magdae, striking me where I was bitten. It is permanent; further warning our people about the curse."

I must be drunk. Her Gensipk tall tales—they're making sense.

Stephan groaned with disbelief at Mariskka's admission as she pulled her nightdress over the mark again. She pressed her hands against his and gazed at the window to their left.

"Full moons are out," she said, smiling. "Our legends say lunathropes become beasts under those. Silly legend—but I still want us—to be together."

The prince squeezed his companion's hands and shifted to face her.

"I don't know if it's your Papa's cider or our - ordeal, but we're connected, Mariskka. Why do you say strange things?"

Nestled closer against Stephan, Mariskka's Gensipk accent was more pronounced.

"My people believe two souls on the kindred journey are

denied joyous union only by death. I sensed your courage before being forced to kill those men, yet trusted you not. But after today's travels, I realized your wolf's heart, and heard its desire, now that we're alone here."

She's trying to seduce me. No, I'm—I'm promised to another woman—Halle.

Shaking his head again to clear it, Stephan focused valiantly on one thing Mariskka had said.

"Whatdja mean before...you killed those men? I don't...don't under..."

Mariskka laughed.

"You're the stubborn fool, despite the evidence. Educated men deny superstition's reality. I've spoken true, Stephan, and will prove it the only way I can now…beloved."

Pouncing atop the prince, Mariskka held him down and bit his clean-shaven upper lip. The startled man cried and struggled to break free, but the Gensipk's might was greater than her size suggested. The lady alternated gentle kisses with licking blood off his mouth. Stephan ignored his pain when becoming aroused by her bizarre seduction. This exotic woman enthralled her startled guest, stripping that nightdress and spreading legs to mount him. The noble responded to this raw passion, freeing his lover's raven hair from the bandana, caressing her golden-tan naked flesh (even as it felt hairier), and slipped his own underwear away for their pleasure.

I want her—Gensipk or not! Is she changing somehow, or is it just the cider?

The couple's heated intercourse was interrupted by panicked neighs from her horses outside. Stephan reluctantly extricated himself from Mariskka, and retrieved his clothes off the floor to investigate. Swiftly donning the purple pants, red tunic, his own black boots and gray cloak, the prince wiped blood trickles off his mouth, lit a lantern and drew the silver-coated long sword, his head clearing from adrenaline as he looked at Mariskka one final time.

"Stay here, Darling, until I return."

Something's stalking our wagon. I'm the only one trained to fight.

Sitting up, Mariskka licked at the prince's blood on her lips, seeming unconcerned about any danger outside. Stephan paused inside the exit, realizing his new love's exposed skin seemed more hair-covered, the ears semi-pointed and her expression almost feral.

It's just that damned Gensipk cider, nothing more.

Entering the frigid night, Prince Stephan trod through snow as wind blew against his back, advancing on that shelter to part the tent flap using the sword. His lantern and the two Wyche-Realms full brilliance moons (the larger gray and its smaller counterpart blue) illuminated this area. The lone man inspected four unnerved, stout Gensipk horses. Stephan's intoxication lessened after minutes in this chill night air.

They smell something lurking out there, but I can't tell where.

Exiting the tent, Stephan saw a large shadow approaching and avoided a blow aimed at his head's right side from some heavy blunt weapon. The prince tumbled across snow and recovered into the defensive crouch, despite cider-slowed reflexes. He lost the lantern, but viewed his large opponent by moonlight now. The hulking thing was half again the size of a man, wearing animal hides made into a hooded cloak and other crude clothing that covered its body. The creature's face was hideous by human standards, its fangs protruding, and matted black hair drooped over that sloping forehead.

It's an ogre. I've seen them in Academy journal illustrations, but this one's—

The ogre bounded across snow toward Stephan, wielding a tree trunk club against the human. Stephan stumbled in attempting to dodge that determined beast's charge when the humanoid was tackled by one black-furred blur. The two figures rolled across the snow, fighting for advantage, and Stephan kept his distance, uncertain which to attack. The green-skinned ogre dropped the club, smashing the black quadruped with its fists while the new pointed-eared arrival clawed and bit the larger creature ferociously.

Wait, it... it's the beast Mariskka said saved her from our captors. Did it follow us?

The brief struggle ended as the black creature ripped the ogre's throat out, and spun toward a confused Stephan still holding his sword. Sniffing the prince, the beast advanced upon him, dark ogre blood covering the lupine thing's claws and muzzle.

The creature did us a service slaying that monster. Why do I almost trust it now?

Lowering the sword when the black-haired creature began walking on hind legs, Stephan felt no instinctive fear against it.

"What are you? I feel almost as though I know—"

He then recognized the creature's green eyes and knew who this was, despite the thought: *No—it can't be.*

Stephan closed his violet eyes in denial, as Mariskka lunged. The prince caught the creature with the sword, but her left paw did not deflect the slicing blow. The silver blade slashed her left side into the central chest, and Mariskka yelped when shoving him down.

This is the woman I love? She's killing me!

Collapsing beneath her attack, Stephan lost consciousness in a pain haze as the shaggy female bit his left shoulder when pinning him on the ground. The prince lost his grip on the long sword and sank into temporary oblivion.

Waking a few hours later, Prince Stephan clutched his once-bleeding shoulder and saw the blood-covered sword and Mariskka's naked, motionless form nearby.

Oh God, what have I done?

Retrieving his weapon out of habit, Stephan felt it burn him. He flung it away, then wrapped the wounded Gensipk in the gray cloak and carried her inside the wagon.

"I love you, Stephan," Mariskka whispered, "and shared my curse. I was uncertain if biting your mouth would be sufficient, so I attacked again."

"Don't talk, Mariskka." Stephan placed her gently across one bed and knelt beside his lover. "Let me help you."

Examining her sword wound, the prince was shocked at the apparent blood loss from a single eight-inch gash between two ribs. Mariskka's golden-tan complexion was paler, but she seemed at peace with impending death.

The books said a silver weapon could kill any lycanthrope. There's nothing I...

"Your blade was coated with silver. I don't blame any misunderstanding. You know I spoke the truth before."

Nodding at her words, Stephan fought anguish about needless death, hating the abandoned sword and reflexive fear using it earlier. The man forgot his own minor injuries.

"I feel different inside, Mariskka, not just because I love you. You slew that big ogre for me. Please, I cannot live without you now."

"You must survive, Stephan, even if you could never marry a Gensipk like..."

Mariskka's eyes stared at the ceiling and her body convulsed. Stephan felt the curse burning within his body, wiped away tears and howled at her passing.

At dawn, Prince Stephan rode from the clearing on one Gensipk horse, leading three others in tow, and leaving Mariskka Pechova's body inside a burning wagon as her funeral pyre.

I understand why her family needed an outside lock and strong chains in their wagon.

The Crown Prince returned to Kronenberg by midday a changed man in more than one way. Stephan personally tracked down Lord Dursten later in secret and gained his eventual confession before death that Serelethia had plotted the young nobleman's kidnapping. Careful to never share his curse with Halle, Stephan's lycanthropy altered the House of Schweitzen's character across several succeeding generations.

Excerpt from the Upcoming Novel Deadfall by Shaun Jeffrey

Hunter lay behind a log and peered through the ATN scope of the Dragunov sniper rifle. He made a couple of adjustments to the rangefinder reticle that allowed him to gauge the target's distance, made another couple of adjustments to compensate for elevation and wind, took a deep inhalation, exhaled until the moment of natural respiratory pause, then squeezed the trigger. The rifle kicked in his hand, but he kept his head in firm contact with the stock, kept the trigger pulled all the way to the rear, continued to look through the sight, and only released the trigger when the recoil stopped. Through the sight, he watched the bullet strike its target with unerring accuracy and the zombie flew back to lie spread-eagled across the ground, its head blown apart.

Hunter couldn't afford to feel remorse when he took someone out, but knowing the targets were already dead made it more monotonous than anything, like shooting inanimate objects. He found another target, a woman this time, readjusted the sight and then went through the previous breathing procedure before he pulled the trigger. The 7.62x54mm bullet struck home, spinning the woman like a top.

Rain trickled through the leafy canopy above, the foliage providing a little relief from the downpour. Despite having a good view of the village, the layout and the buildings provided too many obstacles. From what he could see, the zombies were everywhere. Some were running around like wild things in search of fresh meat, others just stood in ominous silence. He could just about see the building Lars and Six-pack holed up in, but couldn't help from where he was. With the rest of the team scattered, all leadership seemed to have gone out the window. It now seemed to be every man for himself. Hunter could deal with that, could work well enough whether acting on his own or under orders. Sometimes he found his own company preferable to that of others. Those three days in the jungle when he had waited for the rebel leader had shown him that. It took a certain sort of person to be a sniper.

His girlfriend Alice, on the other hand, would probably say he couldn't cope too well on his own, considering the mess he left their flat in on the rare occasions she went away without him to visit relatives or friends. In the army, he had to keep things tidy, had to look smart and follow orders to the letter. Once he left the armed forces, a rebellious streak manifested, and he took a more slovenly approach to his general appearance. He liked to think of himself as laid-back and chilled, a surf bum with a gun who followed the tides of war instead of the waves.

He slotted into the personal security way of life without too much trouble. There were plenty of opportunities for the right people. Sure, there was danger, but that was part of the thrill. He couldn't see himself opting for the quiet life, stacking shelves in the supermarket like his brother, Tony. Getting a rollicking for stacking the cans of baked beans too high wasn't the same as making life or death decisions.

He retargeted, adjusted the range, took a respiratory pause and fired another round. The bullet struck home with devastating effect, taking a man out and almost severing the leg of a man standing a few feet behind. The crippled zombie flopped to the ground and started crawling, pulling himself along like a slug. Hunter decided not to bother wasting a bullet dealing the deathblow, preferring to save each round for those who looked capable of doing damage.

A branch snapped somewhere behind him. He felt his heart

kick like a mule as he swung the gun around, targeting the trees. The sudden adrenaline rush made him feel light-headed as he scanned the area. When he failed to spot anything through the sight, his heart went from a gallop to a trot and then relaxed. Unsure if it was sweat or raindrops on his forehead, he ran the sleeve of his jacket across his brow to wipe it away. He exhaled a shaky breath, couldn't believe how spooked he felt.

He turned back to view the village, grateful for the distance and the rain which helped to dampen the zombies' groans. He felt the darkness pressing at his back and a shiver went down his spine. The hairs on the nape of his neck bristled. He glanced over his shoulder—the darkness absolute. At least it helped as much as it hindered, because if he couldn't see, he couldn't be seen either—or could dead people see in the dark? They couldn't in any of the films he'd seen, but this wasn't a goddamn film. As he equated death with darkness, perhaps they could see as they existed between two worlds, that of the living and that of the dead. The thought sent another shiver coursing through his body.

The sooner they were out of here, the better. This was fucked-up with a capital F.

Although loaded with plenty of ammunition to last a while, he knew taking out one or two zombies wasn't going to help when there were so many of them. A sniper in the field took out selected enemy personnel. But here, no one stood out as a selective target. To Hunter, it now became a case of if-the-face-fits.

He scanned the streets, spotted John and Barry at the edge of the village, hiding behind a low wall. Further movement caught his eye and he saw a large, topless man charging toward their position. From where they were, they wouldn't be able to see the man, drapes of belly fat swaying from side to side as he ran.

Hunter targeted the man, but fired too fast. The bullet missed. He fired again, not taking the time to sight the target, and missed again.

He thumbed his microphone. "John, Barry, there's a man running toward you. Seven o'clock. Coming in fast."

He watched through the scope as Barry poked his head above the bricks in time to see the man plough through the wall at his side. Startled, Barry fell back, his gun sent flying in the confusion. John jumped aside and raised the barrel of his gun to target the zombie, but it straddled Barry, causing him to hold fire, afraid he might hit his companion. Hunter watched Barry wrestle the zombie while John battered its head with the stock of his gun.

Strong and resilient to pain, the zombie seemed unperturbed. The force of John's blows caved half of its head in, but it didn't seem to make any difference. He guessed it didn't feel anything in death.

While watching the fight, Hunter adjusted the scope. He aligned the sight on the zombie, but couldn't take the shot for fear of hitting Barry.

Despite the damp conditions and the rain trickling through the leaves, Hunter's lips felt dry. As he licked them, he thought how Alice liked kissing them. He didn't think she would feel that way now, would no doubt say they felt like sandpaper.

Although he acted macho and a little aloof around Alice, thinking about her caused a slight pain in his stomach. Unused to the unfamiliar sensation, his hands started shaking, disturbing the image through the scope. Hunter released the polymer foregrip and wiped his hand along his trousers before resuming his hold. It took him a couple of seconds to retarget on the zombie.

John had moved aside, was crouched by the wall, fiddling with something Hunter couldn't make out. Next second, the zombie seemed to freeze, its head aloft as it straddled Barry.

Hunter prepared to take the shot. He regulated his breathing, relaxed his muscles. Water trickled into his eye, whether sweat or rain he didn't know. He blinked, blurring his vision, removed his trigger finger to rub his face, then retargeted. With no time left to hesitate, he pulled the trigger, saw half the zombie's head disintegrate.

The sound of breaking branches made Hunter jump. He snapped his head around, saw a figure darker than the surrounding night rushing toward him. He started to bring his weapon around to fire, but the figure crashed into him, knocking the Dragunov aside. It brought with it the smell of death and putrefying flesh. Hunter gagged. Strong hands with sharp nails gouged his face, scoring the flesh from his cheeks. Hunter grunted. Leaves, mulch and clods of earth fell onto his face from the creature. The sweet smell of the mulch entered his nostrils, but the fetid odor of decay proved too overpowering.

He couldn't tell whether it was a man or woman, didn't care. All he knew was that it was trying to kill him. Although he couldn't see clearly, he heard its teeth click together, primed to tear a chunk out of his flesh. The thought spurred him on, fuelling his muscles. He released the gun and threw a punch, his fist striking cold, compliant flesh that felt like the congealed skin of a rice pudding. He grimaced, his stomach as queasy as if he'd awoken from a night of heavy drinking.

The zombie groaned, a sound of anger or pain—Hunter couldn't decide which.

He tried to rise, but the zombie pushed him over the log he'd been using to support the gun. He landed in a mulch of leaves that felt slimy against his skin. He struggled to his feet, pulled the Colt M1911 pistol from the holster around his waist and cocked the hammer, fired blindly into the dark. The pistol bucked in his hand, the automatic movement of the slide cocking the hammer for each subsequent shot. The trees swallowed the roar of the gun. He heard the thud of bullets striking targets, but didn't know what those targets were. The magazine ran dry, all seven bullets fired.

Hoping and praying he'd hit the zombie, he reached for the Maglite on his belt when he heard a groan to his left. He turned, switched on the torch and shone it into the ravaged face of his adversary, taking an involuntary gasp as he surveyed the creature.

Dead eyes stared back from what turned out to be a man's sunken sockets. His skin looked waxy and pale. Leaves and dirt protruded from his black hair, one of his ears looking as though it had been nibbled by a rat, or blasted by a bullet. At a guess, the man hadn't been dead too long. The Colt's bullets had ripped holes in his once white, now filthy, ripped shirt. No blood poured from the wounds, but an internal organ protruded from one, like sausage meat squeezed from a machine. The man's corpse was bloated with gasses, the release of which tainted the air with an even more disgusting aroma.

Hunter ejected the magazine from the pistol and reached for another, but the zombie moved too fast. It lunged forward.

Unable to react quickly enough, Hunter dropped the gun and torch, freeing his hands to wrestle the zombie. But it was too strong. He smelled its fetid, stomach churning odor wash over him, felt its teeth bite down on his wrist as he tried to protect his face. White-hot pain seared through his body, made him feel as though he had been dunked in liquid nitrogen. He gasped, felt the zombie crunch through skin and connective tissue, then bite into bone. He felt its teeth gnawing. Felt bone splinter and break. He squealed. Kicked out. But the zombie didn't react.

He felt warm blood run along his arm, seeping from the cold, dry kiss of the zombie's lips against his flesh.

Hunter punched with his free hand, screamed, kicked, but none of it helped. The zombie shook its head like a dog, tore a chunk of meat from Hunter's arm. He heard it spit the chunk out, making room for more as it pressed itself forward, knocking Hunter to the ground as his feet slipped in the mulch. His breath blasted from his mouth as the zombie landed on his chest, compressing his lungs. He groaned, felt the zombie lower its head, its teeth finding the fresh meat around his throat.

Tears rolled from Hunter's eyes. In his mind he pictured Alice. He wished he could tell her how much he loved her.

For the first time in his life, he envied his brother. Stacking shelves didn't seem such a bad career after all.

Excerpt from the Upcoming Novel
The Rocket's Red Glare
by
David M. Peak

The next day, Isaac woke up at his usual early hour, grabbed his Gillie pole, and went down to the river to meet his friends.

The sky was overcast and the air was still. A light mist, greenish gray in color, had settled over the city, making it difficult, if not impossible, to see far in any direction. The apartment complexes of his neighborhood seemed to vanish into the sky—*a lot* of things seemed to be vanishing these days. The Breathers, for one, were disappearing.

In God We Trust City used to be crawling with lumbering, whispering Breathers. But even as Isaac made his way through his neighborhood, passing the small, lot-sized fenced-in pens that functioned as "Breather Parks," he didn't see a single one. Their chains lay on the ground, coiled and rusting. But no Breathers. They were vanishing—right off the face of the Quarter.

The moisture in the air made Isaac's T-shirt cling to his wide body.

He walked along the bank of the river all the way out of the city, wondering if what he'd seen the night before, that building vanishing in a great burst of sparks, was somehow connected to the disappearing Breathers or the president. It had to be. After all, he'd scoured the newspapers that morning, trying to find some article, no matter how small, mentioning the incident, but he'd come up with nothing—not even a blurb. He felt like the Quarter was dissolving, wearing away to nothing.

By the time he got to the highways his shirt was saturated with water. He was cranky and distracted. Catching Gillies just didn't seem as important as it had a week ago. *And why is that? Why don't I care anymore?*

Isaac stared at the swirling silver waters of the river, licking and sloshing at the gray, muddy bank to his right, and mulled over what the Sage had said to him. *"Isaac, you're a very bright young germ. If anyone can figure that out, perhaps it is you."*

After he'd gotten home from visiting the Sage the night before, Isaac spent all night reading in his bed; he read books from Miss May's reading list, books he'd long been putting off, books with unpronounceable names. His mother had gone to sleep early so Isaac had been able to stay up as late as he wanted. He had been inspired by his discussion with the Sage. When he grew weary of Miss May's books, he read an about the lore of rockets—from ancient times. He'd bought the text a year or two before. It was dense stuff, written in rhyming verse, but still, it wasn't that different from what germs like Sartarian and Spengler—if there still *was* a Spengler—were saying about them: how rockets could be used to launch germs from one side of the quarter to the other, or to be used as weaponry.

He'd fallen asleep that night with the lights on, the book open across his chest, his tentacles splayed out at his sides.

Isaac met up with Glenn and Gus by Plated Road, two or three highway exits outside the city limits. The familiar drone of the highway traffic was loud and clear in the distance. Glenn's propeller was stationary in the still air and he had a frown on his face. His Gillie pole was lying on the ground beside him.

Glenn never was one to take care of his stuff, Isaac thought. *Not at all like Gus.*

Gus had one long arm wrapped several times around the shaft of his pole. He let the handle rest on the ground. Isaac could tell that his line was new.

The delicate rush of the river hissed before them, mixing with the drone of the traffic, sounding like a radio picking up static from two different stations. It felt to Isaac like a strange day, one of those days where everything was a bit off, removed from normal, like everything was buried beneath a layer of gray gauze.

"What's the matter, Glenn?" Isaac said, approaching his friends, his tentacles slapping against the cool mud. Gus reached out his hand and Isaac slapped it. "Hey, Gus," he said. Gus nodded back at him with his long, tube-shaped head.

"Glenn here is getting pissy about walking out here," Gus said.

"Hrumph," Glenn grunted. He had his arms crossed over his gut, his ashy black belly showing between the waist of his pants and his tight T-shirt. Isaac noticed that Glenn hadn't cleaned his shoes, they were still muddy from the little scuffle they'd gotten into during the previous outing. "It's not like the Gillie hooking's any better out here," Glenn said. "And it takes nearly an hour to walk this far."

Isaac rolled his eyes. "Not this again. Look, from now on we don't need to come out this far. I just like coming a little ways outside the city. There's not so many other germs around."

"Not so many Gillies around either," Glenn said.

"Ha ha," Isaac feigned. "We'll see about that." He curled one of his tentacles and prodded Glenn's soft belly. "I'll betcha I catch a Gillie at least twice as big as anything you'll catch."

"Knock it off," Glenn yelled, pushing Isaac's tentacle away, his propeller giving one mighty spin. "You couldn't catch a, a uh—"

Gus and Isaac laughed as Glenn gave up on an adequate comeback, his gray face flushing dark black. The three young germs playfully shoved each other around and made cracks at one another. For a second, Isaac allowed himself to act like a germ his age, eleven-years-old, found himself having fun for the first time in who knows how long. And in the process, he enjoyed being with his friends.

"Come on, now," Gus said, twirling the fleshy propeller on Glenn's head with one of his slinky fingers. "Let's get going. We've got some Gillie hooking to do."

"Right-o," Isaac said.

As they walked along the river, the three young germs continued jostling and harassing one another. Isaac had forgotten all about rockets, about disappearing Breathers, ancient lore. He'd forgotten all about the Sage telling him that there might not be an edge to the Quarter.

"Hey. Let's act like soldiers," Glenn said.

"Yeah," Gus said.

They cradled the handles of their Gillie poles in their elbows and hands—Gus's arms bending and angling in all sorts of directions—and rested the shafts on their shoulders.

"Hut. Hut. Hut." Glenn chanted between labored breaths, sucking in as much air he could between words.

Glenn and Gus started marching—Glenn stomping in the mud, Gus hopping lightly. Glenn kept his back straight and kicked his legs out straight, raising his chin to the sky.

"Forward march," Gus barked.

Isaac had seen his friends do this a thousand times before—had even participated himself many times over. But something was different now. As he watched them march along the bank of the river, Isaac felt like he was going to be sick. A lump lodged itself in his throat.

He thought of Spengler's radio broadcast, his talk of preparation for another Great War. He thought about what he had read in Sartarian's *Duality and Quarter Existence*.

"*That's a dangerous book,*" the Sage had said. And only now, as Isaac watched his friends play soldiers, did he understand what the Sage had meant by that, or how a book could be dangerous, as dangerous as a weapon, a bomb.

"Now charge," Glenn yelled. They dropped their poles down from their shoulders and held them out before them. Glenn ran ahead, Gus hopped, and yelled. "Die. Die. Stab 'em." They stabbed at imaginary enemies.

Isaac watched his friends run up the riverbank, laughing wildly, disappearing into the swirling gray mist, their laughter fading with distance.

"Hey," Isaac yelled. "Wait for me." He slapped after them.

The riverbank was raised from the water level, creating a small, rocky ridge. From atop the ridge, they had a pretty good view of the silver waters churning downstream. The dirt incline of the opposite bank—which was usually reflected on the water's surface—was lost in the fog, and they could only see about halfway across. The city behind them was also lost in the fog. They were floating in the gray, the gauze.

Something out in the water had Gus and Glenn's attention. Isaac reached them, stood behind them. He peered over Glenn's shoulder down into the water.

Two gray, formless shapes were splashing around. Not too far away. The ripples from their splashes rolled across the surface of the water and licked at the muddy riverbank.

"What are those?" Isaac asked. "Are those gillies?" He squinted his eyes, trying to see through the fog. It was no use. He couldn't see a thing.

"There's no Gillie that big," Glenn said. "Those sound like Cloppies splashing around or something. Like maybe they're drowning or something."

"Cloppies in the river?" Gus asked. "Should we go down there?"

The formless shapes started to come into focus, getting closer. They weren't gillies at all—but two adult germs—about thirty or forty-years-old, low-breeds, Zeros. They were both as round as the sun, fleshy and orange, legless, arms only a foot or so long protruding beneath their flat, smeared-looking faces. One was heavier than the other. He had a thick, knotty beard, like a fur that had grown around the pulled-back, red lips of his mouth. His teeth were enormous, yellowed.

"It's a couple of Zeros," Isaac said, squinting even harder. "You never see those things outside the slums."

The Zeros were flipping and turning circles around one another. The heavier one squirted some water out of his mouth at the other one. They both laughed, their voices resounding like great belly-laughs, flapping their short arms, splashing. They gnashed their teeth and giggled. The sound of their laughter carried over the water and reached the three germs on the riverbank.

"What the hell are those freaks doing?" Glenn squealed. "No one ever comes out here."

"It looks like they're swimming," Isaac said.

"Are they naked?" Gus asked.

"You ever heard of a Zero wearing clothes?" Isaac said. "They're too stupid to know how to wear clothes."

"How are we supposed to hook Gillies with them swimming right in front of us?" Glenn asked. He threw his pole down onto the ground. It clattered on the hard dirt.

"Why don't we just head up river a bit?" Isaac asked.

"No way," Glenn said, shaking his head back and forth. The sounds of splashing in the water ceased. The laughter died out. Glenn huffed and puffed, his breathing sounding husky, labored. "There's no way. You hear me? No way."

Isaac's eyes darted from Glenn to the river. The two Zeros had stopped their tumbling and had waded closer to the shore, trying to see what the yelling was about, smiling huge toothy smiles. But as they got closer, their smiles went away. Their faces, stretched over their round bodies, looked worried. Their turned-down lips opened and closed as they murmured to one another. Their little hands—with fingers like fleshy tubes of lipstick—were shaking slightly.

Isaac looked back at Glenn and held his eye contact.

"You made us walk this far already," Glenn said, poking Isaac in the chest with his stubby index finger. "And now you want us to walk even farther? There's no way."

Isaac took a step back. "Relax, will you? It was just an idea."

"Jeez, Glenn," Gus said. "Isaac's right, just relax." He wound up his long arm and lightly socked Glenn in the shoulder.

Glenn swiveled on his heels and threw a punch back at Gus—missing entirely. His torso twisted as his arm completed its arc. His feet tangled on his Gillie pole and he stumbled forward, propeller twirling. There was a loud, sharp cracking noise as his pole snapped in half.

Glenn lost his balance and fell, slowly, like in slow-motion, managing to brace his fall a bit with his left elbow. But his weight was too great. He fell hard. Both Isaac and Gus flinched as Glenn made a loud *ooomph* noise when he hit the ground belly-first, his arms out before him. His outstretched chin slapped the mud and his legs kicked up after him.

And then Isaac and Gus started laughing—for the second time that day, laughing at their friend. They laughed so hard they were howling. Isaac didn't want to be laughing, he knew it would only make Glenn angrier. But he couldn't help it. It was too funny. The whole thing was too funny. Gus bent forward and put his hands on the ground, balancing himself. He was laughing so hard that tears streamed down his face.

Glenn rolled over onto his back, making no attempt to get up. Dirt stained the front of his T-shirt. His mouth was slack and his eyes were shut. "Dammit," he muttered. "That hurt." His voice was quiet, embarrassed. His lips were trembling.

Gus keeled forward. He curled up into a ball and rocked back and forth.

Isaac wiped his eyes with one of his tentacles, his laughter subsiding.

"You gotta be more careful, Glenn," Isaac said, sliding forward and extending a tentacle. Glenn exhaled loudly as he sat forward, his face dark black, blackest black. He grabbed hold of Isaac's tentacle, squeezing hard, and climbed to his feet. Isaac smiled and said, "You should watch out for your stuff. Take better care of it."

"Thanks a lot," Glenn said, sneering. "I'll keep that in mind."

Gus was now laughing so hard that his laughter was silent. His pipe-cleaner arms were wrapped around his sides nearly ten times over, like his guts might fall out if he let go of himself. His small mouth was open wide, his pink tongue lashing about inside.

Glenn shuffled over and prodded Gus with his foot. "Knock it off," he said. "Come on. Let's just get some Gillie-hooking done."

"Okay. Okay," Gus wheezed. "Just. Give. Me. One second."

Glenn bent down and picked up the pieces of his broken pole; it had snapped in half cleanly, the line an awkward tether between the two pieces. They clanked together a few times as he turned them over in his hands. "My dad is gonna kill me," he said.

Isaac walked back to the edge of the ridge. The two Zeros had gone back to their swimming and splashing, indifferent to whatever else was going on. He watched them for a few moments as they took turns doing somersaults, spitting streams of water at each other, clapping their hands, always laughing.

Glenn muttered something under his breath as he tried to brush the dirt off of his shirt.

"Those Zeros are still out there swimming," Isaac said.

Glenn looked up from his shirt. "What the hell? Are those low-breeds just gonna swim out there all day long?"

Gus had collected himself somewhat. He joined his friends on the ridge. "You know," he said, massaging his jaw, "you don't need to call them low-breeds, Dweeb. We always could walk farther up river—"

"No," Glenn screamed. He turned and glared at Gus. "And don't call me a Dweeb. 'Least I got two legs."

"Alright, alright," Gus said. He wiped tears from his eyes. "Fatty here doesn't want to walk anymore then we won't."

"Shut up," Glenn said. He brushed at his shirt again—no result; it was stained. "Dammit, my mom is already mad at me for coming home covered in mud last time I went out to catch Gillies." He crossed his arms over his stomach, looked out into the river, radiating anger, nearly vibrating.

There was a long pause as the three of them watched the Zeros frolicking in the water. The round, legless germs laughed loudly, showing no signs of ending their swim anytime soon.

"Have you guys ever thought," Isaac said slowly, not knowing how his friends were going to react to the question he was going to ask, "that maybe the Quarter isn't flat?"

"Are you serious?" Gus said. "Where the hell did you get that loony idea?"

Glenn remained silent, his arms crossed over his stomach. The corners of his mouth were pulled down in a frown.

"I don't know," Isaac said. "It makes sense though, at least, I think it does."

"What makes sense?" Gus said.

"The Quarter being round."

"How do you figure that makes sense?"

"It's like I was talking about last time we went Gillie-hooking, I've never met anyone that's been to the other side of the Quarter."

"Me neither," Gus snapped. "That doesn't *mean* anything."

"And I've never met anyone that's been to the edge of the Quarter."

Gus shook his head and laughed, his reedy voice letting out a high-pitched whistle. "That's just plain foolish. Just because you've never met anyone that's been to the edge doesn't mean that the Quarter is *round.* It just means that you've never met anyone that's been to the edge. That's all."

"But the Sage said—"

"The *Sage?*" Gus laughed. "You're still spending time with that old weirdo?"

"I *like* talking to the Sage. He's got all sorts of interesting stories. He's lived for so long that he can talk about just about anything."

Gus clucked his tongue. "Just plain foolish."

Isaac was getting frustrated. He didn't think that Gus was listening to reason. His face was getting hot. He wrapped a tentacle even tighter around his pole and smacked his thick lips.

Glenn continued to stare at the water.

"I think stuff is, like, disappearing—like the president. Remember when we had a president? Remember that radio broadcast where he disappeared?"

"What is it with you?" Gus snapped. "All of a sudden it's Lazlow Sartarian this and Lazlow Sartarian that and Sage this and Sage that. You never used to talk about all this stuff."

"I've been a reading a lot, down at the library—"

"And talking to the Sage and thinking about crazy ideas like the Quarter being round," Gus interrupted.

"—Like this guy Coppernickus," Isaac continued.

"Who?"

"Coppernickus."

"Never heard of him."

"He was the one who said that the Quarter was round."

"Then why haven't I heard of him?"

"I don't know. Maybe 'cause you don't read books?"

Gus threw his arms up into the air, they bobbled and bounced, turning and bending. "What's *that* got to do with anything?"

"What the hell are you doing down there?" Glenn screamed into the river, cupping his hands around his mouth, leaning forward. "We want to hook some Gillies."

The splashing and laughing sounds lapsed into silence once again. Isaac looked out into the river but the Zeros were obscured by the thick, silver fog. He thought he could hear them discussing amongst themselves, low mumbles, stifled giggles. Were Zeros dangerous? He didn't know. He'd never really been around any before.

"What the hell is wrong with you?" Isaac said. "Just give them a few minutes."

"We've been here long enough, dammit. I'm ready to *hook*. I didn't walk all the way out here just to watch some legless freaks swim around and splash each other."

"Again with the legs," Gus said beneath his breath.

Glenn's face was blacker than ever. His hands were curled into fists. The propeller on his head was spinning wildly. "I've had enough," he said. "I'm gonna get some Gill-germs whether they're swimming or not. You two can stand around and chuckle your dumb heads off for all I care."

Glenn reached out and yanked Isaac's Gillie pole—his *father's* Gillie pole—right out of his tentacles. Isaac didn't have time to react. He watched, dumbfounded, as his friend quickly drew the pole back over his shoulder, threw his arms forward and released the line. He hadn't even put any bait on the hook.

It happened in a matter of seconds.

Isaac watched the line propel into the fog.

"Hey," one of the Zeros yelled. His voice roaring like a Burly-Germ.

"Watch it," the other yelled.

Glenn reeled in the line. His face was contorted by his anger and frustration: his lips turned down, an exaggerated frown, chin crumpled, cheeks cloudy black, brow furrowed. As soon as he had the line out of the water, Isaac realized he was going to cast off again.

"Glenn," Isaac yelled. "Knock it off." And yet he did not step forward. He did not try to stop him. He just stood there and watched.

"Screw you," Glenn screamed. "It was your stupid idea to walk all the way out here in the first place. I told you I didn't want to."

Glenn jerked the pole back over his shoulder once more. This time, Isaac *did* take a slap forward, stretched a tentacle out to grab the pole—but it was too late. Glenn twisted his torso and threw his arms forward.

The momentum of Glenn's cast carried the Gillie pole right out of his sweaty hands. Isaac watched his pole turn over itself—one time, then two times—and disappear into the fog, heard it splash in the water.

"That's *it,*" one of the Zeros yelled.

Isaac was shocked. He stood there, mouth open. Like a half-witted Mongroid.

Gus said nothing. Just whistled. Low and long.

Glenn turned to Isaac. His face was drained of all color, pale gray—the palest shade of gray that Isaac had ever seen. His eyes were wide and his lips moved soundlessly with silent apologies. "I, I didn't mean to—"

"You did that on purpose," Isaac yelled.

"No. No, I swear, it was an accident." Glenn turned his head back and forth. He put his hands up, palms facing Isaac, waved them back and forth, crossing before his chest. "I swear."

Isaac took a step back with one of his tentacles, bracing himself with three others, ready to dash forward. His eyes darted from Glenn to Gus and then back again. "You guys are supposed to be my friends."

"We *are* your friends," Gus whistled.

"Yeah," Glenn said, "we—"

"No you're not," Isaac wailed. His tentacles were shaking. "You don't understand anything. You don't listen to me." Images of Glenn and Gus wielding their Gillie poles like rifles ran through his mind. He heard Gus's voice: "*Just plain foolish.*"

"You're both idiots," Isaac yelled. He pointed at Glenn. "You don't know *anything.*" He turned to Gus. "You don't listen to anything I say. You don't *read.*"

The larger of the two Zeros suddenly rolled over the ridge, covered in mud, with great momentum. He stopped with precision, facing the three germs. Water dripped from his beard, the tips of his fingers. He was much, much larger than he had appeared before, nearly the size of four Glenns. His forehead was creased with anger. His huge teeth were coated with mossy bits of food, their cracks caked. He held Isaac's pole in both hands.

"Somebody *lose* this?" he barked, his voice like a growl.

Gus whistled. Glenn actually winced.

Isaac lunged forward and snatched the pole out of the Zero's hands. He took off, slapping and lurching, zipping along the riverbank with a speed he almost never used. He wanted to be far away from Glenn and Gus. He wanted to be far away from the river, from all of In God We Trust City, from the Quarter.

All of the thoughts he had been having lately—about the Quarter being round, about wars and Lazlow Sartarian and rockets and Coppernickus—swirled in his mind as he ran.

He didn't know where he was fleeing to, didn't care. He would have been happy just being lost in the fog. Lost somewhere in that gray gauze.

"Isaac," Glenn shouted. "I'm sorry. I didn't mean it."

But it was too late. Isaac was long gone.

The mossy-toothed Zero looked at the remaining two germs. "You ought to be more careful," he said, his voice stern. "Other germs use this river, too." He rolled over a few times, toward the ridge, then righted himself and spun around, "even *low-breeds*."

Glenn and Gus watched him disappear over the ridge, yelling "*Weeeeeee*" on the way down, heard him splash into the water below.

Gus looked at Glenn. "Close call."

"Yeah, that freak was pissed," Glenn said.

"Was that really an accident—throwing Isaac's pole in the river like that? You know that was his dad's pole, right?"

"Of course it was an accident. Who do you think I am? I'm not a total jerk."

"Just thought I'd ask."

The two young germs stood in silence. They watched the river roll by.

The Zeros were splashing and laughing once again. The fog was now so thick that it appeared to be white.

"Isaac sure was mad," Gus said.

"I know," Glenn said. "Where the hell did that come from?"

Breinigsville, PA USA
29 June 2010
240754BV00001B/3/P